A PAIR OF PATIENT
LOVERS

W. D. HOWELLS

1st WORLD
LIBRARY
Literary Society

A Pair of Patient Lovers

William Dean Howells

© 1st World Library, 2006
PO Box 2211
Fairfield, IA 52556
www.1stworldlibrary.com
First Edition

LCCN: 2007901841

Softcover ISBN: 978-1-4218-4312-4
Hardcover ISBN: 978-1-4218-4214-1
eBook ISBN: 978-1-4218-4410-7

Purchase *"A Pair of Patient Lovers"*
as a traditional bound book at:
www.1stWorldLibrary.com/purchase.asp?ISBN=978-1-4218-4312-4

1st World Library is a literary, educational organization
dedicated to:

- Creating a free internet library of downloadable ebooks

  - Hosting writing competitions and offering book
    publishing scholarships.

1ˢᵗ World Library Literary Society

Giving Back to the World

"If you want to work on the core problem, it's early school literacy."

- James Barksdale, former CEO of Netscape

"No skill is more crucial to the future of a child, or to a democratic and prosperous society, than literacy."

- Los Angeles Times

Literacy... means far more than learning how to read and write... The aim is to transmit... knowledge and promote social participation."

- UNESCO

"Literacy is not a luxury, it is a right and a responsibility. If our world is to meet the challenges of the twenty-first century we must harness the energy and creativity of all our citizens."

- President Bill Clinton

"Parents should be encouraged to read to their children, and teachers should be equipped with all available techniques for teaching literacy, so the varying needs and capacities of individual kids can be taken into account."

- Hugh Mackay

CONTENTS

A PAIR OF PATIENT LOVERS

I

We first met Glendenning on the Canadian boat which carries you down the rapids of the St. Lawrence from Kingston and leaves you at Montreal. When we saw a handsome young clergyman across the promenade-deck looking up from his guide-book toward us, now and again, as if in default of knowing any one else he would be very willing to know us, we decided that I must make his acquaintance. He was instantly and cordially responsive to my question whether he had ever made the trip before, and he was amiably grateful when in my quality of old habitue of the route I pointed out some characteristic features of the scenery. I showed him just where we were on the long map of the river hanging over his knee, and I added, with no great relevancy, that my wife and I were renewing the fond emotion of our first trip down the St. Lawrence in the character of bridal pair which we had spurned when it was really ours. I explained that we had left the children with my wife's aunt, so as to render the travesty more lifelike; and when he said, "I suppose you miss them, though," I gave him my card. He tried to find one of his own to give me in return, but he could only find a lot of other people's cards. He wrote his name on the back of one, and handed it to me with a smile. "It won't do for me to put 'reverend' before it, in my own chirography, but that's the way I have it engraved."

"Oh," I said, "the cut of your coat bewrayed you," and we had some laughing talk. But I felt the eye of Mrs. March dwelling upon me with growing impatience, till I suggested, "I should like to make you acquainted with my wife, Mr. Glendenning."

He said, Oh, he should be so happy; and he gathered his dangling map into the book and came over with me to where Mrs. March sat; and, like the good young American husband I was in those days, I stood aside and left the whole talk to her. She interested him so much more than I could that I presently wandered away and amused myself elsewhere. When I came back, she clutched my arm and bade me not speak a word; it was the most romantic thing in the world, and she would tell me about it when we were alone, but now I must go off again; he had just gone to get a book for her which he had been speaking of, and would be back the next instant, and it would not do to let him suppose we had been discussing him.

William Dean Howells

II

I was sometimes disappointed in Mrs. March's mysteries when I came up close to them; but I was always willing to take them on trust; and I submitted to the postponement of a solution in this case with more than my usual faith. She found time, before Mr. Glendenning reappeared, to ask me if I had noticed a mother and daughter on the boat, the mother evidently an invalid, and the daughter very devoted, and both decidedly ladies; and when I said, "No. Why?" she answered, "Oh, nothing," and that she would tell me. Then she drove me away, and we did not meet till I found her in our state-room just before the terrible mid-day meal they used to give you on the *Corinthian*, and called dinner.

She began at once, while she did something to her hair before the morsel of mirror: "Why I wanted to know if you had noticed those people was because they are the reason of his being here."

"Did he tell you that?"

"Of course not. But I knew it, for he asked if I had seen them, or could tell him who they were."

"It seems to me that he made pretty good time to get so far as that."

"I don't say he got so far himself, but you men never know how to take steps for any one else. You can't put two and two together. But to my mind it's as plain as the nose on his face that he's seen that girl somewhere and is taking this trip because she's on board. He said he hadn't decided to come till the last moment."

"What wild leaps of fancy!" I said. "But the nose on his face is handsome rather than plain, and I sha'n't be satisfied till I see him with the lady."

"Yes, he's quite Greek," said Mrs. March, in assent to my opinion of his nose. "Too Greek for a clergyman, almost. But he isn't vain of it. Those beautiful people are often quite modest, and Mr. Glendenning is very modest."

"And I'm very hungry. If you don't hurry your prinking, Isabel, we shall not get any dinner."

"I'm ready," said my wife, and she continued with her eyes still on the glass: "He's got a church out in Ohio, somewhere; but he's a New-Englander, and he's quite wild to get back. He thinks those people are from Boston: I could tell in a moment if I saw them. Well, now, I *am* ready," and with this she really ceased to do something to her hair, and came out into the long saloon with me where the table was set. Rows of passengers stood behind the rows of chairs, with a detaining grasp on nearly all of them. We gazed up and down in despair. Suddenly Mrs. March sped forward, and I found that Mr. Glendenning had made a sign to her from a distant point, where there were two vacant chairs for us next his own. We eagerly laid hands on them, and waited for the gong to sound for dinner. In this interval an elderly lady followed by a young girl came down the saloon toward us, and I saw signs, or rather emotions, of intelligence pass between Mr. Glendenning and Mrs. March concerning them.

The older of these ladies was a tall, handsome matron, who bore her fifty years with a native severity qualified by a certain air of wonder at a world which I could well fancy had not always taken her at her own estimate of her personal and social importance. She had the effect of challenging you to do less, as she advanced slowly between the wall of state-rooms and the backs of the people gripping their chairs, and eyed them with a sort of imperious surprise that they should have left no place for her. So at least I read her glance, while I read in that of the young lady coming after, and showing her beauty first over this shoulder and then over that of her mother, chiefly a present amusement, behind which lay a character of perhaps equal pride, if not equal hardness. She was very beautiful, in the dark

William Dean Howells

style which I cannot help thinking has fallen into unmerited abeyance; and as she passed us I could see that she was very graceful. She was dressed in a lady's acceptance of the fashions of that day, which would be thought so grotesque in this. I have heard contemporaneous young girls laugh at the mere notion of hoops, but in 1870 we thought hoops extremely becoming; and this young lady knew how to hold hers a little on one side so as to give herself room in the narrow avenue, and not betray more than the discreetest hint of a white stocking. I believe the stockings are black now.

They both got by us, and I could see Mr. Glendenning following them with longing but irresolute eyes, until they turned, a long way down the saloon, as if to come toward us again. Then he hurried to meet them, and as he addressed himself first to one and then to the other, I knew him to be offering them his chair. So did my wife, and she said, "You must give up your place too, Basil," and I said I would if she wished to see me starve on the spot. But of course I went and joined Glendenning in his entreaties that they would deprive us of our chances of dinner (I knew what the second table was on the *Corinthian*); and I must say that the elder lady accepted my chair in the spirit which my secret grudge deserved. She made me feel as if I ought to have offered it when they first passed us; but it was some satisfaction to learn afterwards that she gave Mrs. March, for her ready sacrifice of me, as bad a half-hour as she ever had. She sat next to my wife, and the young lady took Glendenning's place, and as soon as we had left them she began trying to find out from Mrs. March who he was, and what his relation to us was. The girl tried to check her at first, and then seemed to give it up, and devoted herself to being rather more amiable than she otherwise might have been, my wife thought, in compensation for the severity of her mother's scrutiny. Her mother appeared disposed to hold Mrs. March responsible for knowing little or nothing about Mr. Glendenning.

"He seems to be an Episcopal clergyman," she said, in a haughty summing up. "From his name I should have supposed he was Scotch and a Presbyterian." She began to patronize the trip we were making, and to abuse it; she said that she did not see what could have induced them to undertake it; but one had to get back from Niagara somehow, and they had been told at the hotel there that the boats were very comfortable. She had never been more uncomfortable in her life; as for the rapids, they made her ill, and they were obviously so dangerous that she should not even look at them again. Then, from having done all the talking and most of the eating, she fell quite silent, and gave her daughter a chance to speak to my wife. She had hitherto spoken only to her mother, but now she asked Mrs. March if she had ever been down the St. Lawrence before.

When my wife explained, and asked her whether she was enjoying it, she answered with a rapture that was quite astonishing, in reference to her mother's expressions of disgust: "Oh, immensely! Every instant of it," and she went on to expatiate on its peculiar charm in terms so intelligent and sympathetic that Mrs. March confessed it had been part of our wedding journey, and that this was the reason why we were now taking the trip.

The young lady did not seem to care so much for this, and when she thanked my wife in leaving the table with her mother, and begged her to thank the gentlemen who had so kindly given up their places, she made no overture to further acquaintance. In fact, we had been so simply and merely made use of that, although we were rather meek people, we decided to avoid our beneficiaries for the rest of the day; and Mr. Glendenning, who could not, as a clergyman, indulge even a just resentment, could as little refuse us his sympathy. He laughed at some hints of my wife's experience, which she dropped before she left us to pick up a meal from the luke-warm leavings of the *Corinthian's* dinner, if we could. She said she was going forward to get a good place on the bow, and would keep two camp-stools for us, which she could assure us no one would get away from her.

We were somewhat surprised then to find her seated by the rail with the younger lady of the two whom she meant to avoid if she meant anything by what she said. She was laughing and talking on quite easy terms with her apparently, and "There!" she triumphed as we came up, "I've kept your camp-stools for you," and she showed them at her side, where she was holding her hand on them. "You had better put them here."

The girl had stiffened a little at our approach, as I could see, but a young girl's stiffness is always rather amusing than otherwise, and I did not mind it. Neither, that I could see, did Mr. Glendenning, and it soon passed. It seemed that she had left her mother lying down in her state-room, where she justly imagined that if she did not see the rapids she should suffer less alarm from them; the young lady had come frankly to the side of Mrs. March as soon as she saw her, and asked if she might sit with her. She now talked to me for a decent space of time, and then presently, without my knowing how, she was talking to Mr. Glendenning, and they were comparing notes of Niagara; he was saying that he thought he had seen her at the Cataract House, and she was owning that she and her mother had at least stopped at that hotel.

III

I have no wish, and if I had the wish I should not have the art, to keep back the fact that these young people were evidently very much taken with each other. They showed their mutual pleasure so plainly that even I could see it. As for Mrs. March, she was as proud of it as if she had invented them and set them going in their advance toward each other, like two mechanical toys.

I confess that with reference to what my wife had told me of this young lady's behavior when she was with her mother, her submissiveness, her entire self-effacement, up to a certain point, I did not know quite what to make of her present independence, not to say freedom. I thought she might perhaps have been kept so strictly in the background, with young men, that she was rather disposed to make the most of any chance at them which offered. If the young man in this case was at no pains to hide his pleasure in her society, one might say that she was almost eager to show her delight in his. If it was a case of love at first sight, the earliest glimpse had been to the girl, who was all eyes for Glendenning. It was very pretty, but it was a little alarming, and perhaps a little droll, even. She was actually making the advances, not consciously, but helplessly; fondly, ignorantly, for I have no belief, nor had my wife (a much more critical observer), that she knew how she was giving herself away.

I thought perhaps that she was in the habit from pride, or something like it, of holding herself in check, and that this blameless excess which I saw was the natural expansion from an inner constraint. But what I really knew was that the young people got on very rapidly, in an acquaintance that prospered up to the last moment I saw them together. This was just before the *Corinthian* drew up to her landing at Montreal, when Miss Bentley (we had learned her name) came to us from the point where she was standing with Glendenning and said that now she must go to her mother, and took a sweet leave of my wife. She asked where we were going to stay in Montreal and whether we were going on to Quebec; and said her mother would wish to send Mrs. March her card.

When she was gone, Glendenning explained, with rather superfluous apology, that he had offered to see the ladies to a hotel, for he was afraid that at this crowded season they might not find it easy to get rooms, and he did not wish Mrs. Bentley, who was an invalid, to have any anxieties about it. He bade us an affectionate, but not a disconsolate adieu, and when we had got into the modest conveyance (if an omnibus is modest) which was to take us to the Ottawa House, we saw him drive off to the St. Lawrence Hall (it was twenty-five years ago) in one of those vitreous and tinkling Montreal landaus, with Mrs. and Miss Bentley and Mrs. Bentley's maid.

We were still so young as to be very much absorbed in the love affairs of other people; I believe women always remain young enough for that; and Mrs. March talked about the one we fancied we had witnessed the beginning of pretty much the whole evening. The next morning we got letters from Boston, telling us how the children were and all that they were doing and saying. We had stood it very well, as long as we did not hear anything about them, and we had lent ourselves in a sort of semi-forgetfulness of them to the associations of the past when they were not; but now to learn that they were hearty and happy, and that they sent love and kisses, was too much. With one mind we renounced the notion of going on to Quebec; we found that we could just get the ten-o'clock train that would reach Boston by eleven that night, and we made all haste and got it. We had not been really at peace, we perceived, till that moment since we had bidden the children good-bye.

IV

Perhaps it was because we left Montreal so abruptly that Mrs. March never received Mrs. Bentley's card. It may be at the Ottawa House to this day, for all I know. What is certain is that we saw and heard nothing more of her or her daughter. Glendenning called to see us as he passed through Boston on his way west from Quebec, but we were neither of us at home and we missed him, to my wife's vivid regret. I rather think we expected him to find some excuse for writing after he reached his place in northern Ohio; but he did not write, and he became more and more the memory of a young clergyman in the beginning of a love-affair, till one summer, while we were still disputing where we should spend the hot weather within business reach, there came a letter from him saying that he was settled at Gormanville, and wishing that he might tempt us up some afternoon before we were off to the mountains or seaside. This revived all my wife's waning interest in him, and it was hard to keep the answer I made him from expressing in a series of crucial inquiries the excitement she felt at his being in New England and so near Boston, and in Gormanville of all places. It was one of the places we had thought of for the summer, and we were yet so far from having relinquished it that we were recurring from time to time in hope and fear to the advertisement of an old village mansion there, with ample grounds, garden, orchard, ice-house, and stables, for a very low rental to an unexceptionable tenant. We had no doubt of our own qualifications, but we had misgivings of the village mansion; and I am afraid that I rather unduly despatched the personal part of my letter, in my haste to ask what Glendenning knew and what he thought of the Conwell place. However, the letter seemed to serve all purposes. There came a reply from Glendenning, most cordial, even affectionate, saying that the Conwell place was delightful, and I must come at once and see it. He professed that he would be glad to have Mrs. March come too, and he declared that if his joy at having us did not fill his modest rectory to bursting, he was sure it could stand the physical strain of our presence, though he confessed that his guest-chamber was tiny.

"He wants *you*, Basil," my wife divined from terms which gave me no sense of any latent design of parting us in his hospitality. "But, evidently, it isn't a chance to be missed, and you must go—instantly. Can you go to-morrow? But telegraph him you're coming, and tell him to hold on to the Conwell place; it may be snapped up any moment if it's so desirable."

I did not go till the following week, when I found that no one had attempted to snap up the Conwell place. In fact, it rather snapped me up, I secured it with so little trouble. I reported it so perfect that all my wife's fears of a latent objection to it were roused again. But when I said I thought we could relinquish it, her terrors subsided; and I thought this the right moment to deliver a stroke that I had been holding in reserve.

"You know," I began, "the Bentleys have their summer place there—the old Bentley homestead. It's their ancestral town, you know."

"Bentleys? What Bentleys?" she demanded, opaquely.

"Why, those people we met on the *Corinthian*, summer before last—you thought he was in love with the girl—"

A simultaneous photograph could alone reproduce Mrs. March's tumultuous and various emotions as she seized the fact conveyed in my words. She poured out a volume of mingled conjectures, assertions, suspicions, conclusions, in which there was nothing final but the decision that we must not dream of going there; that it would look like thrusting ourselves in, and would be in the worst sort of taste; they would all hate us, and we should feel that we were spies upon the young people; for of course the Bentleys had got Glendenning there to marry him, and in effect did not want any one to witness the disgraceful spectacle.

I said, "That may be the nefarious purpose of the young lady, but, as I understood Glendenning, it is no part of her mother's design."

"What do you mean?"

"Miss Bentley may have got him there to marry him, but Mrs. Bentley seems to have meant nothing more than an engagement at the worst."

"What *do* you mean? They're not engaged, are they?"

"They're not married, at any rate, and I suppose they're engaged. I did not have it from Miss Bentley, but I suppose Glendenning may be trusted in such a case."

"Now," said my wife, with a severity that might well have appalled me, "if you will please to explain, Basil, it will be better for you."

"Why, it is simply this. Glendenning seems to have made himself so useful to the mother and pleasing to the daughter after we left them in Montreal that he was tolerated on a pretence that there was reason for his writing back to Mrs. Bentley after he got home, and, as Mrs. Bentley never writes letters, Miss Bentley had the hard task of answering him. This led to a correspondence."

"And to her moving heaven and earth to get him to Gormanville. I see! Of course she did it so that no one knew what she was about!"

"Apparently. Glendenning himself was not in the secret. The Bentleys were in Europe last summer, and he did not know that they had a place at Gormanville till he came to live there. Another proof that Miss Bentley got him there is the fact that she and her mother are Unitarians, and that they would naturally be able to select the rector of the Episcopal church."

"Go on," said Mrs. March, not the least daunted.

William Dean Howells

"Oh, there's nothing more. He is simply rector of St. Michael's at Gormanville; and there is not the slightest proof that any young lady had a hand in getting him there."

"As if I cared in the least whether she had! I suppose you will allow that she had something to do with getting engaged to him, and that is the *great* matter."

"Yes, I must allow that, if we are to suppose that young ladies have anything to do with young men getting engaged to them; it doesn't seem exactly delicate. But the novel phase of this great matter is the position of the young lady's mother in regard to it. From what I could make out she consents to the engagement of her daughter, but she don't and won't consent to her marriage." My wife glared at me with so little speculation in her eyes that I felt obliged to disclaim all responsibility for the fact I had reported. "Thou canst not say *I* did it. *They* did it, and Miss Bentley, if any one, is to blame. It seems, from what Glendenning says, that the young lady and he wrote to each other while she was abroad, and that they became engaged by letter. Then the affair was broken off because of her mother's opposition; but since they have met at Gormanville, the engagement has been renewed. So much they've managed against the old lady's will, but apparently on condition that they won't get married till she says."

"Nonsense! How could she stop them?"

"She couldn't, I dare say, by any of the old romantic methods of a convent or disinheritance; but she is an invalid; she wants to keep her daughter with her, and she avails with the girl's conscience by being simply dependent and obstructive. The young people have carried their engagement through, and now such hope as they have is fixed upon her finally yielding in the matter of their marriage, though Glendenning was obliged to confess that there was no sign of her doing so. They agree— Miss Bentley and he—that they cannot get married as they got engaged, in spite of her mother—it would be unclerical if it wouldn't be unfilial—and they simply have to bide their time."

My wife asked abruptly, "How many chambers are there in the Conwell place?"

I said, and then she asked, "Is there a windmill or a force-pump?" I answered proudly that in Gormanville there was town water, but that if this should give out there were both a windmill and a force-pump on the Conwell place.

"It is very complete," she sighed, as if this had removed all hope from her, and she added, "I suppose we had better take it."

V

We certainly did not take it for the sake of being near the Bentleys, neither of whom had given us particular reason to desire their further acquaintance, though the young lady had agreeably modified herself when apart from her mother. In fact, we went to Gormanville because it was an exceptional chance to get a beautiful place for a very little money, where we could go early and stay late. But no sooner had we acted from this quite personal, not to say selfish, motive than we were rewarded with the sweetest overtures of neighborliness by the Bentleys. They waited, of course, till we were settled in our house before they came to call upon Mrs. March, but they had been preceded by several hospitable offerings from their garden, their dairy, and their hen-house, which were very welcome in the days of our first uncertainty as to trades-people. We analyzed this hospitality as an effect of that sort of nature in Mrs. Bentley which can equally assert its superiority by blessing or banning. Evidently, since chance had again thrown us in her way, she would not go out of it to be offensive, but would continue in it, and make the best of us.

No doubt Glendenning had talked us into the Bentleys; and this my wife said she hated most of all; for we should have to live up to the notion of us imparted by a young man from the impressions of the moment when he saw us purple in the light of his dawning love. In justice to Glendenning, however, I must say that he did nothing, by a show of his own assiduities, to urge us upon the Bentleys after we came to Gormanville. If we had not felt so sure of him, we might have thought he was keeping his regard for us a little too modestly in the back-ground. He made us one cool little call, the evening of our arrival, in which he had the effect of anxiety to get away as soon as possible; and after that we saw him no more until he came with Miss Bentley and her mother a week later. His forbearance was all the more remarkable because his church and his rectory were just across the street from the Conwell place, at the corner of another street, where we could see their wooden gothic in the cold shadow of the maples with which the green in front of them was planted.

During all that time Glendenning's personal elevation remained invisible to us, and we began to wonder if he were not that most lamentable of fellow-creatures, a clerical snob. I am not sure still that he might not have been so in some degree, there was such a mixture of joy that was almost abject in his genuine affection for us when Mrs. Bentley openly approved us on her first visit. I dare say he would not have quite abandoned us in any case; but he must have felt responsible for us, and it must have been such a load off him when she took that turn with us.

She called in the afternoon, and the young people dropped in again the same evening, and took the trouble to win back our simple hearts. That is, Miss Bentley showed herself again as frank and sweet as she had been on the boat when she joined my wife after dinner and left her mother in her state-room. Glendenning was again the Glendenning of our first meeting, and something more. He fearlessly led the way to intimacies of feeling with an expansion uncommon even in an accepted lover, and we made our conclusions that however subject he might be to his indefinitely future mother-in-law, he would not be at all so to his wife, if she could help it. He took the lead, but because she gave it him; and she displayed an aptness for conjugal submissiveness which almost amounted to genius. Whenever she spoke to either of us, it was with one eye on him to see if he liked what she was saying. It was so perfect that I doubted if it could last; but my wife said a girl like that could keep it up till she dropped. I have never been sure that she liked us as well as he did; I think it was part of her intense loyalty to seem to like us a great deal more.

She was deeply in love, and nothing but her ladylike breeding kept her from being openly fond. I figured her in a sort of impassioned incandescence, such as only a pure and perhaps cold nature could burn into; and I amused myself a little with the sense of Glendenning's apparent inadequacy. Sweet he was, and admirably gentle and fine; he had an unfailing good sense, and a very ready wisdom, as I grew more and more to perceive. But he was an inch or so shorter than Miss Bentley, and in his sunny blondness, with his golden red beard and hair, and his pinkish complexion, he wanted still more the effect of an emotional equality with her. He was very handsome, with features excellently regular; his smile was celestially beautiful; innocent gay lights danced in his blue eyes, through lashes and under brows that were a lighter blond than his beard and hair.

VI

The next morning, which was of a Saturday, when I did not go to town, he came over to us again from the shadow of his sombre maples, and fell simply and naturally into talk about his engagement. He was much fuller in my wife's presence than he had been with me alone, and told us the hopes he had of Mrs. Bentley's yielding within a reasonable time. He seemed to gather encouragement from the sort of perspective he got the affair into by putting it before us, and finding her dissent to her daughter's marriage so ridiculous in our eyes after her consent to her engagement that a woman of her great good sense evidently could not persist in it.

"There is no personal objection to myself," he said, with a modest satisfaction. "In fact, I think she really likes me, and only dislikes my engagement to Edith. But she knows that Edith is incapable of marrying against her mother's will, or I of wishing her to do so; though there is nothing else to prevent us."

My wife allowed herself to say, "Isn't it rather cruel of her?"

"Why, no, not altogether; or not so much so as it might be in different circumstances. I make every allowance for her. In the first place, she is a great sufferer."

"Yes, I know," my wife relented.

"She suffers terribly from asthma. I don't suppose she has lain down in bed for ten years. She sleeps in an easy-chair, and she's never quite free from her trouble; when there's a paroxysm of the disease, her anguish is frightful. I've never seen it, of course, but I have heard it; you hear it all through the house. Edith has the constant care of her. Her mother has to be perpetually moved and shifted in her chair, and Edith does this for her; she will let no one else come near her; Edith must look to the ventilation, and burn the pastilles which help her to

William Dean Howells

breathe. She depends upon her every instant." He had grown very solemn in voice and face, and he now said, "When I think of what she endures, it seems to me that it is I who am cruel even to dream of taking her daughter from her."

"Yes," my wife assented.

"But there is really no present question of that We are very happy as it is. We can wait, and wait willingly till Mrs. Bentley wishes us to wait no longer; or—"

He stopped, and we were both aware of something in his mind which he put from him. He became a little pale, and sat looking very grave. Then he rose. "I don't know whether to say how welcome you would be at St. Michael's to-morrow, for you may not be—"

"*We* are Unitarians, too," said Mrs. March. "But we are coming to hear *you*."

"I am glad you are coming *to church*," said Glendenning, putting away the personal tribute implied with a gentle dignity that became him.

VII

We waited a discreet time before returning the call of the Bentley ladies, but not so long as to seem conscious. In fact, we had been softened towards Mrs. Bentley by what Glendenning told us of her suffering, and we were disposed to forgive a great deal of patronage and superiority to her asthma; they were not part of the disease, but still they were somehow to be considered with reference to it in her case.

We were admitted by the maid, who came running down the hall stairway, with a preoccupied air, to the open door where we stood waiting. There were two great syringa-bushes on each hand close to the portal, which were in full flower, and which flung their sweetness through the doorway and the windows; but when we found ourselves in the dim old-fashioned parlor, we were aware of this odor meeting and mixing with another which descended from the floor above—the smell of some medicated pastille. There was a sound of anxious steps overhead, and a hurried closing of doors, with the mechanical sound of labored breathing.

"We have come at a bad time," I suggested.

"Yes, *why* did they let us in?" cried my wife in an anguish of compassion and vexation. She repeated her question to Miss Bentley, who came down almost immediately, looking pale, indeed, but steady, and making a brave show of welcome.

"My mother would have wished it," she said, "and she sent me as soon as she knew who it was. You mustn't be distressed," she entreated, with a pathetic smile. "It's really a kind of relief to her; anything is that takes her mind off herself for a moment. She will be so sorry to miss you, and you must come again as soon as you can."

"Oh, we will, we will!" cried my wife, in nothing less than a passion of meekness; and Miss Bentley went on to comfort her.

"It's dreadful, of course, but it isn't as bad as it sounds, and it isn't nearly so bad as it looks. She is used to it, and there is a great deal in that. Oh, *don't* go!" she begged, at a movement Mrs. March made to rise. "The doctor is with her just now, and I'm not needed. It will be kind if you'll stay; it's a relief to be out of the room with a good excuse!" She even laughed a little as she said this; she went on to lead the talk away from what was so intensely in our minds, and presently I heard her and my wife speaking of other things. The power to do this is from some heroic quality in women's minds that we do not credit them with; we think it their volatility, and I dare say I thought myself much better, or at least more serious in my make, because I could not follow them, and did not lose one of those hoarse gasps of the sufferer overhead. Occasionally there came a stifling cry that made me jump, inwardly if not outwardly, but those women had their drama to play, and they played it to the end.

Miss Bentley came hospitably to the door with us, and waited there till she thought we could not see her turn and run swiftly up-stairs.

"Why *did* you stay, my dear?" I groaned. "I felt as if I were personally smothering Mrs. Bentley every moment we were there."

"I *had* to do it. She wished it, and, as she said, it was a relief to have us there, though she was wishing us at the ends of the earth all the time. But what a ghastly life!"

"Yes; and can you wonder that the poor woman doesn't want to give her up, to lose the help and comfort she gets from her? It's a wicked thing for that girl to think of marrying."

"What are you talking about, Basil? It's a wicked thing for her *not* to think of it! She is wearing her life out, *tearing* it out, and she isn't doing her mother a bit of good. Her mother would be just as well, and better, with a good strong nurse, who could lift her this way and that, and change her about, without feeling her heart-strings wrung at every gasp, as that poor child must. Oh, I *wish* Glendenning was man enough to make her run off with him, and get married, in spite of everything. But, of course, that's impossible—for a clergyman! And her sacrifice began so long ago that it's become part of her life, and she'll simply have to keep on."

William Dean Howells

VIII

When her attack passed off, Mrs. Bentley sent and begged my wife to come again and see her. She went without me, while I was in town, but she was so circumstantial in her report of her visit, when I came home, that I never felt quite sure I had not been present. What most interested us both was the extreme independence which the mother and daughter showed beyond a certain point, and the daughter's great frankness in expressing her difference of feeling. We had already had some hint of this, the first day we met her, and we were not surprised at it now, my wife at first hand, or I at second hand. Mrs. Bentley opened the way for her daughter by saying that the worst of sickness was that it made one such an affliction to others. She lived in an atmosphere of devotion, she said, but her suffering left her so little of life that she could not help clinging selfishly to everything that remained.

My wife perceived that this was meant for Miss Bentley, though it was spoken to herself; and Miss Bentley seemed to take the same view of the fact. She said: "We needn't use any circumlocution with Mrs. March, mother. She knows just how the affair stands. You can say whatever you wish, though I don't know why you should wish to say anything. You have made your own terms with us, and we are keeping them to the letter. What more can you ask? Do you want me to break with Mr. Glendenning? I will do that too, if you ask it. You have got everything *but* that, and you can have that at any time. But Arthur and I are perfectly satisfied as it is, and we can wait as long as you wish us to wait."

Her mother said: "I'm not allowed to forget that for a single hour," and Miss Bentley said, "I never remind you of it unless you make me, mother. You may be thinking of it all the time, but it isn't because of anything I say."

"Or that you *do*?" asked Mrs. Bentley; and her daughter answered, "I can't help existing, of course."

My wife broke off from the account she was giving me of her visit: "You can imagine how pleasant all this was for me, Basil, and how anxious I was to prolong my call!"

"Well," I returned, "there were compensations. It was extremely interesting; it was life. You can't deny that, my dear."

"It was more like death. Several times I was on the point of going, but you know when there's been a painful scene you feel so sorry for the people who've made it that you can't bear to leave them to themselves. I did get up to go, once, in mere self-defence, but they both urged me to stay, and I couldn't help staying till they could talk of other things. But now tell me what you think of it all. Which should your feeling be with the most? That is what I want to get at before I tell you mine."

"Which side was I on when we talked about them last?"

"Oh, when did we talk about them *last*? We are always talking about them! I am getting no good of the summer at all. I shall go home in the fall more jaded and worn out than when I came. To think that we should have this beautiful place, where we could be so happy and comfortable, if it were not for having this abnormal situation under our nose and eyes all the time!"

"Abnormal? I don't call it abnormal," I began, and I was sensible of my wife's thoughts leaving her own injuries for my point of view so swiftly that I could almost hear them whir.

"Not abnormal!" she gasped.

"No; only too natural. Isn't it perfectly natural for an invalid like that to want to keep her daughter with her; and isn't it perfectly natural for a daughter, with a New England sense of duty, to yield to her wish? You might say that she could get married and live at home, and then she and Glendenning could both devote themselves—"

"No, no," my wife broke in, "that wouldn't do. Marriage is marriage; and it puts the husband and wife with each other first; when it doesn't, it's a miserable mockery."

"Even when there's a sick mother in the case?"

"A thousand sick mothers wouldn't alter the case. And that's what they all three instinctively know, and they're doing the only thing they can do."

"Then I don't see what we're complaining of."

"Complaining of? We're complaining of its being all wrong and—romantic. Her mother has asked more than she had any right to ask, and Miss Bentley has tried to do more than she can perform, and that has made them hate each other."

"Should you say *hate*, quite?"

"It must come to that, if Mrs. Bentley lives."

"Then let us hope she—"

"My dear!" cried Mrs. March, warningly.

"Oh, come, now!" I retorted. "Do you mean to say that you haven't thought how very much it would simplify the situation if—"

"Of course I have! And that is the wicked part of it. It's that that is wearing me out. It's perfectly hideous!"

"Well, fortunately we're not actively concerned in the affair, and we needn't take any measures in regard to it. We are mere spectators, and as I see it the situation is not only inevitable for Mrs. Bentley, but it has a sort of heroic propriety for Miss Bentley."

"And Glendenning?"

"Oh, Glendenning isn't provided for in my scheme."

"Then I can tell you that your scheme, Basil, is worse than worthless."

"I didn't brag of it, my dear," I said, meekly enough. "I'm sorry for him, but I can't help him. He must provide for himself out of his religion."

IX

It was, indeed, a trying summer for our emotions, torn as we were between our pity for Mrs. Bentley and our compassion for her daughter. We had no repose, except when we centred our sympathies upon Glendenning, whom we could yearn over in tender regret without doing any one else wrong, or even criticising another. He was our great stay in that respect, and though a mere external witness might have thought that he had the easiest part, we who knew his gentle and affectionate nature could not but feel for him. We never concealed from ourselves certain foibles of his; I have hinted at one, and we should have liked it better if he had not been so sensible of the honor, from a worldly point, of being engaged to Miss Bentley. But this was a very innocent vanity, and he would have been willing to suffer for her mother and for herself, if she had let him. I have tried to insinuate how she would not let him, but freed him as much as possible from the stress of the situation, and assumed for him a mastery, a primacy, which he would never have assumed for himself. We thought this very pretty of her, and in fact she was capable of pretty things. What was hard and arrogant in her, and she was not without something of the kind at times, was like her mother; but even she, poor soul, had her good points, as I have attempted to suggest. We used to dwell upon them, when our talk with Glendenning grew confidential, as it was apt to do; for it seemed to console him to realize that her daughter and he were making their sacrifice to a not wholly unamiable person.

He confided equally in my wife and myself, but there were times when I think he rather preferred the counsel of a man friend. Once when we had gone a walk into the country, which around Gormanville is of the pathetic Mid-Massachusetts loveliness and poverty, we sat down in a hillside orchard to rest, and he began abruptly to talk of his affair. Sometimes, he said, he felt that it was all an error, and he could not rid himself of the fear that an error persisted in was a wrong, and therefore a species of sin.

"That is very interesting," I said. "I wonder if there is anything in it? At first blush it looks so logical; but is it? Or are you simply getting morbid? What is the error? What is your error?"

"You know," he said, with a gentle refusal of my willingness to make light of his trouble. "It is surely an error to allow a woman to give her word when she can promise nothing more, and to let her hold herself to it."

I could have told him that I did not think the error in this case was altogether or mainly his, or the persistence in it; for it had seemed to me from the beginning that the love between him and Miss Bentley was fully as much her affair as his, and that quite within the bounds of maidenly modesty she showed herself as passionately true to their plighted troth. But of course this would not do, and I had to be content with the ironical suggestion that he might try offering to release Miss Bentley.

"Don't laugh at me," he implored, and I confess his tone would have taken from me any heart to do so.

"My dear fellow," I said, "I see your point. But don't you think you are quite needlessly adding to your affliction by pressing it? You two are in the position which isn't at all uncommon with engaged people, of having to wait upon exterior circumstances before you get married. Suppose you were prevented by poverty, as often happens? It would be a hardship as it is now; but in that case would your engagement be any less an error than it is now? I don't think it would, and I don't believe you think so either."

"In that case we should not be opposing our wills to the will of some one else, who has a better claim to her daughter's allegiance than I have. It seems to me that our error was in letting her mother consent to our engagement if she would not or could not consent to our marriage. When it came to that we ought both to have had the strength to say that then there should be no engagement. It was my place to do that. I could have prevented the error which I can't undo."

"I don't see how it could have been easier to prevent than to undo your error. I don't admit it's an error, but I call it so because you do. After all, an engagement is nothing but an open confession between two people that they are in love with each other and wish to marry. There need be no sort of pledge or promise to make the engagement binding, if there is love. It's the love that binds."

"Yes."

"It bound you from your first acknowledgment of it, and unless you could deny your love now, or hereafter, it must always bind you. If you own that you still love each other, you are still engaged, no matter how much you release each other. Could you think of loving her and marrying some one else? Could she love you and marry another? There isn't any error, unless you've mistaken your feeling for each other. If you have, I should decidedly say you couldn't break your engagement too soon. In fact, there wouldn't be any real engagement to break."

"Of course you are right," said Glendenning, but not so strenuously as he might.

I had a feeling that he had not put forward the main cause of his unhappiness, though he had given a true cause; that he had made some lesser sense of wrong stand for a greater, as people often do in confessing themselves; and I was not surprised when he presently added: "It is not merely the fact that she is bound in that way, and that her young life is passing in this sort of hopeless patience, but that—that—I don't know how to put the ugly and wicked thing into words, but I assure you that sometimes when I think—when I'm aware that I know— Ah, I can't say it!"

"I fancy I understand what you mean, my dear boy," I said, and in the right of my ten years' seniority I put my hand caressingly on his shoulder, "and you are no more guilty than I am in knowing that if Mrs. Bentley were not in the way there would be no obstacle to your happiness."

"But such a cognition is of hell," he cried, and he let his face fall into his hands and sobbed heartrendingly.

"Yes," I said, "such a cognition is of hell; you are quite right. So are all evil concepts and knowledges; but so long as they are merely things of our intelligence, they are no part of us, and we are not guilty of them."

"No; I trust not, I trust not," he returned, and I let him sob his trouble out before I spoke again; and then I began with a laugh of unfeigned gayety. Something that my wife had hinted in one of our talks about the lovers freakishly presented itself to my mind, and I said, "There is a way, and a very practical way, to put an end to the anomaly you feel in an engagement which doesn't imply a marriage."

"And what is that?" he asked, not very hopefully; but he dried his eyes and calmed himself.

"Well, speaking after the manner of men, you might run off with Miss Bentley."

All the blood in his body flushed into his face. "Don't!" he gasped, and I divined that what I had said must have been in his thoughts before, and I laughed again. "It wouldn't do," he added, piteously. "The scandal—I am a clergyman, and my parish—"

I perceived that no moral scruple presented itself to him; when it came to the point, he was simply and naturally a lover, like any other man; and I persisted: "It would only be a seven days' wonder. I never heard of a clergyman's running away to be married; but they must have sometimes done it. Come, I don't believe you'd have to plead hard with Miss Bentley, and Mrs. March and I will aid and abet you to the limit of our small ability. I'm sure that if I wrap up warm against the night air, she will let me go and help you hold the rope-ladder taut."

X

It was not very reverent to his cloth, or his recent tragical mood, but Glendenning was not offended; he laughed with a sheepish pleasure, and that evening he came with Miss Bentley to call upon us. The visit passed without unusual confidences until they rose to go, when she said abruptly to me: "I feel that we both owe you a great deal, Mr. March. Arthur has been telling me of your talk this afternoon, and I think that what you said was all so wise and true! I don't mean," she added, "your suggestion about putting an end to the anomaly!" and she and Glendenning both laughed.

My wife said, "That was very wicked, and I have scolded him for thinking of such a thing." She had, indeed, forgotten that she had put it in my head, and made me wholly responsible for it.

"Then you must scold me too a little, Mrs. March," said the girl, "for I've sometimes wondered if I couldn't work Arthur up to the point of making me run away with him," which was a joke that wonderfully amused us all.

I said, "I shouldn't think it would be so difficult;" and she retorted:

"Oh, you've no idea how obdurate clergymen are;" and then she went on, seriously, to thank me for talking Glendenning out of his morbid mood. With the frankness sometimes characteristic of her she said that if he had released her, it would have made no difference—she should still have felt herself bound to him; and until he should tell her that he no longer cared for her, she should feel that he was bound to her. I saw no great originality in this reproduction of my own ideas. But when Miss Bentley added that she believed her mother herself would be shocked and disappointed if they were to give each other up, I was aware of being in the presence of a curious psychological fact. I so wholly lost myself in the inquiry it

William Dean Howells

invited that I let the talk flow on round me unheeded while I questioned whether Mrs. Bentley did not derive a satisfaction from her own and her daughter's mutual opposition which she could never have enjoyed from their perfect agreement. She had made a certain concession in consenting to the engagement, and this justified her to herself in refusing her consent to the marriage, while the ingratitude of the young people in not being content with what she had done formed a grievance of constant avail with a lady of her temperament. From what Miss Bentley let fall, half seriously, half jokingly, as well as what I observed, I divined a not unnatural effect of the strained relations between her and her mother. She concentrated whatever resentment she felt upon Miss Bentley, insomuch that it seemed as though she might altogether have withdrawn her opposition if it had been a question merely of Glendenning's marriage. So far from disliking him, she was rather fond of him, and she had no apparent objection to him except as her daughter's husband. It had not always been so; at first she had an active rancor against him; but this had gradually yielded to his invincible goodness and sweetness.

"Who could hold out against him?" his betrothed demanded, fondly, when these facts had been more or less expressed to us; and it was not the first time that her love had seemed more explicit than his. He smiled round upon her, pressing the hand she put in his arm; for she asked this when they stood on our threshold ready to go, and then he glanced at us with eyes that fell bashfully from ours.

"Oh, of course it will come right in time," said my wife when they were gone, and I agreed that they need only have patience. We had all talked ourselves into a cheerful frame concerning the affair; we had seen it in its amusing aspects, and laughed about it; and that seemed almost in itself to dispose of Mrs. Bentley's opposition. My wife and I decided that this could not long continue; that by-and-by she would become tired of it, and this would happen all the sooner if the lovers submitted absolutely, and did nothing to remind her of their submission.

The Conwells came home from Europe the next summer, and we did not go again to Gormanville. But from time to time we heard of the Bentleys, and we heard to our great amaze that there was no change in the situation, as concerned Miss Bentley and Glendenning. I think that later it would have surprised us if we had learned that there was a change. Their lives all seemed to have adjusted themselves to the conditions, and we who were mere spectators came at last to feel nothing abnormal in them.

Now and then we saw Glendenning, and now and then Miss Bentley came to call upon Mrs. March, when she was in town. Her mother had given up her Boston house, and they lived the whole year round at Gormanville, where the air was good for Mrs. Bentley without her apparently being the better for it; again, we heard in a roundabout way that their circumstances were not so fortunate as they had been, and that they had given up their Boston house partly from motives of economy.

There was no reason why our intimacy with the lovers' affairs should continue, and it did not. Miss Bentley made mention of Glendenning, when my wife saw her, with what Mrs. March decided to be an abiding fealty, but without offer of confidence; and Glendenning, when we happened to meet at rare intervals, did not invite me to more than formal inquiry concerning the well-being of Mrs. Bentley and her daughter.

He was undoubtedly getting older, and he looked it. He was one of those gentle natures which put on fat, not from self-indulgence, but from want of resisting force, and the clerical waistcoat that buttoned black to his throat swayed decidedly beyond a straight line at his waist. His red-gold hair was getting thin, and though he wore it cut close all round, it showed thinner on the crown than on the temples, and his pale eyebrows were waning. He had a settled patience of look which would have been a sadness, if there had not been mixed with it an air of resolute cheerfulness. I am not sure that this kept it from being sad, either.

Miss Bentley, on her part, was no longer the young girl she was when we met on the *Corinthian*. She must then have been about twenty, and she was now twenty-six, but she looked thirty. Dark people show their age early, and she showed hers in cheeks that grew thinner if not paler, and in a purple shadow under her fine eyes. The parting of her black hair was wider than it once was, and she wore it smooth in apparent disdain of those arts of fluffing and fringing which give an air of vivacity, if not of youth. I should say she had always been a serious girl, and now she showed the effect of a life that could not have been gay for any one.

The lovers promised themselves, as we knew, that Mrs. Bentley would relent, and abandon what was more like a whimsical caprice than a settled wish. But as time wore on, and she gave no sign of changing, I have wondered whether some change did not come upon them, which affected them towards each other without affecting their constancy. I fancied their youthful passion taking on the sad color of patience, and contenting itself more and more with such friendly companionship as their fate afforded; it became, without marriage, that affectionate comradery which wedded love passes into with the lapse of as many years as they had been plighted. "What," I once suggested to my wife, in a very darkling mood—"what if they should gradually grow apart, and end in rejoicing that they had never been allowed to join their lives? Wouldn't that be rather Hawthornesque?"

"It wouldn't be true," said Mrs. March, "and I don't see why you should put such a notion upon Hawthorne. If you can't be more cheerful about it, Basil, I wish you wouldn't talk of the affair at all."

"Oh, I'm quite willing to be cheerful about it, my dear," I returned; "and, if you like, we will fancy Mrs. Bentley coming round and ardently wishing their marriage, and their gayly protesting that after having given the matter a great deal of thought they had decided it would be better not to marry, but to live on separately for their own sake, just as they have been doing for hers so long. Wouldn't that be cheerful?"

Mrs. March said that if I wished to tease it was because I had no ideas on the subject, and she would advise me to drop it. I did so, for the better part of the evening, but I could not relinquish it altogether. "Do you think," I asked, finally, "that any sort of character will stand the test of such a prolonged engagement?"

"Why not? Very indifferent characters stand the test of marriage, and that's indefinitely prolonged."

"Yes, but it's not indefinite itself. Marriage is something very distinct and permanent; but such an engagement as this has no sort of future. It is a mere motionless present, without the inspiration of a common life, and with no hope of release from durance except through a chance that it will be sorrow instead of joy. I should think they would go to pieces under the strain."

"But as you see they don't, perhaps the strain isn't so great after all."

"Ah," I confessed, "there is that wonderful adaptation of the human soul to any circumstances. It's the one thing that makes me respect our fallen nature. Fallen? It seems to me that we ought to call it our risen nature; it has steadily mounted with the responsibility that Adam took for it—or Eve."

"I don't see," said my wife, pursuing her momentary advantage, "why they should not be getting as much pleasure or happiness out of life as most married people. Engagements are supposed to be very joyous, though I think they're rather exciting and restless times, as a general thing. If they've settled down to being merely engaged, I've no doubt they've decided to make the best of being merely engaged as long as her

William Dean Howells

mother lives."

"There is that view of it," I assented.

XII

By the following autumn Glendenning had completed the seventh year of his engagement to Miss Bentley, and I reminded my wife that this seemed to be the scriptural length of a betrothal, as typified in the service which Jacob rendered for Rachel. "But *he* had a prospective father-in-law to deal with," I added, "and Glendenning a mother-in-law. That may make a difference."

Mrs. March did not join me in the humorous view of the affair which I took. She asked me if I had heard anything from Glendenning lately; if that were the reason why I mentioned him.

"No," I said; "but I have some office business that will take me to Gormanville to-morrow, and I did not know but you might like to go too, and look the ground over, and see how much we have been suffering for them unnecessarily." The fact was that we had now scarcely spoken of Glendenning or the Bentleys for six months, and our minds were far too full of our own affairs to be given more than very superficially to theirs at any time. "We could both go as well as not," I suggested, "and you could call upon the Bentleys while I looked after the company's business."

"Thank you, Basil, I think I will let you go alone," said my wife. "But try to find out how it is with them. Don't be so terribly straightforward, and let it look as if that was what you came for. Don't make the slightest advance towards their confidence. But do let them open up if they will."

"My dear, you may depend upon my asking no leading questions whatever, and I shall behave with far more discretion than if you were with me. The danger is that I shall behave with too much, for I find that my interest in their affair is very much faded. There is every probability that unless Glendenning speaks of his engagement it won't be spoken of at all."

William Dean Howells

This was putting it rather with the indifference of the past six months than with the feeling of the present moment. Since I had known that I was going to Gormanville, the interest I denied had renewed itself pretty vividly for me, and I was intending not only to get everything out of Glendenning that I decently could, but to give him as much good advice as he would bear. I was going to urge him to move upon the obstructive Mrs. Bentley with all his persuasive force, and I had formulated some arguments for him which I thought he might use with success. I did not tell my wife that this was my purpose, but all the same I cherished it, and I gathered energy for the enforcement of my views for Glendenning's happiness from the very dejection I was cast into by the outward effect of the Gormanville streets. They were all in a funeral blaze of their shade trees, which were mostly maples, but were here and there a stretch of elms meeting in arches almost consciously Gothic over the roadway; the maples were crimson and gold, and the elms the pale yellow that they affect in the fall. A silence hung under their sad splendors which I found deepen when I got into what the inhabitants called the residential part. About the business centre there was some stir, and here in the transaction of my affairs I was in the thick of it for a while. Everybody remembered me in a pleasant way, and I had to stop and pass the time of day, as they would have said, with a good many whom I could not remember at once. It seemed to me that the maples in front of St. Michael's rectory were rather more depressingly gaudy than elsewhere in Gormanville; but I believe they were only thicker. I found Glendenning in his study, and he was so far from being cast down by their blazon that I thought him decidedly cheerfuller than when I saw him last. He met me with what for him was ardor; and as he had asked me most cordially about my family, I thought it fit to inquire how the ladies at the Bentley place were.

"Why, very well, very well indeed," he answered, brightly. "It's very odd, but Edith and I were talking about you all only last night, and wishing we could see you again. Edith is most uncommonly well. During the summer Mrs. Bentley had some rather severer attacks than usual, and the care and anxiety told upon Edith, but since the cooler weather has come she has picked up wonderfully." He did not say that Mrs. Bentley had shared this gain, and I imagined that he had a reluctance to confess she had not. He went on, "You're going to stay and spend the night with me, aren't you?"

"No," I said; "I'm obliged to be off by the four-o'clock train. But if I may be allowed to name the hospitality I could accept, I should say luncheon."

"Good!" cried Glendenning, gayly. "Let us go and have it at the Bentleys'."

"Far be it from me to say where you shall lunch me," I returned. "The question isn't where, but when and how, with me."

He got his hat and stick, and as we started out of his door he began: "You'll be a little surprised at the informality, perhaps, but I'm glad you take it so easily. It makes it easier for me to explain that I'm almost domesticated at the Bentley homestead; I come and go very much as if it were my own house."

"My dear fellow," I said, "I'm not surprised at anything in your relation to the Bentley homestead, and I won't vex you with any glad inferences."

"Why," he returned, a little bashfully, "there's no explicit change. The affair is just where it has been all along. But with the gradual decline in Mrs. Bentley—I'm afraid you'll notice it—she seems rather to want me about, and at times I'm able to be of use to Edith, and so—"

He stopped, and I said, "Exactly."

He went on: "Of course it's rather anomalous, and I oughtn't to let you get the impression that she has actually conceded anything. But she shows herself much more—er, shall I say?—affectionate, and I can't help hoping there may be a change in

William Dean Howells

her mood which will declare itself in an attitude more favorable to—"

I said again, "Exactly," and Glendenning resumed:

"In spite of Edith's not having been quite so well as usual—she's wonderfully well now—it's been a very happy summer with us, on account of this change. It seems to have come about in a very natural way with Mrs. Bentley, and out of a growing regard which I can't specifically account for, as far as anything I've done is concerned."

"I think I could account for it," said I. "She must be a stonier-hearted old lady than I imagine if she hasn't felt your goodness, all along, Glendenning."

"Why, you're very kind," said the gentle creature. "You tempt me to repeat what she said, at the only time she expressed a wish to have me oftener with them: 'You've been very patient with a contrary old woman. But I sha'n't make you wait much longer.'"

"Well, I think that was very encouraging, my dear fellow."

"Do you?" he asked, wistfully. "I thought so too, at first, but when I told Edith she could not take that view of it. She said that she did not believe her mother had changed her mind at all, and that she only meant she was growing older."

"But, at any rate," I argued, "it was pleasant to have her make an open recognition of your patience."

"Yes, that was pleasant," he said, cheerfully again, "And it was the beginning of the kind of relation that I have held ever since to her household. I am afraid I am there a good half of my time, and I believe I dine there oftener than I do at home. I am quite on the footing of a son, with her."

"There are some of the unregenerate, Glendenning," I made

bold to say, "who think it is your own fault that you weren't on the footing of a son-in-law with her long ago. If you'll excuse my saying so, you have been, if anything, too patient. It would have been far better for all if you had taken the bit in your teeth six or seven years back—"

He drew a deep breath. "It wouldn't have done; it wouldn't have done! Edith herself would never have consented to it."

"Did you ever ask her?"

"No," he said, innocently. "How could I?"

"And of course *she* could never ask *you*," I laughed. "My opinion is that you have lost a great deal of time unnecessarily. I haven't the least doubt that if you had brought a little pressure to bear with Mrs. Bentley herself, it would have sufficed."

He looked at me with a kind of dismay, as if my words had carried conviction, or had roused a conviction long dormant in his heart. "It wouldn't have done," he gasped.

"It isn't too late to try, yet," I suggested.

"Yes, it's too late. We must wait now." He hastened to add, "Until she yields entirely of herself."

He gave me a guilty glance when he drew near the Bentley place and we saw a buggy standing at the gate. "The doctor!" he said, and he hurried me up the walk to the door.

The door stood open and we heard the doctor saying to some one within: "No, no, nothing organic at all, I assure you. One of the commonest functional disturbances."

Miss Bentley appeared at the threshold with him, and she and Glendenning had time to exchange a glance of anxiety and of smiling reassurance, before she put out her hand in greeting to me, a very glad and cordial greeting, apparently. The doctor and I shook hands, and he got himself away with what I afterwards remembered as undue quickness, and left us to Miss Bentley.

Glendenning was quite right about her looking better. She looked even gay, and there was a vivid color in her checks such as I had not seen there for many years; her lips were red, her eyes brilliant. Her face was still perhaps as thin as ever, but it was indescribably younger.

I cannot say that there were the materials of a merrymaking amongst us, exactly, and yet I remember that luncheon as rather a gay one, with some laughing. I had not been till now in discovering that Miss Bentley had a certain gift of humor, so shy and proud, if I may so express it, that it would not show itself except upon long acquaintance, and I distinctly perceived now that this enabled her to make light of a burden that might otherwise have been intolerable. It qualified her to treat with cheerfulness the grimness of her mother, which had certainly not grown less since I saw her last, and to turn into something like a joke her valetudinarian austerities of sentiment and opinion. She made a pleasant mock of the amenities which passed between her mother and Glendenning, whose gingerliness in the acceptance of the old lady's condescension would, I confess, have been notably comical without this gloss. It was perfectly evident that Mrs. Bentley's favor was bestowed with a mental reservation, and conditioned upon his forming no expectations from it, and poor Glendenning's eagerness to show that he took it upon these terms was amusing as well as touching. I do not know how to express that Miss Bentley contrived to eliminate herself from the affair, or to have the effect of doing that, and to abandon it to them. I can only say that she left them to be civil to each other, and that, except when she recurred to them in playful sarcasm from time to time, she devoted herself to me.

Evidently, Mrs. Bentley was very much worse than she had been; her breathing was painfully labored. But if her daughter had any anxiety about her condition, she concealed it most effectually from us. I decided that she had perhaps been asking the doctor as to certain symptoms that had alarmed her, and it was in the rebound from her anxiety that her spirits had risen to the height I saw. Glendenning seized the moment of her absence after luncheon, when she helped her mother up to her room, to impart to me that this was his conclusion too. He said that he had not seen her so cheerful for a long time, and when I praised her in every way he basked in my appreciation of her as if it had all been flattery for himself. She came back directly, and then I had a chance to see what she might have been under happier stars. She could not, at any moment, help showing herself an intellectual and cultivated woman, but her opportunities to show herself a woman of rare social gifts had been scanted by circumstances and perhaps by conscience. It seemed to me that even in devoting herself to her mother as she had always done she need not have enslaved herself, and that it was in this excess her inherited puritanism came out. She might sometimes openly rebel against her mother's domination, as my wife and I had now and again seen her do; but inwardly she was almost passionately submissive. Here I thought that Glendenning, if he had been a different sort of man, might have been useful to her; he might have encouraged her in a little wholesome selfishness, and enabled her to withhold sacrifice where it was needless. But I am not sure; perhaps he would have made her more unhappy, if he had attempted this; perhaps he was the only sort of man whom, in her sense of his own utter unselfishness, she could have given her heart to in perfect peace. She now talked brilliantly and joyously to me, but all the time her eye sought his for his approval and sympathy; he, for his part, was content to listen in a sort of beatific pride in her which he did not, in his simple-hearted fondness, make any effort to mask.

When we came away he made himself amends for his silence by a long hymn in worship of her, and I listened with all the acquiescence possible. He asked me questions—whether I had noticed this thing or that about her, or remembered what she had said upon one point or another, and led up to

William Dean Howells

compliments of her which I was glad to pay. In the long ordeal they had undergone they had at least kept all the freshness of their love.

XIII

Glendenning and I went back to the rectory, and sat down in his study, or rather he made me draw a chair to the open door, and sat down himself on a step below the threshold. The day was one of autumnal warmth; the haze of Indian summer blued the still air, and the wind that now and then stirred the stiff panoply of the trees was lullingly soft. This part of Gormanville quite overlooked the busier district about the mills, where the water-power found its way, and it was something of a climb even from the business street of the old hill village, which the rival prosperity of the industrial settlement in the valley had thrown into an aristocratic aloofness. From the upper windows of the rectory one could have seen only the red and yellow of the maples, but from the study door we caught glimpses past their boles of the outlying country, as it showed between the white mansions across the way. One of these, as I have already mentioned, was the Conwell place; and after we had talked of the landscape awhile, Glendenning said: "By the way! Why don't you buy the Conwell place? You liked it so much, and you were all so well in Gormanville. The Conwells want to sell it, and it would be just the thing for you, five or six months of the year."

I explained, almost compassionately, the impossibility of a poor insurance man thinking of a summer residence like the Conwell place, and I combated as well as I could the optimistic reasons of my friend in its favor. I was not very severe with him, for I saw that his optimism was not so much from his wish to have me live in Gormanville as from the new hope that filled him. It was by a perfectly natural, if not very logical transition that we were presently talking of this greater interest again, and Glendenning was going over all the plans that it included. I encouraged him to believe, as he desired, that a sea-voyage would be the thing for Mrs. Bentley, and that it would be his duty to take her to Europe as soon as he was in authority to do so. They should always, he said, live in Gormanville, for they were greatly attached to the place, and they should keep up the old Bentley homestead in the style that he thought they owed to the region where the Bentleys had always lived. It is a comfort to a man to tell his dreams, whether of the night or of the day, and I enjoyed Glendenning's pleasure in rehearsing these fond reveries of his.

He interrupted himself to listen to the sound of hurried steps, and directly a man in his shirt-sleeves came running by on the sidewalk beyond the maples. In a village like Gormanville any passer is of interest to the spectator, and a man running is of thrilling moment. Glendenning started to his feet, and moved forward for a better sight of the flying passer. He called out to the man, who shouted back something I could not understand, and ran on.

"What did he say?"

"I don't know." Glendenning's face as he turned to me again was quite white. "It is Mrs. Bentley's farmer," he added, feebly, and I could see that it was with an effort he kept himself from sinking. "Something has happened."

"Oh, I guess not, or not anything serious," I answered, with an effort to throw off the weight I suddenly felt at my own heart. "People have been known to run for a plumber. But if you're anxious, let us go and see what the matter is."

I turned and got my hat; Glendenning came in for his, but seemed unable to find it, though he stood before the table where it lay. I had to laugh, though I felt so little like it, as I put it in his hand.

"Don't leave me," he entreated, as we hurried out through the maples to the sidewalk. "It has come at last, and I feel, as I always knew I should, like a murderer."

"What rubbish!" I retorted. "You don't know that anything has happened. You don't know what the man's gone for."

"Yes, I do," he said. "Mrs. Bentley is—He's gone for the doctor."

As he spoke a buggy came tearing down the street behind us; the doctor was in it, and the man in shirt-sleeves beside him. We did not try to hail them, but as they whirled by the farmer turned his face, and again called something unintelligible to Glendenning.

We made what speed we could after them, but they were long out of sight in the mile that it seemed to me we were an hour in covering before we reached the Bentley place. The doctor's buggy stood at the gate, and I perceived that I was without authority to enter the house, on which some unknown calamity had fallen, no matter with what good-will I had come; I could see that Glendenning had suffered a sudden estrangement, also, which he had to make a struggle against. But he went in, leaving me without, as if he had forgotten me.

I could not go away, and I walked down the path to the gate, and waited there, in case I should be in any wise wanted. After a very long time the doctor came bolting over the walk towards me, as if he did not see me, but he brought himself up short with an "Oh!" before he actually struck against me. I had known him during our summer at the Conwell place, where we used to have him in for our little ailments, and I would never have believed that his round, optimistic face could look so worried. I read the worst in it; Glendenning was right; but I asked the doctor, quite as if I did not know, whether there was anything serious the matter.

"Serious—yes," he said. "Get in with me; I have to see another patient, but I'll bring you back." We mounted into his buggy, and he went on. "She's in no immediate danger, now. The faint lasted so long I didn't know whether we should bring her out of it, at one time, but the most alarming part is over for the present. There is some trouble with the heart, but I don't think anything organic."

"Yes, I heard you telling her daughter so, just before lunch. Isn't it a frequent complication with asthma?"

"Asthma? Her daughter? Whom are you talking about?"

"Mrs. Bentley. Isn't Mrs. Bentley—"

"No!" shouted the doctor, in disgust, "Mrs. Bentley is as well as ever. It's Miss Bentley. I wish there was a thousandth part of the chance for her that there is for her mother."

XIV

I stayed over for the last train to Boston, and then I had to go home without the hope which Miss Bentley's first rally had given the doctor. My wife and I talked the affair over far into the night, and in the paucity of particulars I was almost driven to their invention. But I managed to keep a good conscience, and at the same time to satisfy the demand for facts in a measure by the indulgence of conjectures which Mrs. March continually took for them. The doctor had let fall, in his talk with me, that he had no doubt Miss Bentley had aggravated the affection of the heart from which she was suffering by her exertions in lifting her mother about so much; and my wife said that it needed only that touch to make the tragedy complete.

"Unless," I suggested, "you could add that her mother had just told her she would not oppose her marriage any longer, and it was the joy that brought on the access of the trouble that is killing her."

"Did the doctor say that?" Mrs. March demanded, severely.

"No. And I haven't the least notion that anything like it happened. But if it had—"

"It would have been too tawdry. I'm ashamed of you for thinking of such a thing, Basil."

Upon reflection, I was rather ashamed myself; but I plucked up courage to venture: "It would be rather fine, wouldn't it, when that poor girl is gone, if Mrs. Bentley had Glendenning come and live with her, and they devoted themselves to each other for her daughter's sake?"

"Fine! It would be ghastly. What are you thinking of, my dear? How would it be fine?"

"Oh, I mean dramatically," I apologized, and, not to make bad worse, I said no more.

The next day, which was Sunday, a telegram came for me, which I decided, without opening it, to be the announcement of the end. But it proved to be a message from Mrs. Bentley, begging in most urgent terms that Mrs. March and I would come to her at once, if possible. These terms left the widest latitude for surmise, but none for choice, in the sad circumstances, and we looked up the Sunday trains for Gormanville, and went.

We found the poor woman piteously grateful, but by no means so prostrated as we had expected. She was rather, as often happens, stayed and held upright by the burden that had been laid upon her, and it was with fortitude if not dignity that she appealed to us for our counsel, and if possible our help, in a matter about which she had already consulted the doctor. "The doctor says that the excitement cannot hurt Edith; it may even help her, to propose it. I should like to do it, but if you do not think well of it, I will not do it. I know it is too late now to make up to her for the past," said Mrs. Bentley, and here she gave way to the grief she had restrained hitherto.

"There is no one else," she went on, "who has been so intimately acquainted with the facts of my daughter's engagement—no one else that I can confide in or appeal to."

We both murmured that she was very good; but she put our politeness somewhat peremptorily aside.

"It is the only thing I can do now, and it is useless to do that now. It will be no reparation for the past, and it will be for myself and not for her, as all that I have done in the past has been; but I wish to know what you think of their getting married now."

I am afraid that if we had said what we thought of such a tardy and futile proof of penitence we should have brought little comfort to the mother's heart, but we looked at each other in the disgust we both felt and said there would be a sacred fitness in it.

She was apparently much consoled.

It was touching enough, and I at least was affected by her tears; I am not so sure my wife was. But she had instantly to consider how best to propose the matter to Miss Bentley, and to act upon her decision.

After all, as she reported the fact to me later, it was very simple to suggest her mother's wish to the girl, who listened to it with a perfect intelligence in which there was no bitterness.

"They think I am going to die," she said, quietly, "and I can understand how she feels. It seems such a mockery; but if she wishes it; and Arthur—"

It was my part to deal with Glendenning, and I did not find it so easy.

"Marriage is for life and for earth," he said, solemnly, and I thought very truly. "In the resurrection we shall be one another's without it. I don't like to go through the form of such a sacrament idly; it seems like a profanation of its mystery."

"But if Miss Bentley—"

"She will think whatever I do; I shall feel as she does," he answered, with dignity.

"Yes, I know," I urged. "It would not be for her; it would not certainly be for yourself. But if you could see it as the only form of reparation which her mother can now offer you both, and the only mode of expressing your own forgiveness— Recollect how you felt when you thought that it was Mrs. Bentley's death; try to recall something of that terrible time—"

William Dean Howells

"I don't forget that," he relented. "It was in mercy to Edith and me that our trial is what it is: we have recognized that in the face of eternity. I can forgive anything in gratitude for that."

*   *   *   *   *

I have often had to criticise life for a certain caprice with which she treats the elements of drama, and mars the finest conditions of tragedy with a touch of farce. No one who witnessed the marriage of Arthur Glendenning and Edith Bentley had any belief that she would survive it twenty-four hours; they themselves were wholly without hope in the moment which for happier lovers is all hope. To me it was like a funeral, but then most weddings are rather ghastly to look upon; and the stroke that life had in reserve perhaps finally restored the lost balance of gayety in this. At any rate, Mrs. Glendenning did live, and she is living yet, and in rather more happiness than comes to most people under brighter auspices. After long contention among many doctors, the original opinion that her heart trouble was functional, not organic, has been elected final, and upon these terms she bids fair to live as long as any of us.

I do not know whether she will live as long as her mother, who seems to have taken a fresh lease of years from her single act of self-sacrifice. I cannot say whether Mrs. Bentley feels herself deceived and defrauded by her daughter's recovery; but I have made my wife observe that it would be just like life if she bore the young couple a sort of grudge for unwittingly outwitting her. Certainly, on the day we lately spent with them all at Gormanville, she seemed, in the slight attack of asthma from which she suffered, to come as heavily and exactingly upon both as she used to come upon her daughter alone. But I was glad to see that Glendenning eagerly bore the greater part of the common burden. He grows stouter and stouter, and will soon be the figure of a bishop.

THE PURSUIT OF THE PIANO

I

Hamilton Gaites sat breakfasting by the window of a restaurant looking out on Park Square, in Boston, at a table which he had chosen after rejecting one on the Boylston Street side of the place because it was too noisy, and another in the little open space, among evergreens in tubs, between the front and rear, because it was too chilly. The wind was east, but at his Park Square window it tempered the summer morning air without being a draught; and he poured out his coffee with a content in his circumstance and provision which he was apt to feel when he had taken all the possible pains, even though the result was not perfect. But now, he had real French bread, as good as he could have got in New York, and the coffee was clear and bright. A growth of crisp green watercress embowered a juicy steak, and in its shade, as it were, lay two long slices of bacon, not stupidly broiled to a crisp, but delicately pink, and exemplarily lean. Gaites had already had a cantaloupe, whose spicy fragrance lingered in the air and mingled with the robuster odors of the coffee, the steak, and the bacon.

He owned to being a fuss, but he contended that he was a cheerful fuss, and when things went reasonably well with him, he was so. They were going well with him now, not only in the small but in the large way. He was sitting there before that capital breakfast in less than half an hour after leaving the sleeping-car, where he had passed a very good night, and he was setting out on his vacation, after very successful work in the June term of court. He was in prime health; he had a good conscience in leaving no interests behind him that could suffer in his absence; and the smile that he bent upon the Italian waiter as he retired, after putting down the breakfast, had some elements of a benediction.

There was a good deal of Gaites's smile, when it was all on: he had a generous mouth, full of handsome teeth, very white and even, which all showed in his smile. His whole face took part in the smile, and it was a charming face, long and rather quaintly narrow, of an amiable aquilinity, and clean-shaven. His figure, tall and thin, comported well with his style of visage, and at a given moment, when he suddenly rose and leaned from the window, eagerly following something outside with his eye, he had an alert movement that was very pleasant.

The thing outside which had caught, and which now kept, his eye as long as he could see it, was a case in the shape of an upright piano, on the end of a long, heavy-laden truck, making its way with a slow, jolting progress among the carts, carriages, and street cars, out of the square round the corner toward Boylston Street. On the sloping front of the case was inscribed an address, which seemed to gaze at Gaites with the eyes of the girl whom it named and placed, and to whom in the young man's willing fancy it attributed a charming quality. Nothing, he felt, could be more suggestive, more expressive of something shy, something proud, something pure, something pastoral yet patrician, something unaffected and yet *chic*, in an unknown personality, than the legend:

Miss Phyllis Desmond,
Lower Merritt,
New Hampshire.

Via S. B. & H. C. R. R.

Like most lawyers, he had a vein of romance, and this now opened in pleasing conjectures concerning the girl. He knew just where Lower Merritt was, and so well what it was like that a vision of its white paint against the dark green curtain of the wooded heights around it filled his sense as agreeably as so much white marble. There was the cottage of some summer people well above the village level, among pines and birches, and overlooking the foamiest rush of the Saco, to which he instantly destined the piano of Phyllis Desmond. He had never known that these people's name was Desmond, and he had certainly never supposed that they had a daughter called Phyllis; but he divined these facts in losing sight of the truck; and he imagined with as logical probability that one of the little girls whom he used to see playing on the hill-slope before the cottage had grown up into the young lady whose name the piano bore. There was quite time enough for this transformation; it was seven years since Gaites had run up into the White Mountains for a month's rest after his last term in the Harvard Law School, and before beginning work in the office of the law firm in New York where he had got a clerkship, and where he had now a junior partnership. The little girl was then just ten years old, and now, of course, the young lady was seventeen, or would be when the piano reached Lower Merritt, for it was clearly meant to arrive on her birthday; it was a birthday-present and a surprise. He had always liked the way those nice people let their children play about barefoot; it would be in character with them to do a fond, pretty thing like that; and Gaites smiled for pleasure in it, and then rather blushed in relating the brown legs of the little girl, as he remembered seeing them in her races over her father's lawn, to the dignified young lady she had now become.

He amused himself in mentally following the piano on its way to the Sea Board & Hill Country R. R. freight-depot, which he was quite able to do from a habit of Boston formed during his four years in the academic course and his three years in the law-school at Harvard. He knew that it would cross Boylston into Charles Street, and keep along that level to Cambridge; then it would turn into McLane Street, and again into Lynde, by this means avoiding the grades as much as possible, and arriving through Causeway Street at the long, low freight-depot of the S. B. & H. C., where it would be the first thing unloaded from the truck. It would stand indefinitely on the outer platform; and then, when the men in flat, narrow-peaked silk caps and grease-splotched overalls got round to it, with an air of as much personal indifference as if they were mere mechanical agencies, it would be pulled and pushed into the dimness of the interior, cool, and pleasantly smelling of pine, and hemp, and flour, and dried fruit, and coffee, and tar, and leather, and fish. There it would abide, indefinitely again, till in the same large impersonal way it was pulled and pushed out on the platform beside the track, where a freight-car marked for the Hill Country division of the road, with devices intelligible to the train-men, had been shunted down by a pony engine in obedience to mystical semaphoric gesticulations, from the brakeman risking his life for the purpose among the rails, addressed to the engineer keeping his hand on the pulse of the locomotive, and his head out of the cab window to see how near he could come to killing the brakeman without doing it.

Gaites witnessed the whole drama with an interest that held him suspended between the gulps and morsels of his breakfast, and at times quite arrested the processes of mastication and deglutition. That pretty girl's name on the slope of the piano-case continued to look at him from the end of the truck; it smiled at him from the outer platform of the freight-house; it entreated him with a charming trepidation from the dim interior; again it smiled on the inner platform; and then, from the safety of the car, where the case found itself ensconced among freight of a neat and agreeable character, the name had the effect of intrepidly blowing him a kiss as the train-man slid the car doors together and fastened them. He drew a long breath when the train had backed and bumped down to the car, and the couplers had clashed together, and the maniac, who had not been mashed in dropping the coupling-pin into its socket, scrambled out from the wheels, and frantically worked his arms to the potential homicide in the locomotive cab, and the train had jolted forward on the beginning of its run.

That was the last of the piano, and Gaites threw it off his mind, and finished his breakfast at his leisure. He was going to spend his vacation at Kent Harbor, where he knew some agreeable people, and where he knew that a young man had many chances of a good time, even if he were not the youngest kind of young man. He had spent two of his Harvard vacations there, and he knew this at first hand. He could not and did not expect to do so much two-ing on the rocks and up the river as he used; the zest of that sort of thing was past, rather; but he had brought his golf stockings with him, and a quiverful of the utensils of the game, in obedience to a lady who had said there were golf-links at Kent, and she knew a young lady who would teach him to play.

He was going to stop off at Burymouth, to see a friend, an old Harvard man, and a mighty good fellow, who had rather surprised people by giving up New York, and settling in the gentle old town on the Piscatamac. They accounted for it as well as they could by his having married a Burymouth girl; and since he had begun, most unexpectedly, to come forward in literature, such of his friends as had seen him there said it was just the place for him. Gaites had not yet seen him there, and he had a romantic curiosity, the survival of an intensified friendship of their Senior year, to do so. He got to thinking of this good fellow rather vividly, when he had cleared his mind of Miss Desmond's piano, and he did not see why he should not take an earlier train to Burymouth than he had intended to take; and so he had them call him a coupe from the restaurant, and he got into it as soon as he left the breakfast-table.

He gave the driver the authoritative address, "Sea Board Depot," and left him to take his own way, after resisting a rather silly impulse to bid him go through Charles Street.

The man drove up Beacon, and down Temple through Staniford, and naturally Gaites saw nothing of Miss Desmond's piano, which had come into his mind again in starting. He did not know the colonnaded structure, with its stately *porte-cochere*, where his driver proposed to leave him, instead of the

William Dean Howells

formless brick box which he remembered as the Sea Board Depot, and he insisted upon that when the fellow got down to open the door.

"Ain't no Sibbod Dippo, now," the driver explained, contemptuously. "Guess Union Dippo'll do, though;" and Gaites, a little overcome with its splendor, found that it would. He faltered a moment in passing the conductor and porter at the end of the Pullman car on his train, and then decided that it would be ridiculous to take a seat in it for the short run to Burymouth. In the common coach he got a very good seat on the shady side, where he put down his hand-bag. Then he looked at his watch, and as it was still fifteen minutes before train-time, he indulged a fantastic impulse. He left the car and hurried back through the station and out through the electrics, hacks, herdics, carts, and string-teams of Causeway Street, and up the sidewalk of the street opening into it, as far as the S. B. & H. C. freight-depot. On the way he bet himself five dollars that Miss Desmond's piano would not be there, and lost; for at the moment he came up it was unloading from the end of the truck which he had seen carrying it past the window of his restaurant.

The fact amused him quite beyond the measure of anything intrinsically humorous in it, and he staid watching the exertions of the heated truckman and two silk-capped, sarcastic-faced freight-men, till the piano was well on the platform. He was so intent upon it that his interest seemed to communicate itself to a young girl coming from the other quarter, with a suburban, cloth-sided, crewel-initialed bag in her hand, as if she were going to a train. She paused in the stare she gave the piano-case, and then slowed her pace with a look over her shoulder after she got by. In this her eyes met his, and she blushed and hurried on; but not so soon that he had not time to see she had a thin face of a pathetic prettiness, gentle brown eyes with wistful brows, under ordinary brown hair. She was rather little, and was dressed with a sort of unaccented propriety, which was as far from distinction as it was from pretension.

When Gaites got back to his car, a few minutes before the train was to start, he found the seat where he had left his hand-bag and light overcoat more than half full of a bulky lady, who looked stupidly up at him, and did not move or attempt any excuse for crowding him from his place. He had to walk the whole length of the car before he came to a vacant seat. It was the last of the transverse seats, and at the moment he dropped into it, the girl who had watched the unloading of the piano with him passed him, and took the sidewise seat next the door.

She took it with a weary resignation which somehow made Gaites ashamed of the haste with which he had pushed forward to the only good place, and he felt as guilty of keeping her out of it as if he had known she was following him. He kept a remorseful eye upon her as she arranged her bag and umbrella about her, with some paper parcels which she must have had sent to her at the station. She breathed quickly, as if from final hurry, but somewhat also as if she were delicate; and tried to look as if she did not know he was watching her. She had taken off one of her gloves, and her hand, though little enough, showed an unexpected vigor with reference to her face, and had a curious air of education.

When the train pulled out of the station into the clearer light, she turned her face from him toward the forward window, and the corner of her mouth, which her half-averted profile gave him, had a kind of piteous droop which smote him to keener regret. Once it lifted in an upward curve, and a gay light came into the corner of her eye; then the mouth drooped again, and the light went out.

Gaites could bear it no longer; he rose and said, with a respectful bow: "Won't you take my seat? That seems such a very inconvenient place for you, with the door opening and shutting."

The girl turned her face promptly round and up, and answered, with a flush in her thin cheek, but no embarrassment in her tone, "No, I thank you. This will do quite well," and then she turned her face away as before.

He had not meant his politeness for an overture to her acquaintance, but he felt as justly snubbed as if he had; and he sank back into his seat in some disorder. He tried to hide his confusion behind the newspaper he opened between them; but from time to time he had a glimpse of her round the side of it, and he saw that the hand which clutched her bag all the while tightened upon it and then loosened nervously.

II

"Ah, I see what you mean," said Gaites, with a kind of finality, as his friend Birkwall walked him homeward through the loveliest of the lovely old Burymouth streets. Something equivalent had been in his mind and on his tongue at every dramatic instant of the afternoon; and, in fact, ever since he had arrived from the station at Birkwall's door, where Mrs. Birkwall met them and welcomed him. He had been sufficiently impressed with the aristocratic quiet of the vast square white old wooden house, standing behind a high white board fence, in two acres of gardened ground; but the fine hallway with its broad low stairway, the stately drawing-room with its carving, the library with its panelling and portraits, and the dining-room with its tall wainscoting, united to give him a sense of the pride of life in old Burymouth such as the raw splendors of the millionaire houses in New York had never imparted to him.

"They knew how to do it, they knew how to do it!" he exclaimed, meaning the people who had such houses built; and he said the same thing of the other Burymouth houses which Birkwall showed him, by grace of their owners, after the midday dinner, which Gaites kept calling luncheon.

"Be sure you get back in good time for *tea*," said Mrs. Birkwall for a parting charge to her husband; and she bade Gaites, "Remember that it *is* tea, please; *not* dinner;" and he was tempted to kiss his hand to her with as much courtly gallantry as he could; for, standing under the transom of the slender-pillared portal to watch them away, she looked most distinctly descended from ancestors, and not merely the daughter of a father and mother, as most women do. Gaites said as much to Birkwall, and when they got home Birkwall repeated it to his wife, without injuring Gaites with her. If he saw what Birkwall had meant in marrying her, and settling down to his literary life with her in the atmosphere of such a quiet place as Burymouth, when he might have chosen money and unrest in

New York, she on her side saw what her husband meant in liking the shrewd, able fellow who had such a vein of gay romance in his practicality, and such an intelligent and respectful sympathy with her tradition and environment.

She sent and asked several of her friends to meet him at tea; and if in that New England disproportion of the sexes which at Burymouth is intensified almost to a pure gynocracy these friends were nearly all women, he found them even more agreeable than if they had been nearly all men. It seemed to him that he had never heard better talk than that of these sequestered ladies, who were so well bred and so well read, so humorous and so dignified, who loved to laugh and who loved to think. It was all like something in a pleasant book, and Gaites was not altogether to blame if it went to his head, and after the talk had been of Burymouth, in which he professed so acceptable an interest, and then of novels, of which he had read about as many as they, he confided to the whole table his experience with Miss Phyllis Desmond's piano. He managed the psychology of the little incident so well that he imparted the very quality he meant them to feel in it.

"How perfectly charming!" said one of the ladies. "I don't wonder you fell in love with the name. It's fit for a shepherdess of high degree."

"If *I* were a man," said the girl across the table who was not less sweetly a girl because she would never see thirty-nine again, "I should simply drop everything and follow that piano to Phyllis Desmond's door."

"It's quite what I should like to do," Gaites responded, with a well-affected air of passionate regret. "But I'm promised at Kent Harbor—"

She did not wait for him to say more, but submitted, "Oh, well, if you're going to Kent *Harbor*, of course!" as if that would excuse and explain any sort of dereliction; and then the talk went on about Kent Harbor till Mrs. Birkwall asked, generally, as if it were part of the Kent Harbor inquiry, "Didn't I hear that the Ashwoods were going to their place at Upper Merritt, this year?"

Then there arose a dispute, which divided the company into nearly equal parties; as to whether the Ashwoods had got home from Europe yet. But it all ended in bringing the talk back to Phyllis Desmond's piano again, and in urging its pursuit upon Gaites, as something he owed to romance; at least he ought to do it for their sake, for now they should all be upon pins and needles till they knew who she was, and what she *could* be doing at Lower Merritt, N. H.

At one time he had it on his tongue to say that there seemed to be something like infection in his interest in that piano, and he was going to speak of the young girl who seemed to share it, simply because she saw him staring at it, and who faltered so long with him before the freight-depot that she came near getting no seat in the train for Burymouth. But just at that moment the dispute about the Ashwoods renewed itself upon some fresh evidence which one of the ladies recollected and offered; and Gaites's chance passed. When it came again he had no longer the wish to seize it. A lingering soreness from his experience with that young girl made itself felt in his nether consciousness. He forbore the more easily because, mixed with this pain, was a certain insecurity as to her quality which he was afraid might impart itself to those patrician presences at the table. They would be nice, and they would be appreciative,—but would they feel that she was a lady, exactly, when he owned to the somewhat poverty-stricken simplicity of her dress in some details, more especially her thread gloves, which he could not consistently make kid? He was all the more bound to keep her from slight because he felt a little, a very little ashamed of her.

He woke next morning in a wide, low, square chamber to the singing of robins in the garden, from which at breakfast he had luscious strawberries, and heaped bowls of June roses. When he started for his train, he parted with Mrs. Birkwall as old

William Dean Howells

friends as he was with her husband; and he completed her conquest by running back to her from the gate, and asking, with a great air of secrecy, but loud enough for Birkwall to hear, whether she thought she could find him another girl in Burymouth, with just such a house and garden, and exactly like herself in every way.

"Hundreds!" she shouted, and stood a graceful figure between the fluted pillars of the portal, waving her hand to them till they were out of sight behind the corner of the high board fence, over which the garden trees hung caressingly, and brushed Gaites's shoulder in a shy, fond farewell.

It had all been as nice as it could be, and he said so again and again to Birkwall, who *would* go to the train with him, and who would *not* let him carry his own hand-bag. The good fellow clung hospitably to it, after Gaites had rechecked his trunk for Kent Harbor, and insisted upon carrying it as they walked up and down the platform together at the station. It seemed that the train from Boston which the Kent Harbor train was to connect with was ten minutes late, and after some turns they prolonged their promenade northward as far as the freight-depot, Birkwall in the abstraction of a plot for a novel which he was seizing these last moments to outline to his friend, and Gaites with a secret shame for the hope which was springing in his breast.

On a side track stood a freight-car, from which the customary men in silk caps were pulling the freight, and standing it about loosely on the platform. The car was detached from the parent train, which had left it not only orphaned on this siding, but apparently disabled; for Gaites heard the men talking about not having cut it out a minute too soon. One of them called, in at the broad low door, to some one inside, "All out?" and a voice from far within responded, "Case here, yet; *I* can't handle it alone."

The others went into the car, and then, with an interval for some heavy bumping and some strong language, they reappeared at the door with the case, which Gaites was by this time not surprised to find inscribed with the name and address of Miss Phyllis Desmond. He remained watching it, while the men got it on the platform, so wholly inattentive to Birkwall's plot that the most besotted young author could not have failed to feel his want of interest. Birkwall then turned his vision outward upon the object which engrossed his friend, and started with an "Oh, hello!" and slapped him on the back.

Gaites nodded in proud assent, and Birkwall went on: "I thought you were faking the name last night; but I didn't want to give you away. It was the real thing, wasn't it, after all."

"The real thing," said Gaites, with his most toothful smile, and he laughed for pleasure in his friend's astonishment.

"Well," Birkwall resumed, "she seems to be following *you* up, old fellow. This will be great for Polly, and for Miss Seaward, who wanted you to follow *her* up; and for all Burymouth, for that matter. Why, Gaites, you'll be the tea-table talk for a week; you'll be married to that girl before you know it. What is the use of flying in the face of Providence? Come! There's time enough to get a ticket, and have your check changed from Kent Harbor to Lower Merritt, and the Hill Country express will be along here at nine o'clock. You can't let that poor thing start off on her travels alone again!"

Gaites flushed in a joyful confusion, and put the joke by as well as he could. But he was beginning to feel it not altogether a joke; it had acquired an element of mystery, of fatality, which flattered while it awed him; and he could not be easy till he had asked one of the freight-handlers what had happened to the car. He got an answer—flung over the man's shoulder—which seemed willing enough, but was wholly unintelligible in the clang and clatter of a passenger-train which came pulling in from the southward.

"Here's the Hill Country express now!" said Birkwall. "You won't change your mind? Well, your Kent Harbor train backs down after this goes out. Don't worry about the piano. I'll find out what's happened to the car it was in, and I'll see that it's put into a good strong one, next time."

"Do! That's a good fellow!" said Gaites, and in repeated promises, demanded and given, to come again, they passed the time till the Hill Country train pulled out and the Kent Harbor train backed down.

III

Gaites was going to stay a week with a friend out on the Point; and after the first day he was so engrossed with the goings-on at Kent Harbor that he pretty well forgot about Burymouth, and the piano of Miss Phyllis Desmond lingered in his mind like the memory of a love one has outlived. He went to the golf links every morning in a red coat, and in plaid stockings which, if they did not show legs of all the desired fulness, attested a length of limb which was perhaps all the more remarkable for that reason. Then he came back to the beach and bathed; at half past one o'clock he dined at somebody's cottage, and afterwards sat smoking seaward in its glazed or canopied veranda till it was time to go to afternoon tea at somebody else's cottage, where he chatted about until he was carried off by his hostess to put on a black coat for seven or eight o'clock supper at the cottage of yet another lady.

There was a great deal more society than there had been in his old college-vacation days, when the Kent Harbor House reigned sole in a perhaps somewhat fabled despotism; but the society was of not less simple instincts, and the black coat which Gaites put on for supper was never of the evening-dress convention. Once when he had been out canoeing on the river very late, his hostess made him go "just as he was," and he was consoled on meeting their bachelor host to find that he had had the inspiration to wear a flannel shirt of much more outing type than Gaites himself had on.

The thing that he had to guard against was not to praise the river sunsets too much at any cottage on the Point; and in cottages on the river, not to say a great deal of the surf on the rocks. But it was easy to respect the amiable local susceptibilities, and Gaites got on so well that he told people he was never going away.

He had arrived at this extreme before he received the note from Mrs. Birkwall, which she made his prompt bread-and-butter letter the excuse of writing him. She wrote mainly to remind him of his promise to stay another day with her husband on his way home through Burymouth; and she alleged an additional claim upon him because of what she said she had made Birkwall do for him. She had made him go down to the freight-depot every day, and see what had become of Phyllis Desmond's piano; and she had not dared write before, because it had been most unaccountably delayed there for the three days that had now passed. Only that morning, however, she had gone down herself with Birkwall; and it showed what a woman could do when she took anything in hand. Without knowing of her approach except by telepathy, the railroad people had bestirred themselves, and she had seen them with her own eyes put the piano-case into a car, and had waited till the train had bumped and jolted off with it towards Mewers Junction. All the ladies of her supper party, she declared, had been keenly distressed at the delay of the piano in Burymouth, and she was now offering him the relief which she had shared already with them.

He laughed aloud in reading this letter at breakfast, and he could not do less than read it to his hostess, who said it was charming, and at once took a vivid interest in the affair of the piano. She accepted in its entirety his theory of its being a birthday-present for the young girl with that pretty name; and she professed to be in a quiver of anxiety at its retarded progress.

"And, by-the-way," she added, with the logic of her sex, "I'm just going to the station to see what's become of a trunk myself that I ordered expressed from Chicago a week ago. If you're not doing anything this morning—the tide isn't in till noon, and there'll be little or no bathing to look at before that—you'd better drive down with me. Or perhaps you're canoeing up the river with somebody?"

Gaites said he was not, and if he were he would plead a providential indisposition rather than miss driving with her to the station.

"Well, anyway," she said, tangentially, "I can get June Alber to go too, and you can take her canoeing afterwards."

But Miss Alber was already engaged for canoeing, and Gaites was obliged to drive off with his hostess alone. She said she did pity him, but she pitied him no longer than it took to get at the express agent. Then she began to pity herself, and much more energetically if not more sincerely, for it seemed that the agent had not been able to learn anything about her trunk, and was unwilling even to prophesy concerning it. Gaites left him to question at her hands, which struck him as combining all the searching effects of a Roentgen-ray examination and the earlier procedure with the rack; and he wandered off, in a habit which he seemed to have formed, toward the freight-house.

He amused himself thinking what he should do if he found Phyllis Desmond's piano there, but he was wholly unprepared to do anything when he actually found it standing on the platform, as if it had just been put out of the freight-car which was still on the siding at the door. He passed instantly from the mood of gay conjecture in which he was playing with the improbable notion of its presence to a violent indignation.

"Why, look here!" he almost shouted to a man in a silk cap and greased overalls who was contemplating the inscription on the slope of its cover, "what's that piano doing *here*?"

The man seemed to accept him as one having authority to make this demand, and responded mildly, "Well, that's just what I was thinking myself."

"That piano," Gaites went on with unabated violence, "started from Boston at the beginning of the week; and I happen to know that it's been lying two or three days at Burymouth, instead of going on to Lower Merritt, as it ought to have done at once. It ought to have been in Lower Merritt Wednesday afternoon at the latest, and here it is at Kent Harbor Saturday morning!"

William Dean Howells

The man in the silk cap scanned Gaites's figure warily, as if it might be that of some official whale in disguise, and answered in a tone of dreamy suggestion: "Must have got shifted into the wrong car at Mewers Junction, somehow. Or maybe they started it wrong from Burymouth."

Mrs. Maze was coming rapidly down the platform toward them, leaving the express agent to crawl flaccidly into his den at the end of the passenger-station, with the air of having had all his joints started.

"Just look at this, Mrs. Maze," said Gaites when she drew near enough to read the address on the piano-case. She did look at it; then she looked at Gaites's face, into which he had thrown a sort of stony calm; and then she looked back at the piano-case.

"No!" she exclaimed and questioned in one.

Gaites nodded confirmation.

"Then it won't be there in time for the poor thing's birthday?"

He nodded again.

Mrs. Maze was a woman who never measured her terms, perhaps because there was nothing large enough to measure them with, and perhaps because in their utmost expansion they were a tight fit for her emotions.

"Well, it's an abominable outrage!" she began. She added: "It's a burning shame! They'll never get over it in the world; and when it comes lagging along after everything's over, she won't care a pin for it! How did it happen?"

Gaites mutely referred her, with a shrug, to the man in the silk cap, and he again hazarded his dreamy conjecture.

"Well, it doesn't matter!" she said, with a bitterness that was a great comfort to Gaites. "What are you going to do about it?"

she asked him.

"I don't know what *can* be done about it," he answered, referring himself to the man in the silk cap.

The man said, "No freight out, now, till Monday."

Mrs. Maze burst forth again: "If I had the least confidence in the world in any human express company, I would send it by express and pay the expressage myself."

"Oh, I couldn't let you do that, Mrs. Maze," Gaites protested. "Besides, I don't suppose they'd allow us to take it out of the freight, here, unless we had the bill of lading."

"Well," cried Mrs. Maze, passionately, "I can't bear to think of that child's suspense. It's perfectly heart-sickening. Why shouldn't they telegraph? They ought to telegraph! If they let things go wandering round the earth at this rate, the least they can do is to telegraph and relieve people's minds. We'll go and make the station-master telegraph!"

But even when the station-master was found, and made to understand the case, and to feel its hardship, he had his scruples. "I don't think I've got any right to do that," he said.

"Of coarse I'll pay for the telegram," Mrs. Maze interpolated.

"It ain't that exactly," said the station-master. "It might look as if I was meddling myself. I rather not, Mrs. Maze."

She took fire. "Then *I'll* meddle myself!" she blazed. "There's nothing to hinder my telegraphing, I suppose!"

"*I* can't hinder you," the station-master admitted.

"Well, then!" She pulled a bunch of yellow telegraph blanks toward her, and consumed three of them in her comprehensive despatch:

William Dean Howells

Miss Phyllis Desmond,

Lower Merritt, N. H.

Piano left Boston Monday P. M. Broke down on way to Burymouth, where delayed four days. Sent by mistake to Kent Harbor from Mewers Junction. Forwarded to Lower Merritt Monday.

"There! How will that do?" she asked Gaites, submitting the telegram to him.

"That seems to cover the ground," he said, not so wholly hiding the misgiving he began to feel but that she demanded,

"It explains everything, doesn't it?"

"Yes—"

"Very well; sign it, then!"

"I?"

"Certainly. She doesn't know me."

"She doesn't know me, either," said Gaites. He added: "And a man's name—"

"To be sure! Why didn't I think of that?" and she affixed a signature in which the baptismal name gave away her romantic and impulsive generation—Elaine W. Maze. "*Now,*" she triumphed, as Gaites helped her into her trap—"*now* I shall have a little peace of my life!"

IV

Mrs. Maze had no great trouble in making Gaites stay over Sunday. The argument she used was, "No freight out till Monday, you know." The inducement was June Alber, whom she said she had already engaged to go canoeing with Gaites Sunday afternoon.

That afternoon was exquisite. The sky was cloudless, and of one blue with the river and the girl's eyes, as Gaites noted while she sat facing him from the bow of the canoe. But the day was of the treacherous serenity of a weather-breeder, and the next morning brought a storm of such violence that Mrs. Maze declared it would be a foolhardy risk of his life for Gaites to go; and again she enforced her logic with Miss Alber, whom she said she had asked to one-o'clock dinner, with a few other friends.

Gaites stayed, of course, but he atoned for his weakness by starting early Tuesday morning, so as to get the first Hill Country train from Boston at Burymouth. He had decided that to get in as much change of air as possible he had better go to Craybrooks for the rest of his vacation.

His course lay through Lower Merritt, and perhaps he would have time to run out from the train and ask the station-master (known to him from his former sojourn) who Miss Phyllis Desmond was. His mind was not so full of Miss June Alber but that he wished to know.

It was still raining heavily, and on the first cut beyond Porchester Junction his train was stopped by a flagman, sent back from a freight-train. There was a wash-out just ahead, and the way would be blocked for several hours yet, if not longer. The express backed down to Porchester, and there seemed no choice for Gaites, if he insisted upon going to Craybrooks, but to take the first train up the old Boston and Montreal line to Wells River and across by the Wing Road through Fabyans; and this was what he did, arriving very late, but quite in time for all he had to do at Craybrooks.

The next day the weather cleared up cold, after the storm, and the fat old ladies, who outnumber everybody but the thin young girls at summer hotels, made the landlord put the steam on in the corridors, and toasted themselves before the log fires on the spectacular hall hearth. Gaites walked all day, and at night he lounged by the lamp, trying to read, and wished himself at Kent Harbor. The blue eyes of June Alber made themselves one with the sky and the river again, and all three laughed at him for his folly in leaving the certain delight they embodied for the vague good of a whim fulfilled. Was this the change he had come to the mountains for? He could throw his hat into the clouds that hung so low in the defile where the hotel lurked, and that was something; but it was not so much to the purpose, now that he had it, as June Alber and the sky and the river, which he had no longer. As he drowsed by the fire in a break of the semicircle of old ladies before it, he suddenly ceased to think of June Alber and the Kent sky and river, and found himself as it were visually confronted with that pale, delicate girl in thread gloves; she was facing him from the bow of a canoe in the train at Boston, where he had first met her, and some one was saying, "Oh, she's a Desmond, through and through."

He woke to the sound of a quick snort, in which he suspected a terminal character when he glanced round the semicircle of old ladies and found them all staring at him. From the pain in his neck he knew that his head had been hanging forward on his breast, and, in the strong belief that he had been publicly disgracing himself, he left the place, and went out on the piazza till his shame should be forgotten. Of course, the sound of the name Desmond had been as much a part of his dream as the sight of that pale girl's face; but he felt, while he paced the veranda, the pull of a strong curiosity to make sure of the fact. From time to time he looked in through the window, without courage to return. At last, when the semicircle was reduced to the bulks of the two ladies who had sat nearest him, he went in, and took a place with a newspaper at the lamp just behind them.

They stopped their talk and recognized him with an exchange of consciousness. Then, as if compelled by an irresistible importance in their topic, they began again; that is, one of them began to talk again, and the other to listen, and Gaites from almost the first word joined the listener with all his might, though he diligently held up his paper between himself and the speaker and pretended to be reading.

"Yes," she said, "they must have had their summer home there nearly twenty years. Lower Merritt was one of the first places opened up in that part of the mountains, and I guess the Desmonds built the first cottage there."

The date given would make the young lady whom he remembered from her childhood romps on her father's lawn somewhat older than he imagined, but not too old for the purposes of his romance.

The speaker began to collect her needlework into the handkerchief on her lap as she went on, and he listened with an intensified abandon.

"I guess," she continued, "that they pass most of the year there. After he lost his money, he had to give up his house in town, and I believe they have no other home now. They did use to travel some, winters, but I guess they don't much any more; if they don't stay there the whole winter through, I don't believe they get much farther now than Portland, or Burymouth, at the furthest. It seems to me as if I heard that one of the girls was going to Boston last winter to take piano lessons at the Conservatory, so as to teach; but—"

She stopped with a definite air, and rolled her knitting up into her handkerchief. Gaites made a merit to himself of rising abruptly and closing his paper with a clash, as if he had been trying to read and had not been able for the talking near him.

The ladies looked round conscience-stricken; when they saw who it was, they looked indignant.

V

In the necessity, which we all feel, of making practical excuses to ourselves for a foolish action, he pretended that he had been at Craybrooks long enough, and that now, since he had derived all the benefit to be got from the west-side air, it was best to begin his homestretch on the other slope of the hills. His real reason was that he wished to stop at Lower Merritt and experience whatever fortuities might happen to him from doing so. He wished, in other words, to see Phyllis Desmond, or, failing this, to find out whether her piano had reached her.

It had now a pathos for him which had been wanting earlier in his romance. It was no longer a gay surprise for a young girl's birthday; it was the sober means of living to a woman who must work for her living. But he found it not the less charming for that; he had even a more romantic interest in it, mingled with the sense of patronage, of protection, which is so agreeable to a successful man.

He began to long for some new occasion of promoting the arrival of the piano in Lower Merritt, and he was so far from regretting his former interventions that at the first junction where his train stopped he employed the time in exploring the freight-house in the vain hope of finding it there, and urging the road to greater speed in its delivery to Miss Desmond. He was now not at all ashamed of the stand he had taken in the matter at former opportunities, and he was not abashed when a man in a silk cap demanded, across the twilight of the freight-house, in accents of the semi-sarcasm appropriate in addressing a person apparently not minding his own business, "Lost something?"

"Yes, I have," answered Gaites with just effrontery. "I've lost an upright piano. I started with it from Boston ten days or a fortnight ago, and I've found it everywhere I've stopped, and sometimes where I didn't stop. How long, in the course of nature, ought an upright piano to take in getting to this point

William Dean Howells

from Boston, anyway?"

The man obviously tasted the sarcasm in Gaites's tone, and dropped it from his own, but he was sulkier if more respectful than before in answering: "'D ought a come right through in a couple of days. 'D ought a been here a week ago."

"Why isn't it here now, then?"

"Might 'a' got off on some branch road, by mistake, and waited there till it was looked up. You see," the man continued, resting an elbow on the tall casing of a chest of drawers, and dropping to a more confidential level in his manner, "an upright piano ain't like a passenger. It don't kick if it's shunted off on the wrong line. As a gene'l rule, freight don't complain of the route it travels by, and it ain't in a hurry to arrive."

"Oh!" said Gaites, with a sympathetic sneer.

"But it ain't likely," said the man, who now pushed his hat far back on his head, in the interest of self-possession, "that it's gone wrong. With all these wash-outs and devilments, the last fo't-night, it might a' been travellin' straight and not got the'a, yet. What d'you say was the address?"

"Lower Merritt," said Gaites, beginning to feel a little uncomfortable.

"Name?" persisted the man.

"Miss Phyllis Desmond," Gaites answered, now feeling really silly, but unable to get away without answering.

"That ain't your name?" the man suggested, with reviving sarcasm.

"No, it isn't!" Gaites retorted, angrily, aware that he was giving himself away in fine shape.

"Oh, I see," the man mocked. "Friend o' the family. Well, I guess you'll find your piano at Lower Merritt, all right, in two-three weeks." He was now openly offensive, as with a sense of having Gaites in his power.

A locomotive-bell rang, and Gaites started toward the doorway. "Is that my train?"

The man openly laughed. "Guess it is, if you're goin' to Lower Merritt." As Gaites shot through the doorway toward his train, he added, in an insolent drawl, "Miss—Des—mond!"

Gaites was so furious when he got back to the smoking-room of the parlor-car that he was sorry for several miles that he had not turned back and kicked the man, even if it lost him his train. But this was only while he was under the impression that he was furious with the man. When he discovered that he was furious with himself, for having been all imaginable kinds of an ass, he perceived that he had done the wisest thing he could in leaving the man to himself, and taking up the line of his journey again. What remained mortifying was that he had bought his ticket and checked his bag to Lower Merritt, which he wished never to hear of again, much less see.

He rang for the porter and consulted him as to what could be done toward changing the check on his bag from Lower Merritt to Middlemount Junction; and as it appeared that this was quite feasible, since his ticket would have carried him two stations beyond the Junction, he had done it. He knew the hotel at Middlemount, and he decided to pass the night there, and the next day to go back to Kent Harbor and June Alber, and let Lower Merritt and Phyllis Desmond take care of themselves from that time forward.

While the driver of the Middlemount House barge was helping the station-master-and-baggage-man (they were one) put the arriving passengers' trunks into the wagon for the Middlemount House, Gaites paced up and down the long platform in the remnant of his excitement, and vowed himself to have nothing more to do with Miss Desmond's piano, even if it should turn up then and there and personally appeal to him for help. In this humor he was not prepared to have anything of the kind happen, and he stood aghast, in looking absently into a freight-car standing on the track, to read, "Miss Phyllis Desmond, Lower Merritt, N. H.," on the slope of the now familiar case just within the open doorway. It was as if the poor girl were personally there pleading for his help with the eyes whose tenderness he remembered.

The united station-master-and-baggage-man, who appeared also to be the freight agent, came lounging down the platform toward him. He was so exactly of the rustic railroad type that he confused Gaites with a doubt as to which functionary, of the many he now knew, this was.

"Go'n' to walk over to the hotel?" he asked.

"Yes," Gaites faltered, and the man abruptly turned, and made the gesture for starting a locomotive to the driver of the Middlemount stage.

"All right, Jim!" he shouted, and the stage drove off.

"What time can I get a train for Lower Merritt this afternoon?" asked Gaites.

"Four o'clock," said the man. "This freight goes out first;" and now Gaites noticed that up on a siding beyond the station an engine with a train of freight-cars was fretfully fizzing. The engineer put a silk-capped head out of the cab window and looked back at the station-master, who began to work his arms like a semaphore telegraph. Then the locomotive tooted, the bell rang, and the freight-train ran forward on the switch to the main track, and commenced backing down to where they stood. Evidently it was going to pick up the car with Phyllis Desmond's piano in it.

"When does this freight go out?" Gaites palpitated.

"'Bout ten minutes," said the station-master.

"Does it stop at Lower Merritt?"

"Leaves this cah the'a," said the man, as if surprised into the admission.

"Can I go on her?" Gaites pursued, breathlessly.

"Well, I guess you'll have to talk to this man about that," and the station-master indicated, with a nod of his head, the freight conductor, who was swinging himself down from the caboose, now come abreast of them on the track. A brakeman had also jumped down, and the train fastened on to the waiting car, under his manipulation, with a final cluck and jolt.

The conductor and station-master exchanged large oblong Manila-paper envelopes, and the station-master said, casually, "Here's a man wants to go to Lower Merritt with you, Bill."

The conductor looked amused and interested. "Eva travel in a caboose?"

"No."

"Well, I guess you can stand it fo' five miles, anyway."

He turned and left Gaites, who understood this for permission, and clambered into the car, where he found himself in a rude but far from comfortless interior. There was a sort of table or desk in the middle, with a heavy chair or two before it; round the side of the car were some leather-covered benches, suitable for the hard naps which seemed to be taken on them, if he could guess from the man in overalls asleep on one.

The conductor came in, after the train started, and seemed disposed to be sociable. He had apparently gathered from the station-master so much of Gaites's personal history as had accumulated since he left the express train at Middlemount.

"Thought you'd try a caboose for a little change from a pahla-cah," he suggested, humorously.

"Well, yes," Gaites partially admitted. "I did intend to stay over at Middlemount when I left the express there, but I changed my mind and decided to go on. It's very good of you to let me come with you."

"'Tain't but a little way to Lowa Merritt," the conductor explained, defensively. "Eva been the'a?"

"Oh, yes; I passed a week or so there once, after I left college. Are you acquainted there?"

"I'm *from* the'a. Used to wo'k fo' the Desmonds—got that summa place up the side of the mountain—before I took to the ro-ad."

"Oh, yes! Have they still got it?"

"Yes. Or it's got *them*. Be glad to sell it, I guess, since the old man lost his money. But Lowa Merritt's kind o' gone down as a summa roso't. Tryin' ha'd to bring it up, though. Know the Desmonds?"

"No, not personally."

"Nice fo-aks," said the conductor, providing himself for conversational purposes with a splinter from the floor. He put it between his teeth and continued: "I took ca' thei' hosses, one while, as long's they *had* any, before I went on the ro-ad. Old gentleman kep' up a show till he died; then the fam'ly found out that they hadn't much of anything but the place left. Girls had to do something, and one of 'em got a place in a school out West—smaht, *all* of 'em; the second one kind o' runs the fahm; and the youngest, here, 's been fittin' for a music-teacha. Why, I've got a piano for her in this cah that we picked up at Middlemount, *now*. Been two wintas at the Conservatory in Boston. Got talent enough, they tell *me*. Undastand 't she means to go to Pohtland in the fall and try to get pupils, *the'a.*"

"Not if *I* can help it!" thought Gaites, with a swelling heart; and then he blushed for his folly.

VI

Gaites found some notable changes in the hotel at Lower Merritt since he had last sojourned there. It no longer called itself a Hotel, but an Inn, and it had a brand-new old-fashioned swinging sign before its door; its front had been cut up into several gables, and shingled to the ground with shingles artificially antiquated, so that it looked much grayer than it naturally ought. Within it was equipped for electric lighting; and there was a low-browed aesthetic parlor, where, when Gaites arrived and passed to a belated dinner in the dining-room, an orchestra, consisting of a lady pianist and a lady violinist, was giving the closing piece of the afternoon concert. The dining-room was painted a self-righteous olive-green; it was thoroughly netted against the flies, which used to roost in myriads on the cut-paper around the tops of the pillars, and a college-student head waiter ushered Gaites through the gloom to his place with a warning and hushing hand which made him feel as if he were being shown to a pew during prayers.

He escaped as soon as possible from the refection which, from the soup to the ice-cream, had hardly grown lukewarm, and went out to walk by a way that he knew well, and which had for him now a romantically pathetic interest. It was, of course, the way past the Desmond cottage, which, when he came in sight of it round the shoulder of upland where it stood, was curiously strange, curiously familiar. It needed painting badly, and the grounds had a sadly neglected air. The naked legs of little girls no longer twinkled over the lawn, which was grown neglectedly up to low-bush blackberries.

Gaites hurried past with a lump in his throat, and returned by another road to the Inn, where his long ramble ended just as the dining-room doors were opened behind their nettings for supper. At this cheerfuler moment he found the head waiter much more conversible than at the hour of his retarded dinner, and Gaites made talk with him, as the young follow lingered beside his chair, with one eye on the door for the behoof of other guests.

Gaites said he had found great changes in Lower Merritt since he had been there some years before, and he artfully led the talk up to the Desmonds. The head waiter was rather vague about their past; but he was distinct enough about their present, and said the young ladies happened all to be at home. "I don't know," he added, "whether you noticed our lady orchestra when you came in to dinner to-day?"

"Yes, I did," said Gaites. "I was very much interested. I thought they played charmingly, and I was sorry that I got in only for the close of the last piece."

"Well," the head waiter consoled him, "you'll have a chance to hear them again to-night; they're going to play for the hop. I don't know," he added again, "whether you noticed the lady at the piano."

"I noticed that she had a pretty head, which she carried gracefully, but it was against the window, and I couldn't make out the face."

"That," said the head waiter, with pride either in the fact or for the effect it must produce, "was Miss Phyllis Desmond."

Gaites started as satisfactorily as could be wished. "Indeed?"

"Yes; she's engaged to play here the whole summer." The head waiter fumbled with the knife and fork at the place opposite, and blushed. "But you'll hear her to-night yourself," he ended incoherently, and hurried away, to show another guest to his, or rather her, place.

Gaites wondered why he felt suddenly angry; why he resented the head waiter's blush as an impertinence and a liberty. After all, the fellow was a student and probably a gentleman; and if he chose to help himself through college by taking that menial role during the summer, rather than come upon the charity of his friends or the hard-earned savings of a poor old father, what had any one to say against it? Gaites had nothing to say against it; and yet that blush, that embarrassment of a man who had pulled out his chair for him, in relation to such a girl as Miss Phyllis Desmond, incensed him so much that he could not enjoy his supper. He did not bow to the head waiter when he held the netting-door open for him to go out, and he felt the necessity of taking the evening air in another stroll to cool himself off.

Of course, if the poor girl was reduced to playing in the hotel orchestra for the money it would give her, she had come down to the level of the head waiter, and they must meet as equals. But the thought was no less intolerable for that, and Gaites set out with the notion of walking away from it. At the station, however, which was in friendly proximity to the Inn, his steps were stayed by the sound of girlish voices, rising like sweetly varied pipes from beyond the freight-depot. Their youth invited his own to look them up, and he followed round to the back of the depot, where he came upon a sight which had, perhaps from the waning light, a heightened charm. Against the curtain of low pines which had been gradually creeping back upon the depot ever since the woods were cut away to make room for it, four girls were posed in attitudes instinctively dramatic and vividly eager, while as many men were employed in getting what Gaites at once saw to be Miss Phyllis Desmond's piano into the wagon backed up to the platform of the depot. Their work was nearly accomplished, but at every moment of what still remained to be done the girls emitted little shrieks, laughs, and moans of intense interest, and fluttered in their light summer dresses against the background of the dark evergreens like anxious birds.

At last the piano was got into the middle of the wagon, the inclined planks withdrawn and loaded into it, and the tail-board snapped to. Three of the men stepped aside, and one of them jumped into the front of the wagon and gathered up the reins from the horses' backs. He called with mocking challenge to the group of girls, "Nobody goin' to git up here and keep this piano from tippin' out?"

A wild clamor rose from the girls, settling at last into staccato cries.

"You've got to *do* it, Phyl!"

"Yes, Phyllis, you *must* get in!"

"It's *your* piano, Phyl. You've got to keep it from tipping out!"

"No, no! I won't! I can't! I'm not going to!" one voice answered to all, but apparently without a single reference to the event; for in the end the speaker gave her hand to the man in the wagon, and with many small laughs and squeaks was pulled up over the hub and tire of a front wheel, and then stood staying herself against the piano-case, with a final lamentation of "Oh, it's a shame! I'll never speak to any of you again! How perfectly mean! *Oh!*" The last exclamation signalized the start of the horses at a brisk mountain trot, which the driver presently sobered to a walk. The three remaining girls followed, mocking and cheering, and after them lounged the three remaining men, at a respectful distance, marking the social interval between them, which was to be bridged only in some such moment of supreme excitement as the present.

It was no question with Gaites whether he should bring up the end of the procession; he could not think of any consideration that would have stayed him. He scarcely troubled himself to keep at a fit remove from the rest; and as he followed in the deepening twilight he felt a sweet, unselfish gladness of heart that the poor girl whom he had seen so wan and sad in Boston should be the gay soul of this pretty triumph.

The wagon drove into the grounds of the Desmond cottage, and backed up to the edge of the veranda. Lights appeared, and voices came from within. One of the men, despatched to the barn for a hatchet, came flickering back with a lantern also; lamps brought out of the house were extinguished by the evening breeze (in spite of luminous hands held near the chimney to shelter them), amidst the joyful applause of all the girls and the laughter of the men. A sound of hammering rose, and then a sound of boards rending from the clutch of nails, and then a sound of pieces thrown loosely into a pile. There was a continual flutter of women's dresses and emotions, and this did not end even when the piano, disclosed from its casing and all its wraps, was pushed indoors, and placed against the parlor wall, where a flash of lamp-light revealed it to Gaites in final position.

He lingered still, in the shelter of some barberry-bushes at the cottage gate, and not till the last cry of gratitude had been answered by the unanimous disclaimer of the men rattling away in the wagon did he feel that his pursuit of the piano had ended.

VII

"Can you tell me, madam," asked Gaites of an obviously approachable tabby next the chimney-corner, "which of the musicians is Miss Desmond?"

He had hurried back to the Inn, and got himself early into a dress suit that proved wholly inessential, and was down among the first at the hop. This function, it seemed, was going on in the parlor, which summed in itself the character of ball-room as well as drawing-room. The hop had now begun, and two young girl couples were doing what they could to rebuke the sparse youth of Lower Merritt Inn for their lack of eagerness in the evening's pleasure by dancing alone. Gaites did not even notice them, he was so intent upon the ladies of the orchestra, concerning whom he was beginning to have a troubled mind, not to say a dark misgiving.

"Oh," the approachable tabby answered, "it's the one at the piano. The violinist is Miss Axewright, of South Newton. They were at the Conservatory together in Boston, and they are such friends! Miss Desmond would never have played here—intends to take pupils in Portland in the winter—if Miss Axewright hadn't come," and the pleasant old tabby purred on, with a velvety pat here, and a delicate scratch there. But Gaites heard with one ear only; the other was more devotedly given to the orchestra, which also claimed both his eyes. While he learned, as with the mind of some one else, that the Desmonds had been very much opposed to Phyllis's playing at the Inn, but had consented partly with their poverty, because they needed everything they could rake and scrape together, and partly with their will, because Miss Axewright was such a nice girl, he was painfully adjusting his consciousness to the fact that the girl at the piano was not the girl whom he had seen at Boston and whom he had so rashly and romantically decided to be Miss Phyllis Desmond. The pianist was indeed Miss Desmond, but to no purpose, if the violinist was some one else; it availed as little that the violinist was the illusion that had lured him to Lower Merritt in pursuit of Miss Desmond's piano, if she were really Miss Axewright of South Newton.

What remained for him to do was to arrange for his departure by the first train in the morning; and he was subjectively accounting to the landlord for his abrupt change of mind after he had engaged his room for a week, while he was intent with all his upper faculties upon the graceful poses and movements of Miss Axewright. There was something so appealing in the pressure of her soft chin as it held the violin in place against her round, girlish throat that Gaites felt a lump in his own larger than his Adam's-apple would account for to the spectator; the delicately arched wrist of the hand that held the bow, and the rhythmical curve and flow of her arm in playing, were means of the spell which wove itself about him, and left him, as it were, bound hand and foot. It was in this helpless condition that he rose at the urgence of a friendly young fellow who had chosen himself master of ceremonies, and took part in the dancing; and at the end of the first half of the programme, while the other dancers streamed out on the verandas and thronged the stairways, he was aware of dangling his chains as he lounged toward the ladies of the orchestra. The volunteer master of ceremonies had half shut himself across the piano in his eager talk with Miss Desmond, and he readily relinquished Miss Axewright to Gaites, who willingly devoted himself to her, after Miss Desmond had risen in acknowledgment of his bow. He had then perceived that she was not nearly so tall as she had seemed when seated; and a woman who sat tall and stood low was as much his aversion as if his own abnormally long legs did not render him guilty of the opposite offence.

Miss Desmond must have had other qualities and characteristics, but in his absorption with Miss Axewright's he did not notice them. He saw again the pretty, pathetic face, the gentle brown eyes, the ordinary brown hair, the sentient hands, the slight, graceful figure, the whole undistinguished, unpretentious presence, which had taken his fancy at Boston, and which he now perceived had kept it, under whatever erring impressions, ever since.

"I think we have met before, Miss Axewright," he said boldly, and he had the pleasure of seeing her pensive little visage light up with a responsive humor.

"I think we have," she replied; and Miss Desmond, whose habitual state seemed to be intense inattention to whatever directly addressed itself to her, cut in with the cry:

"You have met *before*!"

"Yes. Two weeks ago, in Boston," said Gaites. "Miss Axewright and I stopped at the S. B. & H. C. freight-depot to see that your piano started off all right."

He explained himself further, and, "Well, I don't see what you did to it," Miss Desmond pouted. "It just got here this afternoon."

"Probably they 'throwed a spell' on it, as the country people say," suggested the master of ceremonies. "But all's well that end's well. The great thing is to have your piano, Miss Phyllis. I'm coming up to-morrow morning to see if it's got here in good condition."

"That's *some* compensation," said the girl ironically; and she added, with the kind of repellent lure with which women know how to leave men the responsibility of any reciprocal approach, "I don't know whether it won't need tuning first."

"Well, I'm a piano-tunist myself," the young fellow retorted, and their banter took a course that left Miss Axewright and Gaites to themselves. The dancers began to stray in again from the stairways and verandas.

"Dear me!" said Miss Desmond, "it's time already;" and as she dropped upon the piano-stool she called to Miss Axewright with an authority of tone which Gaites thought augured well for her success as a teacher, "Millicent!"

VIII

The next morning when Gaites came down to breakfast he had a question which solved itself contrary to his preference as he entered the dining-room. He was so early that the head waiter had to jump from his own unfinished meal, and run to pull out his chair; and Gaites saw that he left at his table the landlord's family, the clerk, the housekeeper, and Miss Axewright. It appeared that she was not only staying in the hotel, but was there on terms which indeed held her above the servants, but separated her from the guests.

He hardly knew how to dissemble the feeling of humiliation mixed with indignation which flashed up in him, and which, he was afterwards afraid, must have made him seem rather curt in his response to the head waiter's civilities. Miss Axewright left the dining-room first, and he hurried out to look her up as soon as he had despatched the coffee and steak which formed his breakfast, with a wholly unreasoned impulse to offer her some sort of reparation for the slight the conditions put upon her. He found her sitting on the veranda beside the friendly tabby of his last night's acquaintance, and far, apparently, from feeling the need of reparation through him. She was very nice, though, and after chatting a little while she rose, and excused herself to the tabby, with a politeness that included Gaites, upon the ground of a promise to Miss Desmond that she would come up, the first thing after breakfast, and see how the piano was getting along.

When she reappeared, in her hat, at the front of the Inn, Gaites happened to be there, and he asked her if he might walk with her and make his inquiries too about the piano, in which, he urged, they were mutually interested. He had a notion to tell her all about his pursuit of Miss Desmond's piano, as something that would peculiarly interest Miss Desmond's friend; but though she admitted the force of his reasoning as to their common concern in the fate of the piano, and had allowed him to go with her to rejoice over its installation, some subtle instinct kept him from the confidence he had intended, and they walked on in talk (very agreeable talk, Gaites found it) which left the subject of the piano altogether intact.

This was fortunate for Miss Desmond, who wished to talk of nothing else. The piano had arrived in perfect condition. "But I don't know where the poor thing *hasn't* been, on the way," said the girl. "It left Boston fully two weeks ago, and it seems to have been wandering round to the ends of the earth ever since. The first of last week, I heard from it at Kent Harbor, of all places! I got a long despatch from there, from some unknown female, telling me it had broken down on the way to Burymouth, and been sent by mistake to Kent Harbor from Mewers Junction. Have you ever been at Kent Harbor, Mr. Gaites?"

"Oh, yes," said Gaites. This was the moment to come out with the history of his relation to the piano; but he waited.

"And can you tell me whether they happen to have a female freight agent there?"

"Not to my knowledge," said Gaites, with a mystical smile.

"Then *do* you know anybody there by the name of Elaine W. Maze?"

"Mrs. Maze? Yes, I know Mrs. Maze. She has a cottage, there."

"And can you tell me *why* Mrs. Maze should be telegraphing me about my piano?"

There was a note of resentment in Miss Desmond's voice, and it silenced the laughing explanation which Gaites had almost upon his tongue. He fell very grave in answering, "I can't, indeed, Miss Desmond."

"Perhaps she found out that it had been a long time on the way, and did it out of pure good-nature, to relieve your anxiety."

This was what Miss Axewright conjectured, but it seemed to confirm Miss Desmond's worst suspicions.

"That is what I should like to be *sure* of," she said.

Gaites thought of all his own anxieties and interferences in behalf of the piano of this ungrateful girl, and in her presence he resolved that his lips should be forever sealed concerning them. She never would take them in the right way. But he experimented with one suggestion. "Perhaps she was taken with the beautiful name on the piano-case, and couldn't help telegraphing just for the pleasure of writing it."

"Beautiful?" cried Miss Desmond. "It was my grandmother's name; and I wonder they didn't call me for my great-grand-mother, Daphne, and be done with it."

The young man who had chosen himself master of ceremonies at the hop the night before now proposed from the social background where he had hitherto kept himself, "*I* will call you Daphne."

"*You* will call me Miss Desmond, if you please, Mr. Ellett." The owner of the name had been facing her visitors from the piano-stool with her back to the instrument. She now wheeled upon the stool, and struck some chords. "I wish you'd thought to bring your fiddle, Millicent. I should like to try this piece." The piece lay on the music-rest before her.

"I will go and get it for her," said the ex-master of ceremonies.

"Do," said Miss Desmond.

"No, no," Gaites protested. "I brought Miss Axewright, and I have the first claim to bring her fiddle."

"I'm afraid you couldn't either of you find it," Miss

William Dean Howells

Axewright began.

"We'll both try," said the ex-master of ceremonies. "Where do you think it is?"

"Well, it's in the case on the piano."

"That doesn't sound very intricate," said Gaites, and they all laughed.

As soon as the two men were out of the house, the ex-master of ceremonies confided: "That name is a very tender spot with Miss Desmond. She's always hated it since I knew her, and I can't remember when I *didn't* know her."

"Yes, I could see that—too late," said Gaites. "But what I can't understand is, Miss Axewright seemed to hate it, too."

Mr. Ellett appeared greatly edified. "Did *you* notice that?"

"I think I did."

"Well, now I'll tell you just what I think. There aren't any two girls in the world that like each other better than those two. But that shows just how it is. Girls are terribly jealous, the best of them. There isn't a girl living that really likes to have another girl praised by a man, or anything about her, I don't care who the man is. It's a fact, whether you believe it or not, or whether you respect it. I don't respect it myself. It's narrow-minded. I don't deny it: they *are* narrow-minded. All the same, we can't *help* ourselves. At least, *I* can't."

Mr. Ellett broke into a laugh of exhaustive intelligence and clapped Gaites on the back.

IX

Gaites, if he did not wholly accept Ellett's philosophy of the female nature, acted in the light it cast upon the present situation. From that time till the end of his stay at Lower Merritt, which proved to be coeval with the close of the Inn for the season, and with the retirement of the orchestra from duty, he said nothing more of Miss Phyllis Desmond's beautiful name. He went further, and altogether silenced himself concerning his pursuit of her piano; he even sought occasions of being silent concerning her piano in every way, or so it seemed to him, in his anxious avoidance of the topic. In all this matter he was governed a good deal by the advice of Mr. Ellett, to whom he had confessed his pursuit of Miss Desmond's piano in all its particulars, and who showed a highly humorous appreciation of the facts. He was a sort of second (he preferred to say second-hand) cousin of Miss Desmond, and, so far as he could make out, had been born engaged to her; and he showed an intuition in the gingerly handling of her rather uncertain temper which augured well for his future happiness. His future happiness seemed to be otherwise taken care of, for though he was a young man of no particular prospects, and no profession whatever, he had a generous willingness to liberate his affianced to an artistic career; or, at least, there was no talk of her giving up her scheme of teaching the piano-forte because she was engaged to be married, he was exactly fitted to become the husband of a wage-earning wife, and was so far from being offensive in this quality that everybody (including Miss Desmond, rather fitfully) liked him; and he was universally known as Charley Ellett.

After he had quite converted Gaites to his theory of silence concerning his outlived romance, he liked to indulge himself, when he got Gaites alone with the young ladies, in speculations as to the wanderings of Miss Desmond's piano. He could always get a rise out of Miss Desmond by referring to the impertinent person who had telegraphed her about it from Kent Harbor, and he could put Gaites into a quiver of anxiety by asking him whether he had heard Mrs. Maze speak of the piano when he was at Kent Harbor, or whether he had happened to see anything of it at any of the junctions on his way to Lower Merritt. To these questions Gaites felt himself obliged to respond with lies point-blank, though there were times when he was tempted to come out with the truth, Miss Axewright seemed so amiably indifferent, or so sympathetically interested, when Ellett was airing his conjectures or pushing his investigations.

Still Gaites clung to the refuge of his lies, and upon the whole it served him well, or at least enabled him to temporize in safety, while he was making the progress in Miss Axewright's affections which, if he had not been her lover, he never would have imagined difficult. They went every day, between the afternoon and evening concerts, to walk in the Cloister, a colonnade of pines not far from the Inn, which differed from some other cloisters in being so much devoted to love-making. She was in love with him, as he was with her; but in her proud maiden soul she did not dream of bringing him to the confession she longed for. This came the afternoon of the last day they walked in the Cloister, when it seemed as if they might go on walking there forever, and never emerge from their fond, delicious, tremulous, trusting doubt of each other.

She cried upon his shoulder, with her arms round his neck, and owned that she had loved him from the first moment she had seen him in front of the S. B. & H. C. freight-depot in Boston; and Gaites tried to make his passion antedate this moment. To do so, he had to fall back upon the notion of pre-existence, but she gladly admitted his hypothesis.

The next morning brought another mood, a mood of sweet defiance, in which she was still more enrapturing. By this time the engagement was known to their two friends, and Miss Desmond came to the cars with Charley Ellett to see her off. As Gaites was going to Boston on the same train, they made it the occasion of seeing him off, too. Millicent openly declared that they two were going together, that in fact she was taking him home to show him to her family in South Newton and see whether they liked him.

Ellett put this aspect of the affair aside. "Well, then," he said, "if you're going to be in Boston together, I think you ought to see the S. B. & H. C. traffic-manager, and find out all about what kept Phyl's piano so long on the road. *I* think they owe her an explanation, and Gaites is a lawyer, and he's just the man to get it, with damages."

Gaites saw in Ellett's impudent, amusing face that he divined Millicent's continued ignorance of his romance, and was bent on mischief. But the girl paid no heed to his talk, and Gaites could not help laughing. He liked the fellow; he even liked Miss Desmond, who was so much softened by the occasion that she had all the thorny allure of a ripened barberry in his fancy. They both hung about the seat, where he stood ready to take his place beside Millicent, till the conductor shouted, "All aboard!" Then they ran out, and waved to the lovers through the window till the car started.

When they could be seen no longer, Millicent let Gaites arrange their hand-baggage together on the seat in front of them. It was a warm day, and she said she did believe she would take her hat off; and she gave it to him, odorous of her pretty hair, to put in the rack overhead. After he had done this, and sat down definitively, she shrank unconsciously closer to him, knitting her fingers in those of his hand on the seat between them.

"Now," she said, "tell me all about yourself."

"About myself?"

"Yes. About Phyllis Desmond's piano, and why you were so interested in it."

A DIFFICULT CASE

I

It was in the fervor of their first married years that the Ewberts came to live in the little town of Hilbrook, shortly after Hilbrook University had been established there under the name of its founder, Josiah Hilbrook. The town itself had then just changed its name, in compliance with the conditions of his public benefactions, and in recognition of the honor he had done it in making it a seat of learning. Up to a certain day it had been called West Mallow, ever since it was set off from the original town of Mallow; but after a hundred and seventy years of this custom it began on that day to call itself Hilbrook, and thenceforward, with the curious American acquiescence in the accomplished fact, no one within or without its limits called it West Mallow again.

The memory of Josiah Hilbrook himself began to be lost in the name he had given the place; and except for the perfunctory mention of its founder in the ceremonies of Commencement Day, the university hardly remembered him as a man, but rather regarded him as a locality. He had, in fact, never been an important man in West Mallow, up to the time he had left it to seek his fortune in New York; and when he died, somewhat abruptly, and left his money, as it were, out of a clear sky, to his native place in the form of a university, a town hall, a soldiers' monument, a drinking-fountain, and a public library, his fellow-townsmen, in making the due civic acknowledgment and acceptance of his gifts, recalled with effort the obscure family to which he belonged.

He had not tried to characterize the university by his peculiar religious faith, but he had given a church building, a parsonage, and a fund for the support of preaching among them at Hilbrook to the small body of believers to which his people adhered. This sect had a name by which it was officially known to itself; but, like the Shakers, the Quakers, the Moravians, it early received a nickname, which it passively adopted, and even among its own members the body was rarely spoken of or thought of except as the Rixonites.

Mrs. Ewbert fretted under the nickname, with an impatience perhaps the greater because she had merely married into the Rixonite church, and had accepted its doctrine because she loved her husband rather than because she had been convinced of its truth. From the first she complained that the Rixonites were cold; and if there was anything Emily Ewbert had always detested, it was coldness. No one, she once testified, need talk to her of their passive waiting for a sign, as a religious life; if there were not some strong, central belief, some rigorously formulated creed, some—

"Good old herb and root theology," her husband interrupted.

"Yes!" she heedlessly acquiesced. "Unless there is something like *that*, all the waiting in the world won't"—she cast about for some powerful image—"won't keep the cold chills from running down *my* back when I think of my duty as a Christian."

"Then don't think of your duty as a Christian, my dear," he pleaded, with the caressing languor which sometimes made her say, in reprobation of her own pleasure in it, that *he* was a Rixonite, if there ever *was* one. "Think of your duty as a woman, or even as a mortal."

"I believe you're thinking of making a sermon on that," she

retorted; and he gave a sad, consenting laugh, as if it were quite true, though in fact he never really preached a sermon on mere femininity or mere mortality. His sermons were all very good, however; and that was another thing that put her out of patience with his Rixonite parishioners—that they should sit there Sunday after Sunday, year in and year out, and listen to his beautiful sermons, which ought to melt their hearts and bring tears into their eyes, and not seem influenced by them any more than if they were so many dry chips.

"But think how long they've had the gospel," he suggested, in a pensive self-derision which she would not share.

"Well, one thing, Clarence," she summed up, "I'm not going to let you throw yourself away on them; and unless you see some of the university people in the congregation, I want you to use your old sermons from this out. They'll never know the difference; and I'm going to make you take one of the old sermons along every Sunday, so as to be prepared."

II

One good trait of Mrs. Ewbert was that she never meant half she said—she could not; but in this case there was more meaning than usual in her saying. It really vexed her that the university families, who had all received them so nicely, and who appreciated her husband's spiritual and intellectual quality as fully as even she could wish, came some of them so seldom, and some of them never, to hear him at the Rixonite church. They ought, she said, to have been just suited by his preaching, which inculcated with the peculiar grace of his gentle, poetic nature a refinement of the mystical theology of the founder. The Rev. Adoniram Rixon, who had seventy years before formulated his conception of the religious life as a patient waiting upon the divine will, with a constant reference of this world's mysteries and problems to the world to come, had doubtless meant a more strenuous abeyance than Clarence Ewbert was now preaching to a third generation of his followers. He had doubtless meant them to be eager and alert in this patience, but the version of his gospel which his latest apostle gave taught a species of acquiescence which was foreign to the thoughts of the founder. He put as great stress as could be asked upon the importance of a realizing faith in the life to come, and an implicit trust in it for the solution of the problems and perplexities of this life; but so far from wishing his hearers to be constantly taking stock, as it were, of their spiritual condition, and interrogating Providence as to its will concerning them, he besought them to rest in confidence of the divine mindfulness, secure that while they fulfilled all their plain, simple duties toward one another, God would inspire them to act according to his purposes in the more psychological crises and emergencies, if these should ever be part of their experience.

In maintaining, on a certain Sunday evening, that his ideas were much more adapted to the spiritual nourishment of the president, the dean, and the several professors of Hilbrook University than to that of the hereditary Rixonites who

William Dean Howells

nodded in a slumbrous acceptance of them, Mrs. Ewbert failed as usual to rouse her husband to a due sense of his grievance with the university people.

"Well," he said, "you know I can't *make* them come, my dear."

"Of course not. And I would be the last to have you lift a finger. But I know that you feel about it just as I do."

"Perhaps; but I hope not so much as you *think* you feel. Of course, I'm very grateful for your indignation. But I know you don't undervalue the good I may do to my poor sheep— they're *not* an intellectual flock—in trying to lead them in the ways of spiritual modesty and unconsciousness. How do we know but they profit more by my preaching than the faculty would? Perhaps our university friends are spiritually unconscious enough already, if not modest."

"I see what you mean," said Mrs. Ewbert, provisionally suspending her sense of the whimsical quality in his suggestion. "But you need never tell me that they wouldn't appreciate you more."

"More than old Ransom Hilbrook?" he asked.

"Oh, I hope *he* isn't coming here to-night, again!" she implored, with a nervous leap from the point in question. "If he's coming here every Sunday night"—

As he knew she wished, her husband represented that Hilbrook's having come the last Sunday night was no proof that he was going to make a habit of it.

"But he *stayed* so late!" she insisted from the safety of her real belief that he was not coming.

"He came very early, though," said Ewbert, with a gentle sigh, in which her sympathetic penetration detected a retrospective exhaustion.

"I shall tell him you're not well," she went on: "I shall tell him you are lying down. You ought to be, now. You're perfectly worn out with that long walk you took." She rose, and beat up the sofa pillows with a menacing eye upon him.

"Oh, I'm very comfortable here," he said from the depths of his easy-chair. "Hilbrook won't come to-night. It's past the time."

She glanced at the clock with him, and then desisted. "If he does, I'm determined to excuse you somehow. You ought never to have gone near him, Clarence. You've brought it upon yourself."

Ewbert could not deny this, though he did not feel himself so much to blame for it as she would have liked to make out in her pity of him. He owned that if he had never gone to see Hilbrook the old man would probably never have come near them, and that if he had not tried so much to interest him when he did come Hilbrook would not have stayed so long; and even in this contrite mind he would not allow that he ought not to have visited him and ought not to have welcomed him.

William Dean Howells

III

The minister had found his parishioner in the old Hilbrook homestead, which Josiah Hilbrook, while he lived, suffered Ransom Hilbrook to occupy, and when he died bequeathed to him, with a sufficient income for all his simple wants. They were cousins, and they had both gone out into the world about the same time: one had made a success of it, and remained; and the other had made a failure of it, and come back. They were both Rixonites, as the families of both had been in the generation before them. It could be supposed that Josiah Hilbrook, since he had given the money for a Rixonite church and the perpetual pay of a Rixonite minister in his native place, had died in the faith; and it might have been supposed that Ransom Hilbrook, from his constant attendance upon its services, was living in the same faith. What was certain was that the survivor lived alone in the family homestead on the slope of the stony hill overlooking the village. The house was gray with age, and it crouched low on the ground where it had been built a century before, and anchored fast by the great central chimney characteristic of the early New England farmhouse. Below it staggered the trees of an apple orchard belted in with a stone wall, and beside it sagged the sheds whose stretch united the gray old house to the gray old barn, and made it possible for Hilbrook to do his chores in rain or snow without leaving cover. There was a dooryard defined by a picket fence, and near the kitchen door was a well with a high pent roof, where there had once been a long sweep.

These simple features showed to the village on the opposite slope with a distinctness that made the place seem much lonelier than if it had been much more remote. It gained no cheerfulness from its proximity, and when the windows of the house lighted up with the pale gleam of the sunset, they imparted to the village a sense of dreary solitude which its own lamps could do nothing to relieve.

Ransom Hilbrook came and went among the villagers in the

same sort of inaccessible contiguity. He did not shun passing the time of day with people he met; he was in and out at the grocer's, the meat man's, the baker's, upon the ordinary domestic occasions; but he never darkened any other doors, except on his visits to the bank where he cashed the checks for his quarterly allowance. There had been a proposition to use him representatively in the ceremonies celebrating the acceptance of the various gifts of Josiah Hilbrook; but he had not lent himself to this, and upon experiment the authorities found that he was right in his guess that they could get along without him.

He had not said it surlily, but sadly, and with a gentle deprecation of their insistence. While the several monuments that testified to his cousin's wealth and munificence rose in the village beyond the brook, he continued in the old homestead without change, except that when his housekeeper died he began to do for himself the few things that the ailing and aged woman had done for him. How he did them was not known, for he invited no intimacy from his neighbors. But from the extent of his dealings with the grocer it was imagined that he lived mainly upon canned goods. The fish man paid him a weekly visit, and once a week he got from the meat man a piece of salt pork, which it was obvious to the meanest intelligence was for his Sunday baked beans. From his purchase of flour and baking powder it was reasonably inferred that he now and then made himself hot biscuit. Beyond these meagre facts everything was conjecture, in which the local curiosity played somewhat actively, but, for the most part, with a growing acquiescence in the general ignorance none felt authorized to dispel. There had been a time when some fulfilled a fancied duty to the solitary in trying to see him. But the visitors who found him out of doors were not asked within, and were obliged to dismiss themselves, after an interview across the pickets of the dooryard fence or from the trestles or inverted feed pails on which they were invited to seats in the barn or shed. Those who happened to find their host more ceremoniously at home were allowed to come in, but were received in rooms so comfortless from the drawn blinds or

William Dean Howells

fireless hearths that they had not the spirits for the task of cheering him up which they had set themselves, and departed in greater depression than that they left him to.

IV

Ewbert felt all the more impelled to his own first visit by the fame of these failures, but he was not hastened in it. He thought best to wait for some sign or leading from Hilbrook; but when none came, except the apparent attention with which Hilbrook listened to his preaching, and the sympathy which he believed he detected at times in the old eyes blinking upon him through his sermons, he felt urged to the visit which he had vainly delayed.

Hilbrook's reception was wary and non-committal, but it was by no means so grudging as Ewbert had been led to expect. After some ceremonious moments in the cold parlor Hilbrook asked him into the warm kitchen, where apparently he passed most of his own time. There was something cooking in a pot on the stove, and a small room opened out of the kitchen, with a bed in it, which looked as if it were going to be made, as Ewbert handsomely maintained. There was an old dog stretched on the hearth behind the stove, who whimpered with rheumatic apprehension when his master went to put the lamp on the mantel above him.

In describing the incident to his wife Ewbert stopped at this point, and then passed on to say that after they got to talking Hilbrook seemed more and more gratified, and even glad, to see him.

"Everybody's glad to see *you*, Clarence," she broke out, with tender pride. "But why do you say, 'After we got to talking'? Didn't you go to talking at once?"

"Well, no," he answered, with a vague smile; "we did a good deal of listening at first, both of us. I didn't know just where to begin, after I got through my excuses for coming, and Mr. Hilbrook didn't offer any opening. Don't you think he's a very handsome old man?"

"He has a pretty head, and his close-cut white hair gives it a neat effect, like a nice child's. He has a refined face; such a straight nose and a delicate chin. Yes, he is certainly good-looking. But what"—

"Oh, nothing. Only, all at once I realized that he had a sensitive nature. I don't know why I shouldn't have realized it before. I had somehow taken it for granted that he was a self-conscious hermit, who lived in a squalid seclusion because he liked being wondered at. But he did not seem to be anything of the kind. I don't know whether he's a good cook, for he didn't ask me to eat anything; but I don't think he's a bad housekeeper."

"With his bed unmade at eight o'clock in the evening!"

"He may have got up late," said Ewbert. "The house seemed very orderly, otherwise; and what is really the use of making up a bed till you need it!"

Mrs. Ewbert passed the point, and asked, "What did you talk about when you got started?"

"I found he was a reader, or had been. There was a case of good books in the parlor, and I began by talking with him about them."

"Well, what did he say about them?"

"That he wasn't interested in them. He had been once, but he was not now."

"I can understand that," said Mrs. Ewbert philosophically. "Books *are* crowded out after your life fills up with other interests."

"Yes."

"Yes, what?" Mrs. Ewbert followed him up.

"So far as I could make out, Mr. Hilbrook's life hadn't filled up with other interests. He did not care for the events of the day, as far as I tried him on them, and he did not care for the past. I tempted him with autobiography; but he seemed quite indifferent to his own history, though he was not reticent about it. I proposed the history of his cousin in the boyish days which he said they had spent together; but he seemed no more interested in his cousin than in himself. Then I tried his dog and his pathetic sufferings, and I said something about the pity of the poor old fellow's last days being so miserable. That seemed to strike a gleam of interest from him, and he asked me if I thought animals might live again. And I found—I don't know just how to put it so as to give you the right sense of his psychological attitude."

"No matter! Put it any way, and I will take care of the right sense. Go on!" said Mrs. Ewbert.

"I found that his question led up to the question whether men lived again, and to a confession that he didn't or couldn't believe they did."

"Well, upon my word!" Mrs. Ewbert exclaimed. "I don't see what business he has coming to church, then. Doesn't he understand that the idea of immortality is the very essence of Rixonitism! I think it was personally insulting to *you*, Clarence. What did you say?"

"I didn't take a very high hand with him. You know I don't embody the idea of immortality, and the church is no bad place even for unbelievers. The fact is, it struck me as profoundly pathetic. He wasn't arrogant about it, as people sometimes are,—they seem proud of not believing; but he was sufficiently ignorant in his premises. He said he had seen too many dead people. You know he was in the civil war."

"No!"

"Yes,—through it all. It came out on my asking him if he were going to the Decoration Day services. He said that the sight of the first great battlefield deprived him of the power of believing in a life hereafter. He was not very explanatory, but as I understood it the overwhelming presence of death had extinguished his faith in immortality; the dead riders were just like their dead horses"—

"Shocking!" Mrs. Ewbert broke in.

"He said something went out of him." Ewbert waited a moment before adding: "It was very affecting, though Hilbrook himself was as apathetic about it as he was about everything else. He was not interested in not believing, even, but I could see that it had taken the heart out of life for him. If our life here does not mean life elsewhere, the interest of it must end with our activities. When it comes to old age, as it has with poor Hilbrook, it has no meaning at all, unless it has the hope of more life in it. I felt his forlornness, and I strongly wished to help him. I stayed a long time talking; I tried to interest him in the fact that he was not interested, and"—

"Well, what?"

"If I didn't fatigue Hilbrook, I came away feeling perfectly exhausted myself. Were you uneasy at my being out so late?"

V

It was some time after the Ewberts had given up expecting him that old Hilbrook came to return the minister's visit. Then, as if some excuse were necessary, he brought a dozen eggs in a paper bag, which he said he hoped Mrs. Ewbert could use, because his hens were giving him more than he knew what to do with. He came to the back door with them; but Mrs. Ewbert always let her maid of all work go out Sunday evening, and she could receive him in the kitchen herself. She felt obliged to make him the more welcome on account of his humility, and she showed him into the library with perhaps exaggerated hospitality.

It was a chilly evening of April, and so early that the lamp was not lighted; but there was a pleasant glow from the fire on the hearth, and Ewbert made his guest sit down before it. As he lay back in the easy-chair, stretching his thin old hands toward the blaze, the delicacy of his profile was charming, and that senile parting of the lips with which he listened reminded Ewbert of his own father's looks in his last years; so that it was with an affectionate eagerness he set about making Hilbrook feel his presence acceptable, when Mrs. Ewbert left them to finish up the work she had promised herself not to leave for the maid. It was much that Hilbrook had come at all, and he ought to be made to realize that Ewbert appreciated his coming. But Hilbrook seemed indifferent to his efforts, or rather, insensible to them, in the several topics that Ewbert advanced; and there began to be pauses, in which the minister racked his brain for some new thing to say, or found himself saying something he cared nothing for in a voice of hollow resolution, or falling into commonplaces which he tried to give vitality by strenuousness of expression. He heard his wife moving about in the kitchen and dining room, with a clicking of spoons and knives and a faint clash of china, as she put the supper things away, and he wished that she would come in and help him with old Hilbrook; but he could not very well call her, and she kept at her work, with no apparent purpose of leaving it.

William Dean Howells

Hilbrook was a farmer, so far as he was anything industrially, and Ewbert tried him with questions of crops, soils, and fertilizers; but he tried him in vain. The old man said he had never cared much for those things, and now it was too late for him to begin. He generally sold his grass standing, and his apples on the trees; and he had no animals about the place except his chickens,—they took care of themselves. Ewbert urged, for the sake of conversation, even of a disputative character, that poultry were liable to disease, if they were not looked after; but Hilbrook said, Not if there were not too many of them, and so made an end of that subject. Ewbert desperately suggested that he must find them company,—they seemed sociable creatures; and then, in his utter dearth, he asked how the old dog was getting on.

"Oh, he's dead," said Hilbrook, and the minister's heart smote him with a pity for the survivor's forlornness which the old man's apathetic tone had scarcely invited. He inquired how and when the old dog had died, and said how much Hilbrook must miss him.

"Well, I don't know," Hilbrook returned. "He wa'n't much comfort, and he's out of his misery, anyway." After a moment he added, with a gleam of interest: "I've been thinkin', since he went, of what we talked about the other night,—I don't mean animals, but men. I tried to go over what you said, in my own mind, but I couldn't seem to make it."

He lifted his face, sculptured so fine by age, and blinked at Ewbert, who was glad to fancy something appealing in his words and manner.

"You mean as to a life beyond this?"

"Ah!"

"Well, let us see if we can't go over it together."

Ewbert had forgotten the points he had made before, and he

had to take up the whole subject anew, he did so at first in an involuntarily patronizing confidence that Hilbrook was ignorant of the ground; but from time to time the old man let drop a hint of knowledge that surprised the minister. Before they had done, it appeared that Hilbrook was acquainted with the literature of the doctrine of immortality from Plato to Swedenborg, and even to Mr. John Fiske. How well he was acquainted with it Ewbert could not quite make out; but he had recurrently a misgiving, as if he were in the presence of a doubter whose doubt was hopeless through his knowledge. In this bleak air it seemed to him that he at last detected the one thing in which the old man felt an interest: his sole tie with the earth was the belief that when he left it he should cease to be. This affected Ewbert as most interesting, and he set himself, with all his heart and soul, to dislodge Hilbrook from his deplorable conviction. He would not perhaps have found it easy to overcome at once that repugnance which Hilbrook's doubt provoked in him, if it had been less gently, less simply owned. As it was, it was not possible to deal with it in any spirit of mere authority. He must meet it and overcome it in terms of affectionate persuasion.

It should not be difficult to overcome it; but Ewbert had not yet succeeded in arraying his reasons satisfactorily against it when his wife returned from her work in the kitchen, and sat down beside the library table. Her coming operated a total diversion, in which Hilbrook lapsed into his apathy, and was not to be roused from it by the overtures to conversation which she made. He presently got to his feet and said he mast be going, against all her protests that it was very early. Ewbert wished to walk home with him; but Hilbrook would not suffer this, and the minister had to come back from following him to the gate, and watching his figure lose itself in the dark, with a pang in his heart for the solitude which awaited the old man under his own roof. He ran swiftly over their argument in his mind, and questioned himself whether he had used him with unfailing tenderness, whether he had let him think that he regarded him as at all reprobate and culpable. He gave up the quest as he rejoined his wife with a long, unconscious sigh that made her lift her head.

"What is it, Clarence?"

"Nothing"—

"You look perfectly exhausted. You look worried. Was it something you were talking about?"

Then he told her, and he had trouble to keep her resentment in bounds. She held that, as a minister, he ought to have rebuked the wretched creature; that it was nothing short of offensive to him for Hilbrook to take such a position. She said his face was all flushed, and that she knew he would not sleep, and she should get him a glass of warm milk; the fire was out in the stove, but she could heat it over the lamp in a tin cup.

VI

Hilbrook did not come again till Ewbert had been to see him; and in the meantime the minister suffered from the fear that the old man was staying away because of some hurt which he had received in their controversy. Hilbrook came to church as before, and blinked at him through the two sermons which Ewbert preached on significant texts, and the minister hoped he was listening with a sense of personal appeal in them. He had not only sought to make them convincing as to the doctrine of another life, but he had dealt in terms of loving entreaty with those who had not the precious faith of this in their hearts, and he had wished to convey to Hilbrook an assurance of peculiar sympathy.

The day following the last of his sermons, Ewbert had to officiate at the funeral of a little child whose mother had been stricken to the earth by her bereavement. The hapless creature had sent for him again and again, and had clung about his very soul, beseeching him for assurance that she should see her child hereafter, and have it hers, just as it was, forever, he had not had the heart to refuse her this consolation, and he had pushed himself, in giving it, beyond the bounds of imagination. When she confessed her own inability to see how it could be, and yet demanded of him that it should be, he answered her that our inability to realize the fact had nothing to do with its reality. In the few words he said over the little one, at the last, he recurred to this position, and urged it upon all his hearers; but in the moment of doing so a point that old Hilbrook had made in their talk suddenly presented itself. He experienced inwardly such a collapse that he could not be sure he had spoken, and he repeated his declaration in a voice of such harsh defiance that he could scarcely afterwards bring himself down to the meek level of the closing prayer.

As they walked home together, his wife asked, "Why did you repeat yourself in that passage, Clarence, and why did you lift your voice so? It sounded like contradicting some one. I hope

William Dean Howells

you were not thinking of anything that wretched old man said?"

With the mystical sympathy by which the wife divines what is in her husband's mind she had touched the truth, and he could not deny it. "Yes, yes, I was," he owned in a sort of anguish, and she said:—

"Well, then, I wish he wouldn't come about any more. He has perfectly obsessed you. I could see that the last two Sundays you were preaching right at him." He had vainly hoped she had not noticed this, though he had not concealed from her that his talk with Hilbrook had suggested his theme. "What are you going to do about him?" she pursued relentlessly.

"I don't know,—I don't know, indeed," said Ewbert; and perhaps because he did not know, he felt that he must do something, that he must at least not leave him to himself. He hoped that Hilbrook would come to him, and so put him under the necessity of doing something; but Hilbrook did not come, and after waiting a fortnight Ewbert went to him, as was his duty.

VII

The spring had advanced so far that there were now days when it was pleasant to be out in the soft warmth of the afternoons. The day when Ewbert climbed to the Hilbrook homestead it was even a little hot, and he came up to the dooryard mopping his forehead with his handkerchief, and glad of the south-western breeze which he caught at this point over the shoulder of the hill. He had expected to go round to the side door of the house, where he had parted with Hilbrook on his former visit; but he stopped on seeing the old man at his front door, where he was looking vaguely at a mass of Spanish willow fallen dishevelled beside it, as if he had some thought of lifting its tangled spray. The sun shone on his bare head, and struck silvery gleams from his close-cropped white hair; there was something uncommon in his air, though his dress was plain and old-fashioned; and Ewbert wished that his wife were there to share his impression of distinction in Hilbrook's presence.

He turned at Ewbert's cheerful hail, and after a moment of apparent uncertainty as to who he was, he came down the walk of broken brick and opened the gate to his visitor.

"I was just out, looking round at the old things," he said, with an effort of apology. "This sort of weather is apt to make fools of us. It gets into our heads, and before we know we feel as if we had something to do with the season."

"Perhaps we have," said the minister. "The spring is in us, too."

The old man shook his head. "It was once, when we were children; now there's what we remember of it. We like to make believe about it,—that's natural; and it's natural we should make believe that there is going to be a spring for us somewhere else like what we see for the grass and bushes, here, every year; but I guess not. A tree puts out its leaves every spring; but by and by the tree dies, and then it doesn't put out its leaves any more."

"I see what you mean," said Ewbert, "and I allow that there is no real analogy between our life and that of the grass and bushes; yet somehow I feel strengthened in my belief in the hereafter by each renewal of the earth's life. It isn't a proof, it isn't a promise; but it's a suggestion, an intimation."

They were in the midst of a great question, and they sat down on the decaying doorstep to have it out; Hilbrook having gone in for his hat and come out again, with its soft wide brim shading his thin face, frosted with half a week's beard.

"But character," the minister urged at a certain point,—"what becomes of character? You may suppose that life can be lavished by its Origin in the immeasurable superabundance which we see in nature. But character,—that is a different thing; that cannot die."

"The beasts that perish have character; my old dog had. Some are good and some bad; they're kind and they're ugly."

"Ah, excuse me! That isn't character; that's temperament. Men have temperament, too; but the beasts haven't character. Doesn't that fact prove something,—or no, not prove, but give us some reasonable expectation of a hereafter?"

Hilbrook did not say anything for a moment. He broke a bit of fragrant spray from the flowering currant—which guarded the doorway on his side of the steps; Ewbert sat next the Spanish willow—and softly twisted the stem between his thumb and finger.

"Ever hear how I came to leave Hilbrook,—West Mallow, as it was then?" he asked at last.

Ewbert was forced to own that he had heard a story, but he said, mainly in Hilbrook's interest, that he had not paid much attention to it.

"Thought there wa'n't much in it? Well, that's right, generally speakin'. Folks like to make up stories about a man that lives alone like me, here; and they usually get in a disappointment. I ain't goin' to go over it. I don't care any more about it now than if it had happened to somebody else; but it did happen. Josiah got the girl, and I didn't. I presume they like to make out that I've grieved over it ever since. Sho! It's forty years since I gave it a thought, that way." A certain contemptuous indignation supplanted the wonted gentleness of the old man, as if he spurned the notion of such sentimental folly. "I've read of folks mournin' all their lives through, and in their old age goin' back to a thing like that, as if it still meant somethin'. But it ain't true; I don't suppose I care any more for losin' her now than Josiah would for gettin' her if he was alive. It did make a difference for a while; I ain't goin' to deny that. It lasted me four or five years, in all, I guess; but I was married to somebody else when I went to the war,"—Ewbert controlled a start of surprise; he had always taken it for granted that Hilbrook was a bachelor,—"and we had one child. So you may say that I was well over that first thing. *It wore out*; and if it wa'n't that it makes me mad to have folks believin' that I'm sufferin' from it yet, I presume I shouldn't think of it from one year's end to another. My wife and I always got on well together; she was a good woman. She died when I was away at the war, and the little boy died after I got back. I was sorry to lose her, and I thought losin' *him* would kill me. It didn't. It appeared one while as if I couldn't live without him, and I was always contrivin' how I should meet up with him somewhere else. I couldn't figure it out."

Hilbrook stopped, and swallowed dryly. Ewbert noticed how he had dropped more and more into the vernacular, in these reminiscences; in their controversies he had used the language of books and had spoken like a cultivated man, but now he was simply and touchingly rustic.

"Well," he resumed, "that wore out, too. I went into business, and I made money and I lost it. I went through all that experience, and I got enough of it, just as I got enough of fightin'. I guess I was no worse scared than the rest of 'em, but when it came to the end I'd 'bout made up my mind that if there was another war I'd go to Canady; I was sick of it, and I was sick of business even before I lost money. I lost pretty much everything. Josiah—he was always a good enough friend of mine—wanted me to start in again, and he offered to back me, but I said no. I said if he wanted to do something for me, he could let me come home and live on the old place, here; it wouldn't cost him anything like so much, and it would be a safer investment. He agreed, and here I be, to make a long story short."

Hilbrook had stiffened more and more, as he went on, in the sort of defiance he had put on when he first began to speak of himself, and at the end of his confidence Ewbert did not venture any comment. His forbearance seemed to leave the old man freer to resume at the point where he had broken off, and he did so with something of lingering challenge.

"You asked me just now why I didn't think character, as we call it, gave us some right to expect a life after this. Well, I'll try to tell you. I consider that I've been the rounds, as you may say, and that I've got as much character as most men. I've had about everything in my life that most have, and a great deal more than some. I've seen that everything wears out, and that when a thing's worn out it's for good and all. I think it's reasonable to suppose that when I wear out it will be for good and all, too. There isn't anything of us, as I look at it, except the potentiality of experiences. The experiences come through the passions that you can tell on the fingers of one hand: love, hate, hope, grief, and you may say greed for the thumb. When you've had them, that's the end of it; you've exhausted your capacity; you're used up, and so's your character,—that often dies before the body does."

"No, no!" Ewbert protested. "Human capacity is infinite;" but even while he spoke this seemed to him a contradiction in terms. "I mean that the passions renew themselves with new occasions, new opportunities, and character grows continually.

You have loved twice, you have grieved twice; in battle you hated more than once; in business you must have coveted many times. Under different conditions, the passions, the potentiality of experiences, will have a pristine strength. Can't you see it in that light? Can't you draw some hope from that?"

"Hope!" cried Ransom Hilbrook, lifting his fallen head and staring at the minister. "Why, man, you don't suppose I *want* to live hereafter? Do you think I'm anxious to have it all over again, or *any* of it? Is that why you've been trying to convince me of immortality? I know there's something in what you say,—more than what you realize. I've argued annihilation up to this point and that, and almost proved it to my own mind; but there's always some point that I can't quite get over. If I had the certainty, the absolute certainty, that this was all there was to be of it, I wouldn't want to live an hour longer, not a minute! But it's the uncertainty that keeps me. What I'm afraid of is, that if I get out of it here, I might wake up in my old identity, with the potentiality of new experiences in new conditions. That's it I'm tired. I've had enough. I want to be let alone. I don't want to do anything more, or have anything more done to me. I want to *stop*."

Ewbert's first impression was that he was shocked; but he was too honest to remain in this conventional assumption. He was profoundly moved, however, and intensely interested. He realized that Hilbrook was perfectly sincere, and he could put himself in the old man's place, and imagine why he should feel as he did. Ewbert blamed himself for not having conceived of such a case before; and he saw that if he were to do anything for this lonely soul, he must begin far back of the point from which he had started with him. The old man's position had a kind of dignity which did not admit of the sort of pity Ewbert had been feeling for him, and the minister had before him the difficult and delicate task of persuading Hilbrook, not that a man, if he died, should live again, but that he should live upon terms so kind and just that none of the fortuities of mortal life should be repeated in that immortality. He must show the immortal man to be a creature so happily conditioned that he would be in effect newly created, before Hilbrook would consent to accept the idea of living again. He might say to him that he would probably not be consulted in the matter, since he had not been consulted as to his existence here; but such an answer would brutally ignore the claim that such a man's developed consciousness could justly urge to some share in the counsels of omnipotence. Ewbert did not know where to begin, and in his despair he began with a laugh.

"Upon my word," he said, "you've presented a problem that would give any casuist pause, and it's beyond my powers without some further thought. Your doubt, as I now understand it, is not of immortality, but of mortality; and there I can't meet you in argument without entirely forsaking my own ground. If it will not seem harsh, I will confess that your doubt is rather consoling to me; for I have so much faith in the Love which rules the world that I am perfectly willing to accept reexistence on any terms that Love may offer. You may say that this is because I have not yet exhausted the potentialities of experience, and am still interested in my own identity; and one half of this, at least, I can't deny. But even if it were otherwise, I should trust to find among those Many Mansions which we are told of some chamber where I should be at rest without being annihilated; and I can even imagine my being glad to do any sort of work about the House, when I was tired of resting."

VIII

"I am *glad* you said that to him!" cried Ewbert's wife, when he told her of his interview with old Hilbrook. "That will give him something to think about. What did he say?"

Ewbert had been less and less satisfied with his reply to Hilbrook, in which it seemed to him that he had passed from mockery to reproof, with no great credit to himself; and his wife's applause now set the seal to his displeasure with it.

"Oh, he said simply that he could understand a younger person feeling differently, and that he did not wish to set himself up as a censor. But he could not pretend that he was glad to have been called out of nonentity into being, and that he could imagine nothing better than eternal unconsciousness."

"Well?"

"I told him that his very words implied the refusal of his being to accept nonentity again; that they expressed, or adumbrated, the conception of an eternal consciousness of the eternal unconsciousness he imagined himself longing for. I'm not so sure they did, now."

"Of *course* they did. And *then* what did he say?"

"He said nothing in direct reply; he sighed, and dropped his poor old head on his breast, and seemed very tired; so that I tried talking of other things for a while, and then I came away. Emily, I'm afraid I wasn't perfectly candid, perfectly kind, with him."

"I don't see how you could have been more so!" she retorted, in tender indignation with him against himself. "And I think what he said was terrible. It was bad enough for him to pretend to believe that he was not going to live again, but for him to tell you that he was *afraid* he was!" An image sufficiently monstrous to typify Hilbrook's wickedness failed to present itself to Mrs. Ewbert, and she went out to give the maid instructions for something unusually nourishing for Ewbert at their mid-day dinner. "You look fairly fagged out, Clarence," she said, when she came back; "and I insist upon your not going up to that dreadful old man's again,—at least, not till you've got over this shock."

"Oh, I don't think it has affected me seriously," he returned lightly.

"Yes, it has! yes, it has!" she declared. "It's just like your thinking you hadn't taken cold, the other day when you were caught in the rain; and the next morning you got up with a sore throat, and it was Sunday morning, too."

Ewbert could not deny this, and he had no great wish to see Hilbrook soon again. He consented to wait for Hilbrook to come to him, before trying to satisfy these scruples of conscience which he had hinted at; and he reasonably hoped that the painful points would cease to rankle with the lapse of time, if there should be a long interval before they met.

That night, before the Ewberts had finished their tea, there came a ring at the door, from which Mrs. Ewbert disconsolately foreboded a premature evening call. "And just when I was counting on a long, quiet, restful time for you, and getting you to bed early!" she lamented in undertone to her husband; to the maid who passed through the room with an inquiring glance, to the front door, she sighed, still in undertone, "Oh yes, of course we're at *home*."

They both listened for the voice at the door, to make out who was there; but the voice was so low that they were still in ignorance while the maid was showing the visitor into the library, and until she came back to them.

"It's that old gentleman who lives all alone by himself on the hill over the brook," she explained; and Mrs. Ewbert rose with an air of authority, waving her husband to keep his seat.

"Now, Clarence, I am simply not going to *let* you go in. You are sick enough as it is, and if you are going to let that *awful* old man spend the whole evening here, and drain the life out of you! *I* will see him, and tell him"—

"No, no, Emily! It won't do. I *must* see him. It isn't true that I'm sick. He's old, and he has a right to the best we can do for him. Think of his loneliness! I shall certainly not let you send him away." Ewbert was excitedly gulping his second cup of tea; he pushed his chair back, and flung his napkin down as he added, "You can come in, too, and see that I get off alive."

"I shall not come near you," she answered resentfully; but Ewbert had not closed the door behind him, and she felt it her duty to listen.

IX

Mrs. Ewbert heard old Hilbrook begin at once in a high senile key without any form of response to her husband's greeting: "There was one thing you said to-day that I've been thinkin' over, and I've come down to talk with you about it."

"Yes?" Ewbert queried submissively, though he was aware of being quite as fagged as his wife accused him of being, after he spoke.

"Yes," Hilbrook returned. "I guess I ha'n't been exactly up and down with myself. I guess I've been playing fast and loose with myself. I guess you're right about my wantin' to have enough consciousness to enjoy my unconsciousness," and the old gentleman gave a laugh of rather weird enjoyment. "There are things," he resumed seriously, "that are deeper in us than anything we call ourselves. I supposed I had gone to the bottom, but I guess I hadn't. All the while there was something down there that I hadn't got at; but you reached it and touched it, and now I know it's there. I don't know but it's my Soul that's been havin' its say all the time, and me not listenin'. I guess you made your point."

Ewbert was still not so sure of that. He had thrown out that hasty suggestion without much faith in it at the time, and his faith in it had not grown since.

"I'm glad," he began, but Hilbrook pressed on as if he had not spoken.

"I guess we're built like an onion," he said, with a severity that forbade Ewbert to feel anything undignified in the homely illustration. "You can strip away layer after layer till you seem to get to nothing at all; but when you've got to that nothing you've got to the very thing that had the life in it, and that would have grown again if you had put it in the ground."

"Exactly!" said Ewbert.

"You made a point that I can't get round," Hilbrook continued, and it was here that Ewbert enjoyed a little instant of triumph. "But that ain't the point with *me*. I see that I can't prove that we shan't live again any more than you can prove that we shall. What I want you to do *now* is to convince me, or to give me the least reason to believe, that we shan't live again on exactly the same terms that we live now. I don't want to argue immortality any more; we'll take that for granted. But how is it going to be any different from mortality with the hope of death taken away?"

Hilbrook's apathy was gone, and his gentleness; he had suddenly an air and tone of fierce challenge. As he spoke he brought a clenched fist down on the arm of his chair; he pushed his face forward and fixed Ewbert with the vitreous glitter of his old eyes. Ewbert found him terrible, and he had a confused sense of responsibility for him, as if he had spiritually constituted him, in the charnel of unbelief, out of the spoil of death, like some new and fearfuler figment of Frankenstein's. But if he had fortuitously reached him, through the one insincerity of his being, and bidden him live again forever, he must not forsake him or deny him.

"I don't know how far you accept or reject the teachings of Scripture on this matter," he began rather vaguely, but Hilbrook stopped him.

"You didn't go to the Book for the point you made *against* me. But if you go to it now for the point I want you to make *for* me, what are you going to find? Are you going to find the promise of a life any different from the life we have here? I accept it all,—all that the Old Testament says, and all that the New Testament says; and what does it amount to on this point?"

"Nothing but the assurance that if we live rightly here we shall be happy in the keeping of the divine Love there. That assurance is everything to me."

"It isn't to me!" cried the old man. "We are in the keeping of the divine Love here, too, and are we happy? Are those who live rightly happy? It's because we're not conditioned for happiness here; and how are we going to be conditioned differently there? We are going to suffer to all eternity through our passions, our potentialities of experience, there just as we do here."

"There may be other passions, other potentialities of experience," Ewbert suggested, casting about in the void.

"Like what?" Hilbrook demanded. "I've been trying to figure it, and I can't. I should like you to try it. You can't imagine a new passion in the soul any more than you can imagine a new feature in the face. There they are: eyes, ears, nose, mouth, chin; love, hate, greed, hope, fear! You can't add to them or take away from them." The old man dropped from his defiance in an entreaty that was even more terrible to Ewbert. "I wish you could. I should like to have you try. Maybe I haven't been over the whole ground. Maybe there's some principle that I've missed." He hitched his chair closer to Ewbert's, and laid some tremulous fingers on the minister's sleeve. "If I've got to live forever, what have I got to live for?"

"Well," said Ewbert, meeting him fully in his humility, "let us try to make it out together. Let us try to think. Apparently, our way has brought us to a dead wall; but I believe there's light beyond it, if we can only break through. Is it really necessary that we should discover some new principle? Do we know all that love can do from our experience of it here?"

"Have you seen a mother with her child?" Hilbrook retorted.

"Yes, I know. But even that has some alloy of selfishness. Can't we imagine love in which there is no greed,—for greed, and not hate, is the true antithesis of love which is all giving, while greed is all getting,—a love that is absolutely pure?"

"*I* can't," said the old man. "All the love I ever felt had greed in it; I wanted to keep the thing I loved for myself."

"Yes, because you were afraid in the midst of your love. It was fear that alloyed it, not greed. And in easily imaginable conditions in which there is no fear of want, or harm, or death, love would be pure; for it is these things that greed itself wants to save us from. You can imagine conditions in which there shall be no fear, in which love casteth out fear?"

"Well," said Hilbrook provisionally.

Ewbert had not thought of these points himself before, and he was pleased with his discovery, though afterwards he was aware that it was something like an intellectual juggle. "You see," he temporized, "we have got rid of two of the passions already, fear and greed, which are the potentialities of our unhappiest experience in this life. In fact, we have got rid of three, for without fear and greed men cannot hate."

"But how can we exist without them?" Hilbrook urged. "Shall we be made up of two passions,—of love and hope alone?"

"Why not?" Ewbert returned, with what he felt a specious brightness.

"Because we should not be complete beings with these two elements alone."

"Ah, as we know ourselves here, I grant you," said the minister. "But why should we not be far more simply constituted somewhere else? Have you ever read Isaac Taylor's Physical Theory of another Life? He argues that the immortal body would be a far less complex mechanism than the mortal body. Why should not the immortal soul be simple, too? In fact, it would necessarily be so, being one with the body. I think I can put my hand on that book, and if I can I must make you take it with you."

William Dean Howells

He rose briskly from his chair, and went to the shelves, running his fingers along the books with that subtlety of touch by which the student knows a given book in the dark. He had heard Mrs. Ewbert stirring about in the rooms beyond with an activity in which he divined a menacing impatience; and he would have been glad to get rid of old Hilbrook before her impatience burst in an irruption upon them. Perhaps because of this distraction he could not find the book, but he remained on foot, talking with an implication in his tone that they were both preparing to part, and were now merely finishing off some odds and ends of discourse before they said good-night.

Old Hilbrook did not stir. He was far too sincere a nature, Ewbert saw, to conceive of such inhospitality as a hint for his departure, or he was too deeply interested to be aware of it. The minister was obliged to sit down again, and it was eleven o'clock before Hilbrook rose to go.

X

Ewbert went out to the gate with the old man, and when he came back to his study, he found his wife there looking strangely tall and monumental in her reproach. "I supposed you were in bed long ago, my dear," he attempted lightly.

"You *don't* mean that you've been out in the night air without your hat on!" she returned. "Well, this is too *much*!" Her long-pent-up impatience broke in tears, and he strove in vain to comfort her with caresses. "Oh, what a fatal day it was when you stirred that wretched old creature up! *Why* couldn't you leave him alone!"

"To his apathy? To his despair? Emily!" Ewbert dropped his arms from the embrace in which he had folded her woodenly unresponsive frame, and regarded her sadly.

"Oh yes, of course," she answered, rubbing her handkerchief into her eyes. "But you don't know that it was despair; and he was quite happy in his apathy; and as it is, you've got him on your hands; and if he's going to come here every night and stay till morning, it will kill you. You know you're not strong; and you get so excited when you sit up talking. Look how flushed your cheeks are, now, and your eyes—as big! You won't sleep a wink to-night,—I know you won't."

"Oh yes, I shall," he answered bravely. "I believe I've done some good work with poor old Hilbrook; and you mustn't think he's tired me. I feel fresher than I did when he came."

"It's because you're excited," she persisted. "I know you won't sleep."

"Yes, I shall. I shall just stay here, and read my nerves down a little. Then I'll come."

"Oh yes!" Mrs. Ewbert exulted disconsolately, and she left him

William Dean Howells

to his book. She returned to say: "If you *must* take anything to make you sleepy, I've left some warm milk on the back of the stove. Promise me you won't take any sulphonal! You know how you feel the next day!"

"No, no, I won't," said Ewbert; and he kept his word, with the effect of remaining awake all night. Toward morning he did not know but he had drowsed; he was not aware of losing consciousness, and he started from his drowse with the word "consciousness" in his mind, as he had heard Hilbrook speaking it.

XI

Throughout the day, under his wife's watchful eye, he failed of
the naps he tried for, and he had to own himself as haggard,
when night came again, as the fondest anxiety of a wife could
pronounce a husband. He could not think of his talk with old
Hilbrook without an anguish of brain exhaustion; and yet he
could not help thinking of it. He realized what the misery of
mere weakness must be, and the horror of not having the
power to rest. He wished to go to bed before the hour when
Hilbrook commonly appeared, but this was so early that
Ewbert knew he should merely toss about and grow more and
more wakeful from his premature effort to sleep. He trembled
at every step outside, and at the sound of feet approaching the
door on the short brick walk from the gate, he and his wife
arrested themselves with their teacups poised in the air. Ewbert
was aware of feebly hoping the feet might go away again; but
the bell rang, and then he could not meet his wife's eye.

"If it is that old Mr. Hilbrook," she said to the maid in transit
through the room, "tell him that Mr. Ewbert is not well, but *I*
shall be glad to see him," and now Ewbert did not dare to
protest. His forebodings were verified when he heard Hilbrook
asking for him, but though he knew the voice, he detected a
difference in the tone that puzzled him.

His wife did not give Hilbrook time to get away, if he had
wished, without seeing her; she rose at once and went out to
him. Ewbert heard her asking him into the library, and then he
heard them in parley there; and presently they came out into
the hall again, and went to the front door together. Ewbert's
heart misgave him of something summary on her part, and he
did not know what to make of the cheerful parting between
them. "Well, I bid you good-evening, ma'am," he heard old
Hilbrook say briskly, and his wife return sweetly, "Good-night,
Mr. Hilbrook. You must come soon again."

"You may put your mind at rest, Clarence," she said, as she

reentered the dining room and met his face of surprise. "He didn't come to make a call; he just wanted to borrow a book,—Physical Theory of another Life."

"How did you find it?" asked Ewbert, with relief.

"It was where it always was," she returned indifferently. "Mr. Hilbrook seemed to be very much interested in something you said to him about it. I do believe you *have* done him good, Clarence; and now, if you can only get a full night's rest, I shall forgive him. But I hope he won't come *very* soon again, and will never stay so late when he does come. Promise me you won't go near him till he's brought the book back!"

XII

Hilbrook came the night after he had borrowed the book, full of talk about it, to ask if he might keep it a little longer. Ewbert had slept well the intervening night, and had been suffered to see Hilbrook upon promising his wife that he would not encourage the old man to stay; but Hilbrook stayed without encouragement. An interest had come into his apathetic life which renewed it, and gave vitality to a whole dead world of things. He wished to talk, and he wished even more to listen, that he might confirm himself from Ewbert's faith and reason in the conjectures with which his mind was filled. His eagerness as to the conditions of a future life, now that he had begun to imagine them, was insatiable, and Ewbert, who met it with glad sympathy, felt drained of his own spiritual forces by the strength which he supplied to the old man. But the case was so strange, so absorbing, so important, that he could not refuse himself to it. He could not deny Hilbrook's claim to all that he could give him in this sort; he was as helpless to withhold the succor he supplied as he was to hide from Mrs. Ewbert's censoriously anxious eye the nervous exhaustion to which it left him after each visit that Hilbrook paid him. But there was a drain from another source of which he would not speak to her till he could make sure that the effect was not some trick of his own imagination.

He had been aware, in twice urging some reason upon Hilbrook, of a certain perfunctory quality in his performance. It was as if the truth, so vital at first, had perished in its formulation, and in the repetition he was sensible, or he was fearful, of an insincerity, a hollowness in the arguments he had originally employed so earnestly against the old man's doubt. He recognized with dismay a quality of question in his own mind, and he fancied that as Hilbrook waxed in belief he himself waned. The conviction of a life hereafter was not something which he was *sharing* with Hilbrook; he was *giving* it absolutely, and with such entire unreserve that he was impoverishing his own soul of its most precious possession.

So it seemed to him in those flaccid moods to which Hilbrook's visits left him, when mind and body were both spent in the effort he had been making. In the intervals in which his strength renewed itself, he put this fear from him as a hypochondriacal fancy, and he summoned a cheerfulness which he felt less and less to meet the hopeful face of the old man. Hilbrook had renewed himself, apparently, in the measure that the minister had aged and waned. He looked, to Ewbert, younger and stronger. To the conventional question how he did, he one night answered that he never felt better in his life. "But you," he said, casting an eye over the face and figure of the minister, who lay back in his easy-chair, with his hands stretched nerveless on the arms, "*you*, look rather peaked. I don't know as I noticed it before, but come to think, I seemed to feel the same way about it when I saw you in the pulpit yesterday."

"It was a very close day," said Ewbert. "I don't know why I shouldn't be about as well as usual."

"Well, that's right," said Hilbrook, in willing dismissal of the trifle which had delayed him from the great matter in his mind.

Some new thoughts had occurred to him in corroboration of the notions they had agreed upon in their last meeting. But in response Ewbert found himself beset by a strange temptation,—by the wish to take up these notions and expose their fallacy. They were indeed mere toys of their common fancy which they had constructed together in mutual supposition, but Ewbert felt a sacredness in them, while he longed so strangely to break them one by one and cast them in the old man's face. Like all imaginative people, he was at times the prey of morbid self-suggestions, whose nature can scarcely be stated without excess. The more monstrous the thing appeared to his mind and conscience, the more fascinating it became. Once the mere horror of such a conception as catching a comely parishioner about the waist and kissing her, when she had come to him with a case of conscience, had so confused him in her presence as to make him answer her wildly, not because he was really tempted to the wickedness, but because he realized so vividly the hideousness of the impossible temptation. In some such sort he now trembled before old Hilbrook, thinking how dreadful it would be if he were suddenly to begin undoing the work of faith in him, and putting back in its place the doubts which he had uprooted before. In a swift series of dramatic representations he figured the old man's helpless amaze at the demoniacal gayety with which he should mock his own seriousness in the past, the cynical ease with which he should show the vanity of the hopes he had been so fervent in awakening. He had throughout recognized the claim that all the counter-doubts had upon the reason, and he saw how effective he could make these if he were now to become their advocate. He pictured the despair in which he could send his proselyte tottering home to his lonely house through the dark.

He rent himself from the spell, but the last picture remained so real with him that he went to the window and looked out, saying, "Is there a moon?"

"It ain't up yet, I guess," said old Hilbrook, and from something in his manner, rather than from anything he recollected of their talk, Ewbert fancied him to have asked a question, and to be now waiting for some answer. He had not the least notion what the question could have been, and he began to walk up and down, trying to think of something to say, but feeling his legs weak under him and the sweat cold on his forehead. All the time he was aware of Hilbrook following him with an air of cheerful interest, and patiently waiting till he should take up the thread of their discourse again.

He controlled himself at last, and sank into his chair. "Where were we?" he asked. "I had gone off on a train of associations, and I don't just recall our last point."

Hilbrook stated it, and Ewbert said, "Oh, yes," as if he recognized it, and went on from it upon the line of thought which it suggested. He was aware of talking rationally and forcibly; but in the subjective undercurrent paralleling his objective thought he was holding discourse with himself to an effect wholly different from that produced in Hilbrook.

"Well, sir," said the old man when he rose to go at last, "I guess you've settled it for me. You've made me see that there can be an immortal life that's worth living; and I was afraid there wa'n't! I shouldn't care, now, if I woke up any morning in the other world. I guess it would be all right; and that there would be new conditions every way, so that a man could go on and be himself, without feelin' that he was in any danger of bein' wasted. You've made me want to meet my boy again; and I used to dread it; I didn't think I was fit for it. I don't know whether you expect me to thank you; I presume you don't; but I"—he faltered, and his voice shook in sympathy with the old hand that he put trembling into Ewbert's—"I *bless* you!"

XIII

The time had come when the minister must seek refuge and counsel with his wife. He went to her as a troubled child goes to its mother, and she heard the confession of his strange experience with the motherly sympathy which performs the comforting office of perfect intelligence. If she did not grasp its whole significance, she seized what was perhaps the main point, and she put herself in antagonism to the cause of his morbid condition, while administering an inevitable chastisement for the neglect of her own prevision.

"That terrible old man," she said, "has simply been draining the life out of you, Clarence. I saw it from the beginning, and I warned you against it; but you wouldn't listen to me. *Now* I suppose you *will* listen, after the doctor tells you that you're in danger of nervous prostration, and that you've got to give up everything and rest. *I* think you've been in danger of losing your reason, you've overworked it so; and I sha'n't be easy till I've got you safely away at the seaside, and out of the reach of that—that *vampire.*"

"Emily!" the minister protested. "I can't allow you to use such language. At the worst, and supposing that he has really been that drain upon me which you say (though I don't admit it), what is my life for but to give to others?"

"But *my* life isn't for you to give to others, and *your* life *is* mine, and I think I have some right to say what shall be done with it, and I don't choose to have it used up on old Hilbrook." It passed through Ewbert's languid thought, which it stirred to a vague amusement, that the son of an older church than the Rixonite might have found in this thoroughly terrestrial attitude of his wife a potent argument for sacerdotal celibacy; but he did not attempt to formulate it, and he listened submissively while she went on: "*One* thing: I am certainly not going to let you see him again till you've seen the doctor, and I hope he won't come about. If he does, *I* shall see him."

The menace in this declaration moved Ewbert to another protest, which he worded conciliatingly: "I shall have to let you. But I know you won't say anything to convey a sense of responsibility to him. I couldn't forgive myself if he were allowed to feel that he had been preying upon me. The fact is, I've been overdoing in every way, and nobody is to blame for my morbid fancies but myself. I *should* blame myself very severely if you based any sort of superstition on them, and acted from that superstition."

"Oh, you needn't be afraid!" said Mrs. Ewbert. "I shall take care of his feelings, but I shall have my own opinions, all the same, Clarence."

Whether a woman with opinions so strong as Mrs. Ewbert's, and so indistinguishable from her prejudices, could be trusted to keep them to herself, in dealing with the matter in hand, was a question which her husband felt must largely be left to her goodness of heart for its right solution.

When Hilbrook came that night, as usual, she had already had it out with him in several strenuous reveries before they met, and she was able to welcome him gently to the interview which she made very brief. His face fell in visible disappointment when she said that Mr. Ewbert would not be able to see him, and perhaps there was nothing to uplift him in the reasons she gave, though she obscurely resented his continued dejection as a kind of ingratitude. She explained that poor Mr. Ewbert was quite broken down, and that the doctor had advised his going to the seaside for the whole of August, where he promised everything from the air and the bathing. Mr. Ewbert merely needed toning up, she said; but to correct the impression she might be giving that his breakdown was a trifling matter, she added that she felt very anxious about it, and wanted to get him away as soon as possible. She said with a confidential effect, as of something in which Hilbrook could sympathize with her: "You know it isn't merely his church work proper;

it's his giving himself spiritually to all sorts of people so indiscriminately. He can't deny himself to any one; and sometimes he's perfectly exhausted by it. You must come and see him as soon as he gets back, Mr. Hilbrook. He will count upon it, I know; he's so much interested in the discussions he has been having with you."

She gave the old man her hand for good-by, after she had artfully stood him up, in a double hope,—a hope that he would understand that there was some limit to her husband's nervous strength, and a hope that her closing invitation would keep him from feeling anything personal in her hints.

Hilbrook took his leave in the dreamy fashion age has with so many things, as if there were a veil between him and experience which kept him from the full realization of what had happened; and as she watched his bent shoulders down the garden walk, carrying his forward-drooping head at a slant that scarcely left the crown of his hat visible, a fear came upon her which made it impossible for her to recount all the facts of her interview to her husband. It became her duty, rather, to conceal what was painful to herself in it, and she merely told him that Mr. Hilbrook had taken it all in the right way, and she had made him promise to come and see them as soon as they got back.

William Dean Howells

XIV

Events approved the wisdom of Mrs. Ewbert's course in so many respects that she confidently trusted them for the rest. Ewbert picked up wonderfully at the seaside, and she said to him again and again that it was not merely those interviews with old Hilbrook which had drained his vitality, but it was the whole social and religious keeping of the place. Everybody, she said, had thrown themselves upon his sympathies, and he was carrying a load that nobody could bear up under. She addressed these declarations to her lingering consciousness of Ransom Hilbrook, and confirmed herself, by their repetition, in the belief that he had not taken her generalizations personally. She now extended these so as to inculpate the faculty of the university, who ought to have felt it their duty not to let a man of Ewbert's intellectual quality stagger on alone among them, with no sign of appreciation or recognition in the work he was doing, not so much for the Rixonite church as for the whole community. She took several ladies at the hotel into her confidence on this point, and upon study of the situation they said it was a shame. After that she felt more bitter about it, and attributed her husband's collapse to a concealed sense of the indifference of the university people, so galling to a sensitive nature.

She suggested this theory to Ewbert, and he denied it with blithe derision, but she said that he need not tell *her*, and in confirming herself in it she began to relax her belief that old Ransom Hilbrook had preyed upon him. She even went so far as to say that the only intellectual companionship he had ever had in the place was that which he found in the old man's society. When she discovered, after the fact, that Ewbert had written to him since they came away, she was not so severe with him as she might have expected herself to be in view of an act which, if not quite clandestine, was certainly without her privity. She would have considered him fitly punished by Hilbrook's failure to reply, if she had not shared his uneasiness at the old man's silence. But she did not allow this to affect her good spirits, which were essential to her husband's comfort as well as her own. She redoubled her care of him in every sort, and among all the ladies who admired her devotion to him there was none who enjoyed it as much as herself. There was none who believed more implicitly that it was owing to her foresight and oversight that his health mended so rapidly, and that at the end of the bathing season she was, as she said, taking him home quite another man. In her perfect satisfaction she suffered him his small joke about not feeling it quite right to go with her if that were so; and though a woman of little humor, she even professed to find pleasure in his joke after she fully understood it.

"All that I ask," she said, as if it followed, "is that you won't spoil everything by letting old Hilbrook come every night and drain the life out of you again."

"I won't," he retorted, "if you'll promise to make the university people come regularly to my sermons."

He treated the notion of Hilbrook's visits lightly; but with his return to the familiar environment he felt a shrinking from them in an experience which was like something physical. Yet when he sat down the first night in his study, with his lamp in its wonted place, it was with an expectation of old Hilbrook in his usual seat so vivid that its defeat was more a shock than its fulfilment upon supernatural terms would have been. In fact, the absence of the old man was spectral; and though Ewbert employed himself fully the first night in answering an accumulation of letters that required immediate reply, it was with nervous starts from time to time, which he could trace to no other cause. His wife came in and out, with what he knew to be an accusing eye, as she brought up those arrears of housekeeping which always await the housewife on the return from any vacation; and he knew that he did not conceal his guilt from her.

They both ignored the stress which had fallen back upon him, and which accumulated, as the days of the week went by, until the first Sunday came.

Ewbert dreaded to look in the direction of Hilbrook's pew, lest he should find it empty; but the old man was there, and he sat blinking at the minister, as his custom was, through the sermon, and thoughtfully passing the tip of his tongue over the inner edge of his lower lip.

Many came up to shake hands with the minister after church, and to tell him how well he was looking, but Hilbrook was not among them. Some of the university people who had made a point of being there that morning, out of a personal regard for Ewbert, were grouped about his wife, in the church vestibule, where she stood answering their questions about his health. He glimpsed between the heads and shoulders of this gratifying group the figure of Hilbrook dropping from grade to grade on the steps outside, till it ceased to be visible, and he fancied, with a pang, that the old man had lingered to speak with him, and had then given up and started home.

The cordial interest of the university people was hardly a compensation for the disappointment he shared with Hilbrook; but his wife was so happy in it that he could not say anything to damp her joy. "Now," she declared, on their way home, "I am perfectly satisfied that they will keep coming. You never preached so well, Clarence, and if they have any appreciation at all, they simply won't be able to keep away. I wish you could have heard all the nice things they said about you. I guess they've waked up to you, at last, and I do believe that the idea of losing you has had a great deal to do with it. And *that* is something we owe to old Ransom Hilbrook more than to anything else. I saw the poor old fellow hanging about, and I couldn't help feeling for him. I knew he wanted to speak with you, and I'm not afraid that he will be a burden again. It will be such an inspiration, the prospect of having the university people come every Sunday, now, that you can afford to give a little of it to him, and I want you to go and see him soon; he evidently isn't coming till you do."

XV

Ewbert had learned not to inquire too critically for a logical process in his wife's changes of attitude toward any fact. In her present mood he recognized an effect of the exuberant good-will awakened by the handsome behavior of the university people, and he agreed with her that he must go to see old Hilbrook at once. In this good intention his painful feeling concerning him was soothed, and Ewbert did not get up to the Hilbrook place till well into the week. It was Thursday afternoon when he climbed through the orchard, under the yellowing leaves which dappled the green masses of the trees like intenser spots of the September sunshine. He came round by the well to the side door of the house, which stood open, and he did not hesitate to enter when he saw how freely the hens were coming and going through it. They scuttled out around him and between his legs, with guilty screeches, and left him standing alone in the middle of the wide, low kitchen. A certain discomfort of the nerves which their flight gave him was heightened by some details quite insignificant in them-selves. There was no fire in the stove, and the wooden clock on the mantel behind it was stopped; the wind had carried in some red leaves from the maple near the door, and these were swept against the farther wall, where they lay palpitating in the draft.

The neglect in all was evidently too recent to suggest any supposition but that of the master's temporary absence, and Ewbert went to the threshold to look for his coming from the sheds or the barn. But these were all fast shut, and there was no sign of Hilbrook anywhere. Ewbert turned back into the room again, and saw the door of the old man's little bedroom standing slightly ajar. With a chill of apprehension he pushed it open, and he could not have experienced a more disagreeable effect if the dark fear in his mind had been realized than he did to see Hilbrook lying in his bed alive and awake. His face showed like a fine mask above the sheet, and his long, narrow hands rested on the covering across his breast. His eyes met

William Dean Howells

those of Ewbert not only without surprise, but without any apparent emotion.

"Why, Mr. Hilbrook," said the minister, "are you sick?"

"No, I am first-rate," the old man answered.

It was on the point of the minister's tongue to ask him, "Then what in the world are you doing in bed?" but he substituted the less authoritative suggestion, "I am afraid I disturbed you—that I woke you out of a nap. But I found the door open and the hens inside, and I ventured to come in"—

Hilbrook replied calmly, "I heard you; I wa'n't asleep."

"Oh," said Ewbert, apologetically, and he did not know quite what to do; he had an aimless wish for his wife, as if she would have known what to do. In her absence he decided to shut the door against the hens, who were returning adventurously to the threshold, and then he asked, "Is there something I can do for you? Make a fire for you to get up by"—

"I ha'n't got any call to get up," said Hilbrook; and, after giving Ewbert time to make the best of this declaration, he asked abruptly, "What was that you said about my wantin' to be alive enough to know I was dead?"

"The consciousness of unconsciousness?"

"Ah!" the old man assented, as with satisfaction in having got the notion right; and then he added, with a certain defiance: "There ain't anything *in* that. I got to thinking it over, when you was gone, and the whole thing went to pieces. That idea don't prove anything at all, and all that we worked out of it had to go with it."

"Well," the minister returned, with an assumption of cosiness in his tone which he did not feel, and feigning to make himself easy in the hard kitchen chair which he pulled up to the door of Hilbrook's room, "let's see if we can't put that notion together again."

"*You* can, if you want to," said the old man, dryly "I got no interest in it any more; 'twa'n't nothing but a metaphysical toy, anyway." He turned his head apathetically on the pillow, and no longer faced his visitor, who found it impossible in the conditions of tacit dismissal to philosophize further.

"I was sorry," Ewbert began, "not to be able to speak with you after church, the other day. There were so many people"—

"That's all right," said Hilbrook unresentfully. "I hadn't anything to say, in particular."

"But *I* had," the minister persisted. "I thought a great deal about you when I was away, and I went over our talks in my own mind a great many times. The more I thought about them, the more I believed that we had felt our way to some important truth in the matter. I don't say final truth, for I don't suppose that we shall ever reach that in this life."

"Very likely," Hilbrook returned, with his face to the wall. "I don't see as it makes any difference; or if it does, I don't care for it."

Something occurred to Ewbert which seemed to him of more immediate usefulness than the psychological question. "Couldn't I get you something to eat, Mr. Hilbrook? If you haven't had any breakfast to-day, you must be hungry."

"Yes, I'm hungry," the old man assented, "but I don't want to eat anything."

Ewbert had risen hopefully in making his suggestion, but now his heart sank. Here, it seemed to him, a physician rather than a philosopher was needed, and at the sound of wheels on the wagon track to the door his imagination leaped to the miracle of the doctor's providential advent. He hurried to the threshold and met the fish-man, who was about to announce himself with the handle of his whip on the clapboarding. He grasped the situation from the minister's brief statement, and confessed that he had expected to find the old gentleman *dead* in his bed some day, and he volunteered to send some of the women folks from the farm up the road. When these came, concentrated in the person of the farmer's bustling wife, who had a fire kindled in the stove and the kettle on before Ewbert could get away, he went for the doctor, and returned with him to find her in possession of everything in the house except the owner's interest. Her usefulness had been arrested by an invisible but impassable barrier, though she had passed and re-passed the threshold of Hilbrook's chamber with tea and milk toast. He said simply that he saw no object in eating; and he had not been sufficiently interested to turn his head and look at her in speaking to her.

With the doctor's science he was as indifferent as with the farm-wife's service. He submitted to have his pulse felt, and he could not help being prescribed for, but he would have no agency in taking his medicine. He said, as he had said to Mrs. Stephson about eating, that he saw no object in it.

The doctor retorted, with the temper of a man not used to having his will crossed, that he had better take it, if he had any object in living, and Hilbrook answered that he had none. In his absolute apathy he did not even ask to be let alone.

"You see," the baffled doctor fumed in the conference that he had with Ewbert apart, "he doesn't really need any medicine. There's nothing the matter with him, and I only wanted to give him something to put an edge to his appetite. He's got cranky living here alone; but there *is* such a thing as starving to death, and that's the only thing Hilbrook's in danger of. If you're going to stay with him—he oughtn't to be left alone"—

"I can come up, yes, certainly, after supper," said Ewbert, and he fortified himself inwardly for the question this would raise with his wife.

"Then you must try to interest him in something. Get him to talking, and then let Mrs. Stephson come in with a good bowl of broth, and I guess we may trust Nature to do the rest."

William Dean Howells

XVI

When we speak of Nature, we figure her as one thing, with a fixed purpose and office in the universal economy; but she is an immense number of things, and her functions are inexpressibly varied. She includes decay as well as growth; she compasses death as well as birth. We call certain phenomena unnatural; but in a natural world how can anything be unnatural, except the supernatural? These facts gave Ewbert pause in view of the obstinate behavior of Ransom Hilbrook in dying for no obvious reason, and kept him from pronouncing it unnatural. The old man, he reflected, had really less reason to live than to die, if it came to reasons; for everything that had made the world home to him had gone out of it, and left him in exile here. The motives had ceased; the interests had perished; the strong personality that had persisted was solitary amid the familiar environment grown alien.

The wonder was that he should ever have been roused from his apathetic unfaith to inquiry concerning the world beyond this, and to a certain degree of belief in possibilities long abandoned by his imagination. Ewbert had assisted at the miracle of this resuscitation upon terms which, until he was himself much older, he could not question as to their beneficence, and in fact it never came to his being quite frank with himself concerning them. He kept his thoughts on this point in that state of solution which holds so many conjectures from precipitation in actual conviction.

But his wife had no misgivings. Her dread was that in his devotion to that miserable old man (as she called him, not always in compassion) he should again contribute to Hilbrook's vitality at the expense, if not the danger, of his own. She of course expressed her joy that Ewbert had at last prevailed upon him to eat something, when the entreaty of his nurse and the authority of his doctor availed nothing; and of course she felt the pathos of his doing it out of affection for Ewbert, and merely to please him, as Hilbrook declared. It did not surprise her that any one should do anything for the love of Ewbert, but it is doubtful if she fully recognized the beauty of this last efflorescence of the aged life; and she perceived it her duty not to sympathize entirely with Ewbert's morbid regret that it came too late. She was much more resigned than he to the will of Providence, and she urged a like submissiveness upon him.

"Don't talk so!" he burst out. "It's horrible!" It was in the first hours after Ewbert's return from Hilbrook's death-bed, and his spent nerves gave way in a gush of tears.

"I see what you mean," she said, after a pause in which he controlled his sobs. "And I suppose," she added, with a touch of bitterness, "that you blame *me* for taking you away from him here when he was coming every night and sapping your very life. You were very glad to have me do it at the time! And what use would there have been in your killing yourself, anyway? It wasn't as if he were a young man with a career of usefulness before him, that might have been marred by his not believing this or that. He had been a complete failure every way, and the end of the world had come for him. What did it matter whether such a man believed that there was another world or not?"

"Emily! Emily!" the minister cried out. "What are you saying?"

Mrs. Ewbert broke down in her turn. "I don't know *what* I'm saying!" she retorted from behind her handkerchief. "I'm trying to show you that it's your duty to yourself—and to me—and to people who can know how to profit by your teaching and your example, not to give way as you're doing, simply because a wornout old agnostic couldn't keep his hold on the truth. I don't know what your Rixonitism is for if it won't let you wait upon the divine will in such a thing, *too*. You're more conscientious than the worst kind of Congregationalist. And now for you to blame me"—

"Emily, I don't blame *you*," said her husband. "I blame myself."

"And you see that that's the same thing! You ought to thank me for saving your life; for it was just as if you were pouring your heart's blood into him, and I could see you getting more anaemic every day. Even now you're not half as well as when you got home! And yet I do believe that if you could bring old Hilbrook back into a world that he was sick and tired of, you'd give your own life to do it."

XVII

There was reason and there was justice in what she said, though they were so chaotic in form, and Ewbert could not refuse to acquiesce.

After all, he had done what he could, and he would not abandon himself to a useless remorse. He rather set himself to study the lesson of old Hilbrook's life, and in the funeral sermon that he preached he urged upon his hearers the necessity of keeping themselves alive through some relation to the undying frame of things, which they could do only by cherishing earthly ties; and when these were snapped in the removal of their objects, by attaching the broken threads through an effort of the will to yet other objects: the world could furnish these inexhaustibly. He touched delicately upon the peculiarities, the eccentricities, of the deceased, and he did cordial justice to his gentleness, his blameless, harmless life, his heroism on the battlefields of his country. He declared that he would not be the one to deny an inner piety, and certainly not a steadfast courage, in Hilbrook's acceptance of whatever his sincere doubts implied.

The sermon apparently made a strong impression on all who heard it. Mrs. Ewbert was afraid that it was rather abstruse in certain passages, but she felt sure that all the university people would appreciate these. The university people, to testify their respect for their founder, had come in a body to the obsequies of his kinsman; and Mrs. Ewbert augured the best things for her husband's future usefulness from their presence.

THE MAGIC OF A VOICE

I

There was a full moon, and Langbourne walked about the town, unable to come into the hotel and go to bed. The deep yards of the houses gave out the scent of syringas and June roses; the light of lamps came through the fragrant bushes from the open doors and windows, with the sound of playing and singing and bursts of young laughter. Where the houses stood near the street, he could see people lounging on the thresholds, and their heads silhouetted against the luminous interiors. Other houses, both those which stood further back and those that stood nearer, were dark and still, and to these he attributed the happiness of love in fruition, safe from unrest and longing.

His own heart was tenderly oppressed, not with desire, but with the memory of desire. It was almost as if in his faded melancholy he were sorry for the disappointment of some one else.

At last he turned and walked back through the streets of dwellings to the business centre of the town, where a gush of light came from the veranda of his hotel, and the druggist's window cast purple and yellow blurs out upon the footway. The other stores were shut, and he alone seemed to be abroad. The church clock struck ten as he mounted the steps of his hotel and dropped the remnant of his cigar over the side.

He had slept badly on the train the night before, and he had promised himself to make up his lost sleep in the good conditions that seemed to offer themselves. But when he sat down in the hotel office he was more wakeful than he had been when he started out to walk himself drowsy.

The clerk gave him the New York paper which had come by the evening train, and he thanked him, but remained musing in his chair. At times he thought he would light another cigar, but the hand that he carried to his breast pocket dropped nervelessly to his knee again, and he did not smoke. Through his memories of disappointment pierced a self-reproach which did not permit him the perfect self-complacency of regret; and yet he could not have been sure, if he had asked himself, that this pang did not heighten the luxury of his psychological experience.

He rose and asked the clerk for a lamp, but he turned back from the stairs to inquire when there would be another New York mail. The clerk said there was a train from the south due at eleven-forty, but it seldom brought any mail; the principal mail was at seven. Langbourne thanked him, and came back again to beg the clerk to be careful and not have him called in the morning, for he wished to sleep. Then he went up to his room, where he opened his window to let in the night air. He heard a dog barking; a cow lowed; from a stable somewhere the soft thumping of the horses' feet came at intervals lullingly.

II

Langbourne fell asleep so quickly that he was aware of no moment of waking after his head touched the fragrant pillow. He woke so much refreshed by his first sound, soft sleep that he thought it must be nearly morning. He got his watch into a ray of the moonlight and made out that it was only a little after midnight, and he perceived that it must have been the sound of low murmuring voices and broken laughter in the next room which had wakened him. But he was rather glad to have been roused to a sense of his absolute comfort, and he turned unresentfully to sleep again. All his heaviness of heart was gone; he felt curiously glad and young; he had somehow forgiven the wrong he had suffered and the wrong he had done. The subdued murmuring went on in the next room, and he kept himself awake to enjoy it for a while. Then he let himself go, and drifted away into gulfs of slumber, where, suddenly, he seemed to strike against something, and started up in bed.

A laugh came from the next room. It was not muffled, as before, but frank and clear. It was woman's laughter, and Langbourne easily inferred girlhood as well as womanhood from it. His neighbors must have come by the late train, and they had probably begun to talk as soon as they got into their room. He imagined their having spoken low at first for fear of disturbing some one, and then, in their forgetfulness, or their belief that there was no one near, allowed themselves greater freedom. There were survivals of their earlier caution at times, when their voices sank so low as scarcely to be heard; then there was a break from it when they rose clearly distinguishable from each other. They were never so distinct that he could make out what was said; but each voice unmistakably conveyed character.

Friendship between girls is never equal; they may equally love each other, but one must worship and one must suffer worship. Langbourne read the differing temperaments necessary to this relation in the differing voices. That which bore mastery was a low, thick murmur, coming from deep in the throat, and flowing out in a steady stream of indescribable coaxing and drolling. The owner of that voice had imagination and humor which could charm with absolute control her companion's lighter nature, as it betrayed itself in a gay tinkle of amusement and a succession of nervous whispers. Langbourne did not wonder at her subjection; with the first sounds of that rich, tender voice, he had fallen under its spell too; and he listened intensely, trying to make out some phrase, some word, some syllable. But the talk kept its sub-audible flow, and he had to content himself as he could with the sound of the voice.

As he lay eavesdropping with all his might he tried to construct an image of the two girls from their voices. The one with the crystalline laugh was little and lithe, quick in movement, of a mobile face, with gray eyes and fair hair; the other was tall and pale, with full, blue eyes and a regular face, and lips that trembled with humor; very demure and yet very honest; very shy and yet very frank; there was something almost mannish in her essential honesty; there was nothing of feminine coquetry in her, though everything of feminine charm. She was a girl who looked like her father, Langbourne perceived with a flash of divination. She dressed simply in dark blue, and her hair was of a dark mahogany color. The smaller girl wore light gray checks or stripes, and the shades of silver.

The talk began to be less continuous in the next room, from which there came the sound of sighs and yawns, and then of mingled laughter at these. Then the talk ran unbrokenly on for a while, and again dropped into laughs that recognized the drowse creeping upon the talkers. Suddenly it stopped altogether, and left Langbourne, as he felt, definitively awake for the rest of the night.

He had received an impression which he could not fully analyze. With some inner sense he kept hearing that voice, low and deep, and rich with whimsical suggestion. Its owner must have a strange, complex nature, which would perpetually provoke and satisfy. Her companionship would be as easy and reasonable as a man's, while it had the charm of a woman's. At the moment it seemed to him that life without this companionship would be something poorer and thinner than he had yet known, and that he could not endure to forego it. Somehow he must manage to see the girl and make her acquaintance. He did not know how it could be contrived, but it could certainly be contrived, and he began to dramatize their meeting on these various terms. It was interesting and it was delightful, and it always came, in its safe impossibility, to his telling her that he loved her, and to her consenting to be his wife. He resolved to take no chance of losing her, but to remain awake, and somehow see her before she could leave the hotel in the morning. The resolution gave him calm; he felt that the affair so far was settled.

Suddenly he started from his pillow; and again he heard that mellow laugh, warm and rich as the cooing of doves on sunlit eaves. The sun was shining through the crevices of his window-blinds; he looked at his watch; it was half-past eight. The sound of fluttering skirts and flying feet in the corridor shook his heart. A voice, the voice of the mellow laugh, called as if to some one on the stairs, "I must have put it in my bag. It doesn't matter, anyway."

He hurried on his clothes, in the vain hope of finding his late neighbors at breakfast; but before he had finished dressing he heard wheels before the veranda below, and he saw the hotel barge drive away, as if to the station. There were two passengers in it; two women, whose faces were hidden by the fringe of the barge-roof, but whose slender figures showed themselves from their necks down. It seemed to him that one was tall and slight, and the other slight and little.

III

He stopped in the hall, and then, tempted by his despair, he stepped within the open door of the next room and looked vaguely over it, with shame at being there. What was it that the girl had missed, and had come back to look for? Some trifle, no doubt, which she had not cared to lose, and yet had not wished to leave behind. He failed to find anything in the search, which he could not make very thorough, and he was going guiltily out when his eye fell upon an envelope, perversely fallen beside the door and almost indiscernible against the white paint, with the addressed surface inward.

This must be the object of her search, and he could understand why she was not very anxious when he found it a circular from a nursery-man, containing nothing more valuable than a list of flowering shrubs. He satisfied himself that this was all without satisfying himself that he had quite a right to do so; and he stood abashed in the presence of the superscription on the envelope somewhat as if Miss Barbara F. Simpson, Upper Ashton Falls, N. H., were there to see him tampering with her correspondence. It was indelicate, and he felt that his whole behavior had been indelicate, from the moment her laugh had wakened him in the night till now, when he had invaded her room. He had no more doubt that she was the taller of the two girls than that this was her name on the envelope. He liked Barbara; and Simpson could be changed. He seemed to hear her soft throaty laugh in response to the suggestion, and with a leap of the heart he slipped the circular into his breast pocket.

After breakfast he went to the hotel office, and stood leaning on the long counter and talking with the clerk till he could gather courage to look at the register, where he knew the names of these girls must be written. He asked where Upper Ashton Falls was, and whether it would be a pleasant place to spend a week.

The clerk said that it was about thirty miles up the road, and was one of the nicest places in the mountains; Langbourne could not go to a nicer; and there was a very good little hotel. "Why," he said, "there were two ladies here overnight that just left for there, on the seven-forty. Odd you should ask about it."

Langbourne owned that it was odd, and then he asked if the ladies lived at Upper Ashton Falls, or were merely summer folks.

"Well, a little of both," said the clerk. "They're cousins, and they've got an aunt living there that they stay with. They used to go away winters,—teaching, I guess,—but this last year they stayed right through. Been down to Springfield, they said, and just stopped the night because the accommodation don't go any farther. Wake you up last night? I had to put 'em into the room next to yours, and girls usually talk."

Langbourne answered that it would have taken a good deal of talking to wake him the night before, and then he lounged across to the time-table hanging on the wall, and began to look up the trains for Upper Ashton Falls.

"If you want to go to the Falls," said the clerk, "there's a through train at four, with a drawing-room on it, that will get you there by five."

"Oh, I fancy I was looking up the New York trains," Langbourne returned. He did not like these evasions, but in his consciousness of Miss Simpson he seemed unable to avoid them. The clerk went out on the veranda to talk with a farmer bringing supplies, and Langbourne ran to the register, and read there the names of Barbara F. Simpson and Juliet D. Bingham. It was Miss Simpson who had registered for both, since her name came first, and the entry was in a good, simple hand, which was like a man's in its firmness and clearness. He turned from the register decided to take the four-o'clock train for Upper Ashton Falls, and met a messenger with a telegram which he knew was for himself before the boy could ask his name. His partner had fallen suddenly sick; his recall was absolute, his vacation was at an end; nothing remained for him but to take the first train back to New York. He thought how little prescient he had been in his pretence that he was looking the New York trains up; but the need of one had come already, and apparently he should never have any use for a train to Upper Ashton Falls.

William Dean Howells

IV

All the way back to New York Langbourne was oppressed by a
sense of loss such as his old disappointment in love now
seemed to him never to have inflicted. He found that his
whole being had set toward the unseen owner of the voice
which had charmed him, and it was like a stretching and
tearing of the nerves to be going from her instead of going to
her. He was as much under duress as if he were bound by a
hypnotic spell. The voice continually sounded, not in his ears,
which were filled with the noises of the train, as usual, but in
the inmost of his spirit, where it was a low, cooing, coaxing
murmur. He realized now how intensely he must have listened
for it in the night, how every tone of it must have pervaded
him and possessed him. He was in love with it, he was as
entirely fascinated by it as if it were the girl's whole presence,
her looks, her qualities. The remnant of the summer passed in
the fret of business, which was doubly irksome through his
feeling of injury in being kept from the girl whose personality
he constructed from the sound of her voice, and set over his
fancy in an absolute sovereignty. The image he had created of
her remained a dim and blurred vision throughout the day, but
by night it became distinct and compelling. One evening, late
in the fall, he could endure the stress no longer, and he yielded
to the temptation which had beset him from the first moment
he renounced his purpose of returning in person the circular
addressed to her as a means of her acquaintance. He wrote to
her, and in terms as dignified as he could contrive, and as free
from any ulterior import, he told her he had found it in the
hotel hallway and had meant to send it to her at once, thinking
it might be of some slight use to her. He had failed to do this,
and now, having come upon it among some other papers, he
sent it with an explanation which he hoped she would excuse
him for troubling her with.

This was not true, but he did not see how he could begin with
her by saying that he had found the circular in her room, and
had kept it by him ever since, looking at it every day, and

leaving it where he could see it the last thing before he slept at night and the first thing after he woke in the morning. As to her reception of his story, he had to trust to his knowledge that she was, like himself, of country birth and breeding, and to his belief that she would not take alarm at his overture. He did not go much into the world and was little acquainted with its usages, yet he knew enough to suspect that a woman of the world would either ignore his letter, or would return a cold and snubbing expression of Miss Simpson's thanks for Mr. Stephen M. Langbourne's kindness.

He had not only signed his name and given his address carefully in hopes of a reply, but he had enclosed the business card of his firm as a token of his responsibility. The partner in a wholesale stationery house ought to be an impressive figure in the imagination of a village girl; but it was some weeks before any answer came to Langbourne's letter. The reply began with an apology for the delay, and Langbourne perceived that he had gained rather than lost by the writer's hesitation; clearly she believed that she had put herself in the wrong, and that she owed him a certain reparation. For the rest, her letter was discreetly confined to an acknowledgment of the trouble he had taken.

But this spare return was richly enough for Langbourne; it would have sufficed, if there had been nothing in the letter, that the handwriting proved Miss Simpson to have been the one who had made the entry of her name and her friend's in the hotel register. This was most important as one step in corroboration of the fact that he had rightly divined her; that the rest should come true was almost a logical necessity. Still, he was puzzled to contrive a pretext for writing again, and he remained without one for a fortnight. Then, in passing a seedsman's store which he used to pass every day without thinking, he one day suddenly perceived his opportunity. He went in and got a number of the catalogues and other advertisements, and addressed them then and there, in a wrapper the seedsman gave him, to Miss Barbara F. Simpson, Upper Ashton Falls, N. H.

Now the response came with a promptness which at least testified of the lingering compunction of Miss Simpson. She asked if she were right in supposing the seedsman's catalogues and folders had come to her from Langbourne, and begged to know from him whether the seedsman in question was reliable: it was so difficult to get garden seeds that one could trust.

The correspondence now established itself, and with one excuse or another it prospered throughout the winter. Langbourne was not only willing, he was most eager, to give her proof of his reliability; he spoke of stationers in Springfield and Greenfield to whom he was personally known; and he secretly hoped she would satisfy herself through friends in those places that he was an upright and trustworthy person.

Miss Simpson wrote delightful letters, with that whimsical quality which had enchanted him in her voice. The coaxing and caressing was not there, and could not be expected to impart itself, unless in those refuges of deep feeling supposed to lurk between the lines. But he hoped to provoke it from these in time, and his own letters grew the more earnest the more ironical hers became. He wrote to her about a book he was reading, and when she said she had not seen it, he sent it her; in one of her letters she casually betrayed that she sang contralto in the choir, and then he sent her some new songs, which he had heard in the theatre, and which he had informed himself from a friend were contralto. He was always tending to an expression of the feeling which swayed him; but on her part there was no sentiment. Only in the fact that she was willing to continue this exchange of letters with a man personally unknown to her did she betray that romantic tradition which underlies all our young life, and in those unused to the world tempts to things blameless in themselves, but of the sort shunned by the worldlier wise. There was no great wisdom of any kind in Miss Simpson's letters; but Langbourne did not miss it; he was content with her mere words, as they related the little events of her simple daily life. These repeated themselves from the page in the tones of her voice and filled him with a passionate intoxication.

Towards spring he had his photograph taken, for no reason that he could have given; but since it was done he sent one to his mother in Vermont, and then he wrote his name on another, and sent it to Miss Simpson in New Hampshire. He hoped, of course, that she would return a photograph of herself; but she merely acknowledged his with some dry playfulness. Then, after disappointing him so long that he ceased to expect anything, she enclosed a picture. The face was so far averted that Langbourne could get nothing but the curve of a longish cheek, the point of a nose, the segment of a crescent eyebrow. The girl said that as they should probably never meet, it was not necessary he should know her when he saw her; she explained that she was looking away because she had been attracted by something on the other side of the photograph gallery just at the moment the artist took the cap off the tube of his camera, and she could not turn back without breaking the plate.

Langbourne replied that he was going up to Springfield on business the first week in May, and that he thought he might push on as far north as Upper Ashton Falls. To this there came no rejoinder whatever, but he did not lose courage. It was now the end of April, and he could bear to wait for a further verification of his ideal; the photograph had confirmed him in its evasive fashion at every point of his conjecture concerning her. It was the face he had imagined her having, or so he now imagined, and it was just such a long oval face as would go with the figure he attributed to her. She must have the healthy palor of skin which associates itself with masses of dark, mahogany-colored hair.

V

It was so long since he had known a Northern spring that he had forgotten how much later the beginning of May was in New Hampshire; but as his train ran up from Springfield he realized the difference of the season from that which he had left in New York. The meadows were green only in the damp hollows; most of the trees were as bare as in midwinter; the willows in the swamplands hung out their catkins, and the white birches showed faint signs of returning life. In the woods were long drifts of snow, though he knew that in the brown leaves along their edges the pale pink flowers of the trailing arbutus were hiding their wet faces. A vernal mildness overhung the landscape. A blue haze filled the distances and veiled the hills; from the farm door-yards the smell of burning leaf-heaps and garden-stalks came through the window which he lifted to let in the dull, warm air. The sun shone down from a pale sky, in which the crows called to one another.

By the time he arrived at Upper Ashton Falls the afternoon had waned so far towards evening that the first robins were singing their vespers from the leafless choirs of the maples before the hotel. He indulged the landlord in his natural supposition that he had come up to make a timely engagement for summer board; after supper he even asked what the price of such rooms as his would be by the week in July, while he tried to lead the talk round to the fact which he wished to learn.

He did not know where Miss Simpson lived; and the courage with which he had set out on his adventure totally lapsed, leaving in its place an accusing sense of silliness. He was where he was without reason, and in defiance of the tacit unwillingness of the person he had come to see; she certainly had given him no invitation, she had given him no permission to come. For the moment, in his shame, it seemed to him that the only thing for him was to go back to New York by the first train in the morning. But what then would the girl think of him? Such an act must forever end the intercourse which had now become an essential part of his life. That voice which had haunted him so long, was he never to hear it again? Was he willing to renounce forever the hope of hearing it?

He sat at his supper so long, nervelessly turning his doubts over in his mind, that the waitress came out of the kitchen and drove him from the table with her severe, impatient stare.

He put on his hat, and with his overcoat on his arm he started out for a walk which was hopeless, but not so aimless as he feigned to himself. The air was lullingly warm still as he followed the long village street down the hill toward the river, where the lunge of rapids filled the dusk with a sort of humid uproar; then he turned and followed it back past the hotel as far as it led towards the open country. At the edge of the village he came to a large, old-fashioned house, which struck him as typical, with its outward swaying fence of the Greek border pattern, and its gate-posts topped by tilting urns of painted wood. The house itself stood rather far back from the street, and as he passed it he saw that it was approached by a pathway of brick which was bordered with box. Stalks of last year's hollyhocks and lilacs from garden beds on either hand lifted their sharp points, here and there broken and hanging down. It was curious how these details insisted through the twilight.

He walked on until the wooden village pathway ended in the country mud, and then again he returned up upon his steps. As he reapproached the house he saw lights. A brighter radiance streamed from the hall door, which was apparently open, and a softer glow flushed the windows of one of the rooms that flanked the hall.

As Langbourne came abreast of the gate the tinkle of a gay laugh rang out to him; then ensued a murmur of girls' voices in the room, and suddenly this stopped, and the voice that he knew, the voice that seemed never to have ceased to sound in his nerves and pulses, rose in singing words set to the Spanish air of *La Paloma*.

It was one of the songs he had sent to Miss Simpson, but he did not need this material proof that it was she whom he now heard. There was no question of what he should do. All doubt, all fear, had vanished; he had again but one impulse, one desire, one purpose. But he lingered at the gate till the song ended, and then he unlatched it and started up the walk towards the door. It seemed to him a long way; he almost reeled as he went; he fumbled tremulously for the bell-pull beside the door, while a confusion of voices in the adjoining room—the voices which had waked him from his sleep, and which now sounded like voices in a dream—came out to him.

The light from the lamp hanging in the hall shone full in his face, and the girl who came from that room beside it to answer his ring gave a sort of conscious jump at sight of him as he uncovered and stood bare-headed before her.

VI

She must have recognized him from the photograph he had sent, and in stature and figure he recognized her as the ideal he had cherished, though her head was gilded with the light from the lamp, and he could not make out whether her hair was dark or fair; her face was, of course, a mere outline, without color or detail against the luminous interior.

He managed to ask, dry-tongued and with a heart that beat into his throat, "Is Miss Simpson at home?" and the girl answered, with a high, gay tinkle:

"Yes, she's at home. Won't you walk in?"

He obeyed, but at the sound of her silvery voice his heart dropped back into his breast. He put his hat and coat on an entry chair, and prepared to follow her into the room she had come out of. The door stood ajar, and he said, as she put out her hand to push it open, "I am Mr. Langbourne."

"Oh, yes," she answered in the same high, gay tinkle, which he fancied had now a note of laughter in it.

An elderly woman of a ladylike village type was sitting with some needlework beside a little table, and a young girl turned on the piano-stool and rose to receive him. "My aunt, Mrs. Simpson, Mr. Langbourne," said the girl who introduced him to these presences, and she added, indicating the girl at the piano, "Miss Simpson."

They all three bowed silently, and in the hush the sheet on the music frame slid from the piano with a sharp clash, and skated across the floor to Langbourne's feet. It was the song of *La Paloma* which she had been singing; he picked it up, and she received it from him with a drooping head, and an effect of guilty embarrassment.

She was short and of rather a full figure, though not too full. She was not plain, but she was by no means the sort of beauty who had lived in Langbourne's fancy for the year past. The oval of her face was squared; her nose was arched; she had a pretty, pouting mouth, and below it a deep dimple in her chin; her eyes were large and dark, and they had the questioning look of near-sighted eyes; her hair was brown. There was a humorous tremor in her lips, even with the prim stress she put upon them in saying, "Oh, thank you," in a thick whisper of the voice he knew.

"And I," said the other girl, "am Juliet Bingham. Won't you sit down, Mr. Langbourne!" She pushed towards him the arm-chair before her, and he dropped into it. She took her place on the hair-cloth sofa, and Miss Simpson sank back upon the piano-stool with a painful provisionality, while her eyes sought Miss Bingham's in a sort of admiring terror.

Miss Bingham was easily mistress of the situation; she did not try to bring Miss Simpson into the conversation, but she contrived to make Mrs. Simpson ask Langbourne when he arrived at Upper Ashton Falls; and she herself asked him when he had left New York, with many apposite suppositions concerning the difference in the season in the two latitudes. She presumed he was staying at the Falls House, and she said, always in her high, gay tinkle, that it was very pleasant there in the summer time. He did not know what he answered. He was aware that from time to time Miss Simpson said something in a frightened undertone. He did not know how long it was before Mrs. Simpson made an errand out of the room, in the abeyance which age practises before youthful society in the country; he did not know how much longer it was before Miss Bingham herself jumped actively up, and said, Now she would run over to Jenny's, if Mr. Langbourne would excuse her, and tell her that they could not go the next day.

"It will do just as well in the morning," Miss Simpson pitifully entreated.

"No, she's got to know to-night," said Miss Bingham, and she said she should find Mr. Langbourne there when she got back. He knew that in compliance with the simple village tradition he was being purposely left alone with Miss Simpson, as rightfully belonging to her. Miss Bingham betrayed no intentionality to him, but he caught a glimpse of mocking consciousness in the sidelong look she gave Miss Simpson as she went out; and if he had not known before he perceived then, in the vanishing oval of her cheek, the corner of her arched eyebrow, the point of her classic nose, the original of the photograph he had been treasuring as Miss Simpson's.

William Dean Howells

VII

"It was *her* picture I sent you," said Miss Simpson. She was the first to break the silence to which Miss Bingham abandoned them, but she did not speak till her friend had closed the outer door behind her and was tripping down the brick walk to the gate.

"Yes," said Langbourne, in a dryness which he could not keep himself from using.

The girl must have felt it, and her voice faltered a very little as she continued. "We—I—did it for fun. I meant to tell you. I—"

"Oh, that's all right," said Langbourne. "I had no business to expect yours, or to send you mine." But he believed that he had; that his faithful infatuation had somehow earned him the right to do what he had done, and to hope for what he had not got; without formulating the fact, he divined that she believed it too. Between the man-soul and the woman-soul it can never go so far as it had gone in their case without giving them claims upon each other which neither can justly deny.

She did not attempt to deny it. "I oughtn't to have done it, and I ought to have told you at once—the next letter—but I— you said you were coming, and I thought if you did come—I didn't really expect you to; and it was all a joke,—off-hand."

It was very lame, but it was true, and it was piteous; yet Langbourne could not relent. His grievance was not with what she had done, but what she was; not what she really was, but what she materially was; her looks, her figure, her stature, her whole presence, so different from that which he had been carrying in his mind, and adoring for a year past.

If it was ridiculous, and if with her sense of the ridiculous she felt it so, she was unable to take it lightly, or to make him take it lightly. At some faint gleams which passed over her face he felt himself invited to regard it less seriously; but he did not try, even provisionally, and they fell into a silence that neither seemed to have the power of breaking.

It must be broken, however; something must be done; they could not sit there dumb forever. He looked at the sheet of music on the piano and said, "I see you have been trying that song. Do you like it?"

"Yes, very much," and now for the first time she got her voice fairly above a whisper. She took the sheet down from the music-rest and looked at the picture of the lithographed title. It was of a tiled roof lifted among cypresses and laurels with pigeons strutting on it and sailing over it.

"It was that picture," said Langbourne, since he must say something, "that I believe I got the song for; it made me think of the roof of an old Spanish house I saw in Southern California."

"It must be nice, out there," said Miss Simpson, absently staring at the picture. She gathered herself together to add, pointlessly, "Juliet says she's going to Europe. Have you ever been?"

"Not to Europe, no. I always feel as if I wanted to see my own country first. Is she going soon?"

"Who? Juliet? Oh, no! She was just saying so. I don't believe she's engaged her passage yet."

There was invitation to greater ease in this, and her voice began to have the tender, coaxing quality which had thrilled his heart when he heard it first. But the space of her variance from his ideal was between them, and the voice reached him faintly across it.

The situation grew more and more painful for her, he could

William Dean Howells

see, as well as for him. She too was feeling the anomaly of their having been intimates without being acquaintances. They necessarily met as strangers after the exchange of letters in which they had spoken with the confidence of friends.

Langbourne cast about in his mind for some middle ground where they could come together without that effect of chance encounter which had reduced them to silence. He could not recur to any of the things they had written about; so far from wishing to do this, he had almost a terror of touching upon them by accident, and he felt that she shrank from them too, as if they involved a painful misunderstanding which could not be put straight.

He asked questions about Upper Ashton Falls, but these led up to what she had said of it in her letters; he tried to speak of the winter in New York, and he remembered that every week he had given her a full account of his life there. They must go beyond their letters or they must fall far back of them.

VIII

In their attempts to talk he was aware that she was seconding all his endeavors with intelligence, and with a humorous subtlety to which he could not pretend. She was suffering from their anomalous position as much as he, but she had the means of enjoying it while he had not. After half an hour of these defeats Mrs. Simpson operated a diversion by coming in with two glasses of lemonade on a tray and some slices of sponge-cake. She offered this refreshment first to Langbourne and then to her niece, and they both obediently took a glass, and put a slice of cake in the saucer which supported the glass. She said to each in turn, "Won't you take some lemonade? Won't you have a piece of cake?" and then went out with her empty tray, and the air of having fulfilled the duties of hospitality to her niece's company.

"I don't know," said Miss Simpson, "but it's rather early in the season for *cold* lemonade," and Langbourne, instead of laughing, as her tone invited him to do, said:

"It's very good, I'm sure." But this seemed too stiffly ungracious, and he added: "What delicious sponge-cake! You never get this out of New England."

"We have to do something to make up for our doughnuts," Miss Simpson suggested.

"Oh, I like doughnuts too," said Langbourne. "But you can't get the right kind of doughnuts, either, in New York."

They began to talk about cooking. He told her of the tamales which he had first tasted in San Francisco, and afterward found superabundantly in New York; they both made a great deal of the topic; Miss Simpson had never heard of tamales. He became solemnly animated in their exegesis, and she showed a resolute interest in them.

William Dean Howells

They were in the midst of the forced discussion, when they heard a quick foot on the brick walk, but they had both fallen silent when Miss Bingham flounced elastically in upon them. She seemed to take in with a keen glance which swept them from her lively eyes that they had not been getting on, and she had the air of taking them at once in hand.

"Well, it's all right about Jenny," she said to Miss Simpson. "She'd a good deal rather go day after to-morrow, anyway. What have you been talking about? I don't want to make you go over the same ground. Have you got through with the weather? The moon's out, and it feels more like the beginning of June than the last of April. I shut the front door against dor-bugs; I couldn't help it, though they won't be here for six weeks yet. Do you have dor-bugs in New York, Mr. Langbourne?"

"I don't know. There may be some in the Park," he answered.

"We think a great deal of our dor-bugs in Upper Ashton," said Miss Simpson demurely, looking down. "We don't know what we should do without them."

"Lemonade!" exclaimed Miss Bingham, catching sight of the glasses and saucers on the corner of the piano, where Miss Simpson had allowed Langbourne to put them. "Has Aunt Elmira been giving you lemonade while I was gone? I will just see about that!" She whipped out of the room, and was back in a minute with a glass in one hand and a bit of sponge-cake between the fingers of the other. "She had kept some for me! Have you sung *Paloma* for Mr. Langbourne, Barbara?"

"No," said Barbara, "we hadn't got round to it, quite."

"Oh, do!" Langbourne entreated, and he wondered that he had not asked her before; it would have saved them from each ether.

"Wait a moment," cried Juliet Bingham, and she gulped the

last draught of her lemonade upon a final morsel of sponge-cake, and was down at the piano while still dusting the crumbs from her fingers. She struck the refractory sheet of music flat upon the rack with her palm, and then tilted her head over her shoulder towards Langbourne, who had risen with some vague notion of turning the sheets of the song. "Do you sing?"

"Oh, no. But I like—"

"Are you ready, Bab?" she asked, ignoring him; and she dashed into the accompaniment.

He sat down in his chair behind the two girls, where they could not see his face.

Barbara began rather weakly, but her voice gathered strength, and then poured full volume to the end, where it weakened again. He knew that she was taking refuge from him in the song, and in the magic of her voice he escaped from the disappointment he had been suffering. He let his head drop and his eyelids fall, and in the rapture of her singing he got back what he had lost; or rather, he lost himself again to the illusion which had grown so precious to him.

Juliet Bingham sounded the last note almost as she rose from the piano; Barbara passed her handkerchief over her forehead, as if to wipe the heat from it, but he believed that this was a ruse to dry her eyes in it: they shone with a moist brightness in the glimpse he caught of them. He had risen, and they all stood talking; or they all stood, and Juliet talked. She did not offer to sit down again, and after stiffly thanking them both, he said he must be going, and took leave of them. Juliet gave his hand a nervous grip; Barbara's touch was lax and cold; the parting with her was painful; he believed that she felt it so as much as he.

The girls' voices followed him down the walk,—Juliet's treble, and Barbara's contralto,—and he believed that they were making talk purposely against a pressure of silence, and did not know what they were saying. It occurred to him that they had not asked how long he was staying, or invited him to come again: he had not thought to ask if he might; and in the intolerable inconclusiveness of this ending he faltered at the gate till the lights in the windows of the parlor disappeared, as if carried into the hall, and then they twinkled into darkness. From an upper entry window, which reddened with a momentary flush and was then darkened, a burst of mingled laughter came. The girls must have thought him beyond hearing, and he fancied the laugh a burst of hysterical feeling in them both.

IX

Langbourne went to bed as soon as he reached his hotel because he found himself spent with the experience of the evening; but as he rested from his fatigue he grew wakeful, and he tried to get its whole measure and meaning before him. He had a methodical nature, with a necessity for order in his motions, and he now balanced one fact against another none the less passionately because the process was a series of careful recognitions. He perceived that the dream in which he had lived for the year past was not wholly an illusion. One of the girls whom he had heard but not seen was what he had divined her to be: a dominant influence, a control to which the other was passively obedient. He had not erred greatly as to the face or figure of the superior, but he had given all the advantages to the wrong person. The voice, indeed, the spell which had bound him, belonged with the one to whom he had attributed it, and the qualities with which it was inextricably blended in his fancy were hers; she was more like his ideal than the other, though he owned that the other was a charming girl too, and that in the thin treble of her voice lurked a potential fascination which might have made itself ascendently felt if he had happened to feel it first.

There was a dangerous instant in which he had a perverse question of changing his allegiance. This passed into another moment, almost as perilous, of confusion through a primal instinct of the man's by which he yields a double or a divided allegiance and simultaneously worships at two shrines; in still another breath he was aware that this was madness.

If he had been younger, he would have had no doubt as to his right in the circumstances. He had simply corresponded all winter with Miss Simpson; but though he had opened his heart freely and had invited her to the same confidence with him, he had not committed himself, and he had a right to drop the whole affair. She would have no right to complain; she had not committed herself either: they could both come off unscathed. But he was now thirty-five, and life had taught him something concerning the rights of others which he could not ignore. By seeking her confidence and by offering her his, he had given her a claim which was none the less binding because it was wholly tacit. There had been a time when he might have justified himself in dropping the affair; that was when she had failed to answer his letter; but he had come to see her in defiance of her silence, and now he could not withdraw, simply because he was disappointed, without cruelty, without atrocity.

This was what the girl's wistful eyes said to him; this was the reproach of her trembling lips; this was the accusation of her dejected figure, as she drooped in vision before him on the piano-stool and passed her hand soundlessly over the keyboard. He tried to own to her that he was disappointed, but he could not get the words out of his throat; and now in her presence, as it were, he was not sure that he was disappointed.

X

He woke late, with a longing to put his two senses of her to the proof of day; and as early in the forenoon as he could hope to see her, he walked out towards her aunt's house. It was a mild, dull morning, with a misted sunshine; in the little crimson tassels of the budded maples overhead the bees were droning.

The street was straight, and while he was yet a good way off he saw the gate open before the house, and a girl whom he recognized as Miss Bingham close it behind her. She then came down under the maples towards him, at first swiftly, and then more and more slowly, until finally she faltered to a stop. He quickened his own pace and came up to her with a "Good-morning" called to her and a lift of his hat. She returned neither salutation, and said, "I was coming to see you, Mr. Langbourne." Her voice was still a silver bell, but it was not gay, and her face was severely unsmiling.

"To see *me*?" he returned. "Has anything—"

"No, there's nothing the matter. But—I should like to talk with you." She held a little packet, tied with blue ribbon, in her intertwined hands, and she looked urgently at him.

"I shall be very glad," Langbourne began, but she interrupted,—

"Should you mind walking down to the Falls?"

He understood that for some reason she did not wish him to pass the house, and he bowed. "Wherever you like. I hope Mrs. Simpson is well? And Miss Simpson?"

"Oh, perfectly," said Miss Bingham, and they fenced with some questions and answers of no interest till they had walked back through the village to the Falls at the other end of it, where the saw in a mill was whirring through a long pine log, and the water, streaked with sawdust, was spreading over the rocks below and flowing away with a smooth swiftness. The ground near the mill was piled with fresh-sawed, fragrant lumber and strewn with logs.

Miss Bingham found a comfortable place on one of the logs, and began abruptly:

"You may think it's pretty strange, Mr. Langbourne, but I want to talk with you about Miss Simpson." She seemed to satisfy a duty to convention by saying Miss Simpson at the outset, and after that she called her friend Barbara. "I've brought you your letters to her," and she handed him the packet she had been holding. "Have you got hers with you?"

"They are at the hotel," answered Langbourne.

"Well, that's right, then. I thought perhaps you had brought them. You see," Miss Bingham continued, much more cold-bloodedly than Langbourne thought she need, "we talked it over last night, and it's too silly. That's the way Barbara feels herself. The fact is," she went on confidingly, and with the air of saying something that he would appreciate, "I always thought it was some *young* man, and so did Barbara; or I don't believe she would ever have answered your first letter."

Langbourne knew that he was not a young man in a young girl's sense; but no man likes to have it said that he is old. Besides, Miss Bingham herself was not apparently in her first quarter of a century, and probably Miss Simpson would not see the earliest twenties again. He thought none the worse of her for that; but he felt that he was not so unequally matched in time with her that she need take the attitude with regard to him which Miss Bingham indicated. He was not the least gray nor the least bald, and his tall figure had kept its youthful lines.

Perhaps his face manifested something of his suppressed resentment. At any rate, Miss Bingham said apologetically, "I mean that if we had known it was a *serious* person we should have acted differently. I oughtn't to have let her thank you for those seedsman's catalogues; but I thought it couldn't do any harm. And then, after your letters began to come, we didn't know just when to stop them. To tell you the truth, Mr. Langbourne, we got so interested we couldn't *bear* to stop them. You wrote so much about your life in New York, that it was like a visit there every week; and it's pretty quiet at Upper Ashton in the winter time."

She seemed to refer this fact to Langbourne for sympathetic appreciation; he said mechanically, "Yes."

She resumed: "But when your picture came, I said it had *got* to stop; and so we just sent back my picture,—or I don't know but what Barbara did it without asking me,—and we did suppose that would be the last of it; when you wrote back you were coming here, we didn't believe you really would unless we said so. That's all there is about it; and if there is anybody to blame, I am the one. Barbara would never have done it in the world if I hadn't put her up to it."

In those words the implication that Miss Bingham had operated the whole affair finally unfolded itself. But distasteful as the fact was to Langbourne, and wounding as was the realization that he had been led on by this witness of his infatuation for the sake of the entertainment which his letters gave two girls in the dull winter of a mountain village, there was still greater pain, with an additional embarrassment, in the regret which the words conveyed. It appeared that it was not he who had done the wrong; he had suffered it, and so far from having to offer reparation to a young girl for having unwarrantably wrought her up expect of him a step from which he afterwards recoiled, he had the duty of forgiving her a trespass on his own invaded sensibilities. It was humiliating to his vanity; it inflicted a hurt to something better than his vanity. He began very uncomfortably: "It's all right, as far as I'm concerned. I had no business to address Miss Simpson in the first place—"

"Well," Miss Bingham interrupted, "that's what I told Barbara; but she got to feeling badly about it; she thought if you had taken the trouble to send back the circular that she dropped in the hotel, she couldn't do less than acknowledge it, and she kept on so about it that I had to let her. That was the first false step."

These words, while they showed Miss Simpson in a more amiable light, did not enable Langbourne to see Miss Bingham's merit so clearly. In the methodical and consecutive working of his emotions, he was aware that it was no longer a question of divided allegiance, and that there could never be any such question again. He perceived that Miss Bingham had not such a good figure as he had fancied the night before, and that her eyes were set rather too near together. While he dropped his own eyes, and stood trying to think what he should say in answer to her last speech, her high, sweet voice tinkled out in gay challenge, "How do, John?"

He looked up and saw a square-set, brown-faced young man advancing towards them in his shirt-sleeves; he came deliberately, finding his way in and out among the logs, till he stood smiling down, through a heavy mustache and thick black lashes, into the face of the girl, as if she were some sort of joke. The sun struck into her face as she looked up at him, and made her frown with a knot between her brows that pulled her eyes still closer together, and she asked, with no direct reference to his shirt-sleeves,—"A'n't you forcing the season?"

"Don't want to let the summer get the start of you," the young man generalized, and Miss Bingham said,—

"Mr. Langbourne, Mr. Dickery." The young man silently shook hands with Langbourne, whom he took into the joke of Miss Bingham with another smile; and she went on: "Say, John, I wish you'd tell Jenny I don't see why we shouldn't go this afternoon, after all."

"All right," said the young man.

"I suppose you're coming too?" she suggested.

"Hadn't heard of it," he returned.

"Well, you have now. You've got to be ready at two o'clock."

"That so?" the young fellow inquired. Then he walked away among the logs, as casually as he had arrived, and Miss Bingham rose and shook some bits of bark from her skirt.

"Mr. Dickery is owner of the mills," she explained, and she explored Langbourne's face for an intelligence which she did not seem to find there. He thought, indifferently enough, that this young man had heard the two girls speak of him, and had satisfied a natural curiosity in coming to look him over; it did not occur to him that he had any especial relation to Miss Bingham.

She walked up into the village with Langbourne, and he did not know whether he was to accompany her home or not. But she gave him no sign of dismissal till she put her hand upon her gate to pull it open without asking him to come in. Then he said, "I will send Miss Simpson's letters to her at once."

"Oh, any time will do, Mr. Langbourne," she returned sweetly. Then, as if it had just occurred to her, she added, "We're going after May-flowers this afternoon. Wouldn't you like to come too?"

"I don't know," he began, "whether I shall have the time—"

"Why, you're not going away to-day!"

"I expected—I—But if you don't think I shall be intruding—"

"Why, *I* should be delighted to have you. Mr. Dickery's going, and Jenny Dickery, and Barbara. I don't *believe* it will rain."

"Then, if I may," said Langbourne.

William Dean Howells

"Why, certainly, Mr. Langbourne!" she cried, and he started away. But he had gone only a few rods when he wheeled about and hurried back. The girl was going up the walk to the house, looking over her shoulder after him; at his hurried return she stopped and came down to the gate again.

"Miss Bingham, I think—I think I had better not go."

"Why, just as you feel about it, Mr. Langbourne," she assented.

"I will bring the letters this evening, if you will let me—if Miss Simpson—if you will be at home."

"We shall be very happy to see you, Mr. Langbourne," said the girl formally, and then he went back to his hotel.

XI

Langbourne could not have told just why he had withdrawn his acceptance of Miss Bingham's invitation. If at the moment it was the effect of a quite reasonless panic, he decided later that it was because he wished to think. It could not be said, however, that he did think, unless thinking consists of a series of dramatic representations which the mind makes to itself from a given impulse, and which it is quite powerless to end. All the afternoon, which Langbourne spent in his room, his mind was the theatre of scenes with Miss Simpson, in which he perpetually evolved the motives governing him from the beginning, and triumphed out of his difficulties and embarrassments. Her voice, as it acquiesced in all, no longer related itself to that imaginary personality which had inhabited his fancy. That was gone irrevocably; and the voice belonged to the likeness of Barbara, and no other; from her similitude, little, quaint, with her hair of cloudy red and her large, dim-sighted eyes, it played upon the spiritual sense within him with the coaxing, drolling, mocking charm which he had felt from the first. It blessed him with intelligent and joyous forgiveness. But as he stood at her gate that evening this unmerited felicity fell from him. He now really heard her voice, through the open doorway, but perhaps because it was mixed with other voices—the treble of Miss Bingham, and the bass of a man who must be the Mr. Dickery he had seen at the saw mills—he turned and hurried back to his hotel, where he wrote a short letter saying that he had decided to take the express for New York that night. With an instinctive recognition of her authority in the affair, or with a cowardly shrinking from direct dealing with Barbara, he wrote to Juliet Bingham, and he addressed to her the packet of letters which he sent for Barbara. Superficially, he had done what he had no choice but to do. He had been asked to return her letters, and he had returned them, and brought the affair to an end.

In his long ride to the city he assured himself in vain that he was doing right if he was not sure of his feelings towards the girl. It was quite because he was not sure of his feeling that he could not be sure he was not acting falsely and cruelly.

The fear grew upon him through the summer, which he spent in the heat and stress of the town. In his work he could forget a little the despair in which he lived; but in a double consciousness like that of the hypochondriac, the girl whom it seemed to him he had deserted was visibly and audibly present with him. Her voice was always in his inner ear, and it visualized her looks and movements to his inner eye.

Now he saw and understood at last that what his heart had more than once misgiven him might be the truth, and that though she had sent back his letters, and asked her own in return, it was not necessarily her wish that he should obey her request. It might very well have been an experiment of his feeling towards her, a mute quest of the impression she had made upon him, a test of his will and purpose, an overture to a clearer and truer understanding between them. This misgiving became a conviction from which he could not escape.

He believed too late that he had made a mistake, that he had thrown away the supreme chance of his life. But was it too late? When he could bear it no longer, he began to deny that it was too late. He denied it even to the pathetic presence which haunted him, and in which the magic of her voice itself was merged at last, so that he saw her more than he heard her. He overbore her weak will with his stronger will, and set himself strenuously to protest to her real presence what he now always said to her phantom. When his partner came back from his vacation, Langbourne told him that he was going to take a day or two off.

XII

He arrived at Upper Ashton Falls long enough before the early autumnal dusk to note that the crimson buds of the maples were now their crimson leaves, but he kept as close to the past as he could by not going to find Barbara before the hour of the evening when he had turned from her gate without daring to see her. It was a soft October evening now, as it was a soft May evening then; and there was a mystical hint of unity in the like feel of the dull, mild air. Again voices were coming out of the open doors and windows of the house, and they were the same voices that he had last heard there.

He knocked, and after a moment of startled hush within Juliet Bingham came to the door. "Why, Mr. Langbourne!" she screamed.

"I—I should like to come in, if you will let me," he gasped out.

"Why, certainly, Mr. Langbourne," she returned.

He had not dwelt so long and so intently on the meeting at hand without considering how he should account for his coming, and he had formulated a confession of his motives. But he had never meant to make it to Juliet Bingham, and he now found himself unable to allege a word in explanation of his presence. He followed her into the parlor. Barbara silently gave him her hand and then remained passive in the background, where Dickery held aloof, smiling in what seemed his perpetual enjoyment of the Juliet Bingham joke. She at once put herself in authority over the situation; she made Langbourne let her have his hat; she seated him when and where she chose; she removed and put back the lampshades; she pulled up and pulled down the window-blinds; she shut the outer door because of the night air, and opened it because of the unseasonable warmth within. She excused Mrs. Simpson's absence on account of a headache, and asked him if he would not have a fan; when he refused it she made him take it, and while he sat helplessly dangling it from his hand, she asked him about the summer he had had, and whether he had passed it in New York. She was very intelligent about the heat in New York, and tactful in keeping the one-sided talk from falling. Barbara said nothing after a few faint attempts to take part in it, and Langbourne made briefer and briefer answers. His reticence seemed only to heighten Juliet Bingham's satisfaction, and she said, with a final supremacy, that she had been intending to go out with Mr. Dickery to a business meeting of the book-club, but they would be back before Langbourne could get away; she made him promise to wait for them. He did not know if Barbara looked any protest,—at least she spoke none,—and Juliet went out with Dickery. She turned at the door to bid Barbara say, if any one called, that she was at the book-club meeting. Then she disappeared, but reappeared and called, "See here, a minute, Bab!" and at the outer threshold she detained Barbara in vivid whisper, ending aloud, "Now you be sure to do both, Bab! Aunt Elmira will tell you where the things are." Again she vanished, and was gone long enough to have reached the gate and come back from it. She was renewing all her whispered and out-spoken charges when Dickery showed himself at her side, put his hand under her elbow, and wheeled her about, and while she called gayly over her shoulder to the others, "Did you ever?" walked her definitively out of the house.

Langbourne did not suffer the silence which followed her going to possess him. What he had to do he must do quickly, and he said, "Miss Simpson, may I ask you one question?"

"Why, if you won't expect me to answer it," she suggested quaintly.

"You must do as you please about that. It has to come before I try to excuse myself for being here; it's the only excuse I can offer. It's this: Did you send Miss Bingham to get back your letters from me last spring?"

"Why, of course!"

"I mean, was it your idea?"

"We thought it would be better."

The evasion satisfied Langbourne, but he asked, "Had I given you some cause to distrust me at that time?"

"Oh, no," she protested. "We got to talking it over, and—and we thought we had better."

"Because I had come here without being asked?"

"No, no; it wasn't that," the girl protested.

"I know I oughtn't to have come. I know I oughtn't to have written to you in the beginning, but you had let me write, and I thought you would let me come. I tried always to be sincere with you; to make you feel that you could trust me. I believe that I am an honest man; I thought I was a better man for having known you through your letters. I couldn't tell you how much they had been to me. You seemed to think, because I lived in a large place, that I had a great many friends; but I have very few; I might say I hadn't any—such as I thought I had when I was writing to you. Most of the men I know belong to some sort of clubs; but I don't. I went to New York when I was feeling alone in the world,—it was from something that had happened to me partly through my own fault,—and I've never got over being alone there. I've never gone into society; I don't know what society is, and I suppose that's why I am acting differently from a society man now. The only change I ever had from business was reading at night: I've got a pretty good library. After I began to get your letters, I went out more—to the theatre, and lectures, and concerts, and all sorts of things—so that I could have something interesting to write about; I thought you'd get tired of always hearing about me. And your letters filled up my life, so that I didn't seem alone any more. I read them all hundreds of times; I should have said that I knew them by heart, if they had not been as fresh at last as they were at first. I seemed to hear you talking in them." He stopped as if withholding himself from what he had nearly said without intending, and resumed: "It's some comfort to know that you didn't want them back because you doubted me, or my good faith."

"Oh, no, indeed, Mr. Langbourne," said Barbara compassionately.

"Then why did you?"

"I don't know. We—"

"No; *not* 'we.' *You!*"

She did not answer for so long that he believed she resented his speaking so peremptorily and was not going to answer him at all. At last she said, "I thought you would rather give them back." She turned and looked at him, with the eyes which he knew saw his face dimly, but saw his thought clearly.

"What made you think that?"

"Oh, I don't know. Didn't you want to?"

He knew that the fact which their words veiled was now the first thing in their mutual consciousness. He spoke the truth in saying, "No, I never wanted to," but this was only a mechanical truth, and he knew it. He had an impulse to put the burden of the situation on her, and press her to say why she thought he wished to do so; but his next emotion was shame for this impulse. A thousand times, in these reveries in which he had imagined meeting her, he had told her first of all how he had overheard her talking in the room next his own in the hotel, and of the power her voice had instantly and lastingly had upon him. But now, with a sense spiritualized by her presence, he perceived that this, if it was not unworthy, was secondary, and that the right to say it was not yet established.

There was something that must come before this,—something that could alone justify him in any further step. If she could answer him first as he wished, then he might open his whole heart to her, at whatever cost; he was not greatly to blame, if he did not realize that the cost could not be wholly his, as he asked, remotely enough from her question, "After I wrote that I was coming up here, and you did not answer me, did you think I was coming?"

She did not answer, and he felt that he had been seeking a mean advantage. He went on: "If you didn't expect it, if you never thought that I was coming, there's no need for me to tell you anything else."

Her face turned towards him a very little, but not so much as even to get a sidelong glimpse of him; it was as if it were drawn by a magnetic attraction; and she said, "I didn't know but you would come."

"Then I will tell you why I came—the only thing that gave me the right to come against your will, if it *was* against it. I came to ask you to marry me. Will you?"

She now turned and looked fully at him, though he was aware of being a mere blur in her near-sighted vision.

"Do you mean to ask it now?"

"Yes."

"And have you wished to ask it ever since you first saw me?"

He tried to say that he had, but he could not; he could only say, "I wish to ask it now more than ever."

She shook her head slowly. "I'm not sure how you want me to answer you."

"Not sure?"

William Dean Howells

"No. I'm afraid I might disappoint you again."

He could not make out whether she was laughing at him. He sat, not knowing what to say, and he blurted out, "Do you mean that you won't?"

"I shouldn't want you to make another mistake."

"I don't know what you"—he was going to say "mean," but he substituted—"wish. If you wish for more time, I can wait as long as you choose."

"No, I might wish for time, if there was anything more. But if there's nothing else you have to tell me—then, no, I cannot marry you."

Langbourne rose, feeling justly punished, somehow, but bewildered as much as humbled, and stood stupidly unable to go. "I don't know what you could expect me to say after you've refused me—"

"Oh, I don't expect anything."

"But there *is* something I should like to tell you. I know that I behaved that night as if—as if I hadn't come to ask you—what I have; I don't blame you for not trusting me now. But it is no use to tell you what I intended if it is all over."

He looked down into his hat, and she said in a low voice, "I think I ought to know. Won't you—sit down?"

He sat down again. "Then I will tell you at the risk of—But there's nothing left to lose! You know how it is, when we think about a person or a place before we've seen them: we make some sort of picture of them, and expect them to be like it. I don't know how to say it; you do look more like what I thought than you did at first. I suppose I must seem a fool to say it; but I thought you were tall, and that you were—well!—rather masterful—"

"Like Juliet Bingham?" she suggested, with a gleam in the eye next him.

"Yes, like Juliet Bingham. It was your voice made me think—it was your voice that first made me want to see you, that made me write to you, in the beginning. I heard you talking that night in the hotel, where you left that circular; you were in the room next to mine; and I wanted to come right up here then; but I had to go back to New York, and so I wrote to you. When your letters came, I always seemed to hear you speaking in them."

"And when you saw me you were disappointed. I knew it."

"No; not disappointed—"

"Why not? My voice didn't go with my looks; it belonged to a tall, strong-willed girl."

"No," he protested. "As soon as I got away it was just as it always had been. I mean that your voice and your looks went together again."

"As soon as you got away?" the girl questioned.

"I mean—What do you care for it, anyway!" he cried, in self-scornful exasperation.

"I know," she said thoughtfully, "that my voice isn't like me; I'm not good enough for it. It ought to be Juliet Bingham's—"

"No, no!" he interrupted, with a sort of disgust that seemed not to displease her, "I can't imagine it!"

"But we can't any of us have everything, and she's got enough as it is. She's a head higher than I am, and she wants to have her way ten times as bad."

"I didn't mean that," Langbourne began. "I—but you must

William Dean Howells

think me enough of a simpleton already."

"Oh, no, not near," she declared. "I'm a good deal of a simpleton myself at times."

"It doesn't matter," he said desperately; "I love you."

"Ah, that belongs to the time when you thought I looked differently."

"I don't want you to look differently. I—"

"You can't expect me to believe that now. It will take time for me to do that."

"I will give you time," he said, so simply that she smiled.

"If it was my voice you cared for I should have to live up to it, somehow, before you cared for me. I'm not certain that I ever could. And if I couldn't? You see, don't you?"

"I see that I was a fool to tell you what I have," he so far asserted himself. "But I thought I ought to be honest."

"Oh, you've been *honest!*" she said.

"You have a right to think that I am a flighty, romantic person," he resumed, "and I don't blame you. But if I could explain, it has been a very real experience to me. It was your nature that I cared for in your voice. I can't tell you just how it was; it seemed to me that unless I could hear it again, and always, my life would not be worth much. This was something deeper and better than I could make you understand. It wasn't merely a fancy; I do not want you to believe that."

"I don't know whether fancies are such very bad things. I've had some of my own," Barbara suggested.

He sat still with his hat between his hands, as if he could not find a chance of dismissing himself, and she remained looking down at her skirt where it tented itself over the toe of her shoe. The tall clock in the hall ticked second after second. It counted thirty of them at least before he spoke, after a preliminary noise in his throat.

"There is one thing I should like to ask: If you had cared for me, would you have been offended at my having thought you looked differently?"

She took time to consider this. "I might have been vexed, or hurt, I suppose, but I don't see how I could really have been offended."

"Then I understand," he began, in one of his inductive emotions; but she rose nervously, as if she could not sit still, and went to the piano. The Spanish song he had given her was lying open upon it, and she struck some of the chords absently, and then let her fingers rest on the keys.

"Miss Simpson," he said, coming stiffly forward, "I should like to hear you sing that song once more before I—Won't you sing it?"

"Why, yes," she said, and she slipped laterally into the piano-seat.

At the end of the first stanza he gave a long sigh, and then he was silent to the close.

As she sounded the last notes of the accompaniment Juliet Bingham burst into the room with somehow the effect to Langbourne of having lain in wait outside for that moment.

"Oh, I just *knew* it!" she shouted, running upon them. "I bet John anything! Oh, I'm so happy it's come out all right; and now I'm going to have the first—"

She lifted her arms as if to put them round his neck; he stood dazed, and Barbara rose from the piano-stool and confronted her with nothing less than horror in her face.

Juliet Bingham was beginning again, "Why, haven't you—"

"*No*" cried Barbara. "I forgot all about what you said! I just happened to sing it because he asked me," and she ran from the room.

"Well, if I ever!" said Juliet Bingham, following her with astonished eyes. Then she turned to Langbourne. "It's perfectly ridiculous, and I don't see how I can ever explain it. I don't think Barbara has shown a great deal of tact," and Juliet Bingham was evidently prepared to make up the defect by a diplomacy which she enjoyed. "I don't know where to begin exactly; but you must certainly excuse my—manner, when I came in."

"Oh, certainly," said Langbourne in polite mystification.

"It was all through a misunderstanding that I don't think *I* was to blame for, to say the least; but I can't explain it without making Barbara appear perfectly—Mr. Langbourne, *will* you tell whether you are engaged?"

"No! Miss Simpson has declined my offer," he answered.

"Oh, then it's all right," said Juliet Bingham, but Langbourne looked as if he did not see why she should say that. "Then I can understand; I see the whole thing now; and I didn't want to make *another* mistake. Ah—won't you—sit down?"

"Thank you. I believe I will go."

"But you have a right to know—"

"Would my knowing alter the main facts?" he asked dryly.

"Well, no, I can't say it would," Juliet Bingham replied with an air of candor. "And, as you *say*, perhaps it's just as well," she added with an air of relief.

Langbourne had not said it, but he acquiesced with a faint sigh, and absently took the hand of farewell which Juliet Bingham gave him. "I know Barbara will be very sorry not to see you; but I guess it's better."

In spite of the supremacy which the turn of affairs had given her, Juliet Bingham looked far from satisfied, and she let Langbourne go with a sense of inconclusiveness which showed in the parting inclination towards him; she kept the effect of this after he turned from her.

He crept light-headedly down the brick walk with a feeling that the darkness was not half thick enough, though it was so thick that it hid from him a figure that leaned upon the gate and held it shut, as if forcibly to interrupt his going.

"Mr. Langbourne," said the voice of this figure, which, though so unnaturally strained, he knew for Barbara's voice, "you have got to *know*! I'm ashamed to tell you, but I should be more ashamed not to, after what's happened. Juliet made me promise when she went out to the book-club meeting that if I—if you—if it turned out as *you* wanted, I would sing that song as a sign—It was just a joke—like my sending her picture. It was my mistake and I am sorry, and I beg your pardon—I—"

She stopped with a quick catch in her breath, and the darkness round them seemed to become luminous with the light of hope that broke upon him within.

"But if there really was no mistake," he began. He could not get further.

She did not answer, and for the first time her silence was sweeter than her voice. He lifted her tip-toe in his embrace, but he did not wish her taller; her yielding spirit lost itself in his own, and he did not regret the absence of the strong will which he had once imagined hers.

A CIRCLE IN THE WATER

I

The sunset struck its hard red light through the fringe of leafless trees to the westward, and gave their outlines that black definition which a French school of landscape saw a few years ago, and now seems to see no longer. In the whole scene there was the pathetic repose which we feel in some dying day of the dying year, and a sort of impersonal melancholy weighed me down as I dragged myself through the woods toward that dreary November sunset.

Presently I came in sight of the place I was seeking, and partly because of the insensate pleasure of having found it, and partly because of the cheerful opening in the boscage made by the pool, which cleared its space to the sky, my heart lifted. I perceived that it was not so late as I had thought, and that there was much more of the day left than I had supposed from the crimson glare in the west. I threw myself down on one of the grassy gradines of the amphitheatre, and comforted myself with the antiquity of the work, which was so great as to involve its origin in a somewhat impassioned question among the local authorities. Whether it was a Norse work, a temple for the celebration of the earliest Christian, or the latest heathen, rites among the first discoverers of New England, or whether it was a cockpit where the English officers who were billeted in the old tavern near by fought their mains at the time of our Revolution, it had the charm of a ruin, and appealed to the

William Dean Howells

fancy with whatever potency belongs to the mouldering monuments of the past. The hands that shaped it were all dust, and there was no record of the minds that willed it to prove that it was a hundred, or that it was a thousand, years old. There were young oaks and pines growing up to the border of the amphitheatre on all sides; blackberry vines and sumach bushes overran the gradines almost to the margin of the pool which filled the centre; at the edge of the water some clumps of willow and white birch leaned outward as if to mirror their tracery in its steely surface. But of the life that the thing inarticulately recorded, there was not the slightest impulse left.

I began to think how everything ends at last. Love ends, sorrow ends, and to our mortal sense everything that is mortal ends, whether that which is spiritual has a perpetual effect beyond these eyes or not. The very name of things passes with the things themselves, and

> "Glory is like a circle in the water,
> Which never ceaseth to enlarge itself,
> Till by broad spreading, it disperse to naught."

But if fame ended, did not infamy end, too? If glory, why not shame? What was it, I mused, that made an evil deed so much more memorable than a good one? Why should a crime have so much longer lodgment in our minds, and be of consequences so much more lasting than the sort of action which is the opposite of a crime, but has no precise name with us? Was it because the want of positive quality which left it nameless, characterized its effects with a kind of essential debility? Was evil then a greater force than good in the moral world? I tried to recall personalities, virtuous and vicious, and I found a fatal want of distinctness in the return of those I classed as virtuous, and a lurid vividness in those I classed as vicious. Images, knowledges, concepts, zigzagged through my brain, as they do when we are thinking, or believe we are thinking; perhaps there is no such thing as we call thinking, except when we are talking. I did not hold myself responsible in this will-less revery for the question which asked itself, Whether, then, evil and not good was the lasting principle, and whether that which should remain recognizable to all eternity was not the good effect but the evil effect?

Something broke the perfect stillness of the pool near the opposite shore. A fish had leaped at some unseasonable insect on the surface, or one of the overhanging trees had dropped a dead twig upon it, and in the lazy doubt which it might be, I lay and watched the ever-widening circle fade out into fainter and fainter ripples toward the shore, till it weakened to nothing in the eye, and, so far as the senses were concerned, actually ceased to be. The want of visible agency in it made me feel it all the more a providential illustration; and because the thing itself was so pretty, and because it was so apt as a case in point, I pleased myself a great deal with it. Suddenly it repeated itself; but this time I grew a little impatient of it, before the circle died out in the wider circle of the pool. I said whimsically to myself that this was rubbing it in; that I was convinced already, and needed no further proof; and at the same moment the thing happened a third time. Then I saw that there was a man standing at the top of the amphitheatre just across from me, who was throwing stones into the water. He cast a fourth pebble into the centre of the pool, and then a fifth and a sixth; I began to wonder what he was throwing at; I thought it too childish for him to be amusing himself with the circle that dispersed itself to naught, after it had done so several times already. I was sure that he saw something in the pool, and was trying to hit it, or frighten it. His figure showed black against the sunset light, and I could not make it out very well, but it held itself something like that of a workman, and yet with a difference, with an effect as of some sort of discipline; and I thought of an ex-recruit, returning to civil life, after serving his five years in the army; though I do not know why I should have gone so far afield for this notion; I certainly had never seen an ex-recruit, and I did not really know how one would look. I rose up, and we both stood still, as if he were abashed in his sport by my presence. The man made a little cast forward with his hand, and I heard the rattle as of pebbles dropped among the dead leaves.

Then he called over to me, "Is that you, Mr. March?"

"Yes," I called back, "what is wanted?"

"Oh, nothing. I was just looking for you." He did not move, and after a moment I began to walk round the top of the amphitheatre toward him. When I came near him I saw that he had a clean-shaven face, and he wore a soft hat that seemed large for his close-cropped head; he had on a sack coat buttoned to the throat, and of one dark color with his loose trousers. I knew him now, but I did not know what terms to put my recognition in, and I faltered. "What do you want with me?" I asked, as if I did not know him.

"I was at your house," he answered, "and they told me that you had walked out this way." He hesitated a moment, and then he added, rather huskily, "You don't know me!"

"Yes," I said. "It is Tedham," and I held out my hand, with no definite intention, I believe, but merely because I did know him, and this was the usual form of greeting between acquaintances after a long separation, or even a short one, for that matter. But he seemed to find a special significance in my civility, and he took my hand and held it silently, while he was trying to speak. Evidently, he could not, and I said aimlessly, "What were you throwing at?"

"Nothing. I saw you lying down, over there, and I wanted to attract your attention." He let my hand go, and looked at me apologetically.

"Oh! was that all?" I said. "I thought you saw something in the water."

"No," he answered, as if he felt the censure which I had not been able to keep out of my voice.

II

I do not know why I should have chosen to take this simple fact as proof of an abiding want of straight-forwardness in Tedham's nature. I do not know why I should have expected him to change, or why I should have felt authorized at that moment to renew his punishment for it. I certainly had said and thought very often that he had been punished enough, and more than enough. In fact, his punishment, like all the other punishments that I have witnessed in life, seemed to me wholly out of proportion to the offence; it seemed monstrous, atrocious, and when I got to talking of it I used to become so warm that my wife would warn me people would think I wanted to do something like Tedham myself if I went on in that way about him. Yet here I was, at my very first encounter with the man, after his long expiation had ended, willing to add at least a little self-reproach to his suffering. I suppose, as nearly as I can analyse my mood, I must have been expecting, in spite of all reason and experience, that his anguish would have wrung that foible out of him, and left him strong where it had found him weak. Tragedy befalls the light and foolish as well as the wise and weighty natures, but it does not render them wise and weighty; I had often made this sage reflection, but I failed to apply it to the case before me now.

After waiting a little for the displeasure to clear away from my face, Tedham smiled as if in humorous appreciation, and I perceived, as nothing else could have shown me so well, that he was still the old Tedham. There was an offer of propitiation in this smile, too, and I did not like that, either; but I was touched when I saw a certain hope die out of his eye at the failure of his appeal to me.

"Who told you I was here?" I asked, more kindly. "Did you see Mrs. March?"

"No, I think it must have been your children. I found them in front of your house, and I asked them for you, without going to the door."

"Oh," I said, and I hid the disappointment I felt that he had not seen my wife; for I should have liked such a leading as her behavior toward him would have given me for my own. I was sure she would have known him at once, and would not have told him where to find me, if she had not wished me to be friendly with him.

"I am glad to see you," I said, in the absence of this leading; and then I did not know what else to say. Tedham seemed to me to be looking very well, but I could not notify this fact to him, in the circumstances; he even looked very handsome; he had aged becomingly, and a clean-shaven face suited him as well as the full beard he used to wear; but I could speak of these things as little as of his apparent health. I did not feel that I ought even to ask him what I could do for him. I did not want to have anything to do with him, and, besides, I have always regarded this formula as tantamount to saying that you cannot, or will not, do anything for the man you employ it upon.

The silence which ensued was awkward, but it was better than anything I could think of to say, and Tedham himself seemed to feel it so. He said, presently, "Thank you. I was sure you would not take my coming to you the wrong way. In fact I had no one else to come to—after I—" Tedham stopped, and then, "I don't know," he went on, "whether you've kept run of me; I don't suppose you have; I got out to-day at noon."

I could not say anything to that, either; there were very few openings for me, it appeared, in the conversation, which remained one-sided as before.

"I went to the cemetery," he continued. "I wanted to realize that those who had died were dead, it was all one thing as long as I was in there; everybody was dead; and then I came on to your house."

The house he meant was a place I had taken for the summer a little out of town, so that I could run in to business every day, and yet have my mornings and evenings in the country; the fall had been so mild that we were still eking out the summer there.

"How did you know where I was staying?" I asked, with a willingness to make any occasion serve for saying something.

Tedham hesitated. "Well, I stopped at the office in Boston on my way out, and inquired. I was sure nobody would know me there." He said this apologetically, as if he had been taking a liberty, and explained: "I wanted to see you very much, and I was afraid that if I let the day go by I should miss you somehow."

"Oh, all right," I said.

We had remained standing at the point where I had gone round to meet him, and it seemed, in the awkward silence that now followed, as if I were rooted there. I would very willingly have said something leading, for my own sake, if not for his, but I had nothing in mind but that I had better keep there, and so I waited for him to speak. I believed he was beating about the bush in his own thoughts, to find some indirect or sinuous way of getting at what he wanted to know, and that it was only because he failed that he asked bluntly, "March, do you know where my daughter is?"

"No, Tedham, I don't," I said, and I was glad that I could say it both with honesty and with compassion. I was truly sorry for the man; in a way, I did pity him; at the same time I did not wish to be mixed up in his affairs; in washing my hands of them, I preferred that there should be no stain of falsehood left on them.

"Where is my sister-in-law?" he asked next, and now at least I could not censure him for indirection.

"I haven't met her for several years," I answered. "I couldn t say from my own knowledge where she was."

"But you haven't heard of her leaving Somerville?"

"No, I haven't."

"Do you ever meet her husband?"

"Yes, sometimes, on the street; but I think not lately; we don't often meet."

"The last time you saw *her*, did she speak of me?"

"I don't know—I believe—yes. It was a good many years ago."

"Was she changed toward me at all?"

This was a hard question to answer, but I thought I had better answer it with the exact truth. "No, she seemed to feel just the same as ever about it."

I do not believe Tedham cared for this, after all, though he made a show of having to collect himself before he went on. "Then you think my daughter is with her?"

"I didn't say that. I don't know anything about it."

"March," he urged, "don't *you* think I have a right to see my daughter?"

"That's something I can't enter into, Tedham."

"Good God!" said the man. "If you were in my place, wouldn't you want to see her? You know how fond I used to be of her; and she is all that I have got left in the world."

I did indeed remember Tedham's affection for his daughter, whom I remembered as in short frocks when I last saw them together. It was before my own door in town. Tedham had driven up in a smart buggy behind a slim sorrel, and I came out, at a sign he made me through the bow-window with his whip, and saw the little maid on the seat there beside him. They were both very well dressed, though still in mourning for the child's mother, and the whole turnout was handsomely set up. Tedham was then about thirty-five, and the child looked about nine. The color of her hair was the color of his fine brown beard, which had as yet no trace of gray in it; but the light in her eyes was another light, and her smile, which was of the same shape as his, was of another quality, as she leaned across him and gave me her pretty little gloved hand with a gay laugh. "I should think you would be afraid of such a fiery sorrel dragon as that," I said, in recognition of the colt's lifting and twitching with impatience as we talked.

"Oh, I'm not afraid with papa!" she said, and she laughed again as he took her hand in one of his and covered it out of sight.

I recalled, now, looking at him there in the twilight of the woods, how happy they had both seemed that sunny afternoon in the city square, as they flashed away from my door and glanced back at me and smiled together. I went into the house and said to my wife with a formulation of the case which pleased me, "If there is anything in the world that Tedham likes better than to ride after a good horse, it is to ride after a good horse with that little girl of his." "Yes," said my wife, "but a good horse means a good deal of money; even when a little girl goes with it." "That is so," I assented, "but Tedham has made a lot lately in real estate, they say, and I don't know what better he could do with his money; or, I don't believe *he* does." We said no more, but we both felt, with the ardor of young parents, that it was a great virtue, a saving virtue, in Tedham to love his little girl so much; I was afterward not always sure that it was. Still, when Tedham appealed to me now in the name of his love for her, he moved my heart, if not my reason, in his favor; those old superstitions persist.

William Dean Howells

"Why, of course, you want to see her. But I couldn't tell you where she is."

"You could find out for me."

"I don't see how," I said; but I did see how, and I knew as well as he what his next approach would be. I felt strong against it, however, and I did not perceive the necessity of being short with him in a matter not involving my own security or comfort.

"I could find out where Hasketh is," he said, naming the husband of his sister-in-law; "but it would be of no use for me to go there. They wouldn't see me." He put this like a question, but I chose to let it be its own answer, and he went on. "There is no one that I can ask to act for me in the matter but you, and I ask *you*, March, to go to my sister-in-law for me."

I shook my head. "That I can't do, Tedham."

"Ah!" he urged, "what harm could it do you?"

"Look here, Tedham!" I said. "I don't know why you feel authorized to come to me at all. It is useless your saying that there is no one else. You know very well that the authorities, some of them—the chaplain—would go and see Mrs. Hasketh for you. He could have a great deal more influence with her than any one else could, if he felt like saying a good word for you. As far as I am concerned, you have expiated your offence fully; but I should think you yourself would see that you ought not to come to me with this request; or you ought to come to me last of all men."

"It is just because of that part of my offence which concerned you that I come to you. I knew how generous you were, and after you told me that you had no resentment—I acknowledge that it is indelicate, if you choose to look at it in that light, but a man like me can't afford to let delicacy stand in his way. I don't want to flatter you, or get you to do this thing for me on false pretences. But I thought that if you went to Mrs. Hasketh for me, she would remember that you had overlooked something, and she would be more disposed to—to—be considerate."

"I can't do it, Tedham," I returned. "It would be of no use. Besides, I don't like the errand. I'm not sure that I have any business to interfere. I am not sure that you have any right to disturb the shape that their lives have settled into. I'm sorry for you, I pity you with all my heart. But there are others to be considered as well as you. And—simply, I can't."

"How do you know," he entreated, "that my daughter wouldn't be as glad to see me as I to see her?"

"I don't know it. I don't know anything about it. That's the reason I can't have anything to do with it. I can't justify myself in meddling with what doesn't concern me, and in what I'm not sure I should do more harm than good. I must say good-night. It's getting late, and they will be anxious about me at home." My heart smote me as I spoke the last word, which seemed a cruel recognition of Tedham's homelessness. But I held out my hand to him for parting, and braced myself against my inward weakness.

He might well have failed to see my hand. At any rate he did not take it. He turned and started to walk out of the woods by my side. We came presently to some open fields. Beyond them was the road, and after we had climbed the first wall, and found ourselves in a somewhat lighter place, he began to speak again.

"I thought," he said, "that if you had forgiven me, I could take it as a sign that I had suffered enough to satisfy everybody."

"We needn't dwell upon my share in the matter, Tedham," I answered, as kindly as I could. "That was entirely my own affair."

"You can't think," he pursued, "how much your letter was to me. It came when I was in perfect despair—in those awful first days when it seemed as if I could *not* bear it, and yet death itself would be no relief. Oh, they don't *know* how much we suffer! If they did, they would forgive us anything, everything! Your letter was the first gleam of hope I had. I don't know how you came to write it!"

"Why, of course, Tedham, I felt sorry for you—"

"Oh, did you, did you?" He began to cry, and as we hurried along over the fields, he sobbed with the wrenching, rending sobs of a man. "I *knew* you did, and I believe it was God himself that put it into your heart to write me that letter and take off that much of the blame from me. I said to myself that if I ever lived through it, I would try to tell you how much you had done for me. I don't blame you for refusing to do what I've asked you now. I can see how you may think it isn't best, and I thank you all the same for that letter. I've got it here." He took a letter out of his breast-pocket, and showed it to me. "It isn't the first time I've cried over it."

I did not say anything, for my heart was in my throat, and we stumbled along in silence till we climbed the last wall, and stood on the sidewalk that skirted the suburban highway. There, under the street-lamp, we stopped a moment, and it was he who now offered me his hand for parting. I took it, and we said, together, "Well, good-by," and moved in different directions. I knew very well that I should turn back, and I had not gone a hundred feet away when I faced about. He was shambling off into the dusk, a most hapless figure. "Tedham!" I called after him.

"Well?" he answered, and he halted instantly; he had evidently known what I would do as well as I had.

We reapproached each other, and when we were again under the lamp I asked, a little awkwardly, "Are you in need of money, Tedham?"

"I've got my ten years' wages with me," he said, with a lightness that must have come from his reviving hope in me. He drew his hand out of his pocket, and showed me the few dollars with which the State inhumanly turns society's outcasts back into the world again.

"Oh, that won't do." I said. "You must let me lend you something."

"Thank you," he said, with perfect simplicity. "But you know I can't tell when I shall be able to pay you."

"Oh, that's all right." I gave him a ten-dollar note which I had loose in my pocket; it was one that my wife had told me to get changed at the grocery near the station, and I had walked off to the old temple, or the old cockpit, and forgotten about it.

Tedham took the note, but he said, holding it in his hand, "I would a million times rather you would let me go home with you and see Mrs. March a moment."

"I can't do that, Tedham," I answered, not unkindly, I hope. "I know what you mean, and I assure you that it wouldn't be the least use. It's because I feel so sure that my wife wouldn't like my going to see Mrs. Hasketh, that I—"

"Yes, I know that," said Tedham. "That is the reason why I should like to see Mrs. March. I believe that if I could see her, I could convince her."

"She wouldn't see you, my dear fellow," said I, strangely finding myself on these caressing terms with him. "She entirely approved of what I did, the letter I wrote you, but I don't believe she will ever feel just as I do about it. Women are different, you know."

"Yes," he said, drawing a long, quivering breath.

We stood there, helpless to part. He did not offer to leave me, and I could not find it in my heart to abandon him. After a most painful time, he drew another long breath, and asked, "Would you be willing to let me take the chances?"

"Why, Tedham," I began, weakly; and upon that he began walking with me again.

III

I went to my wife's room, after I reached the house, and faced her with considerable trepidation. I had to begin rather far off, but I certainly began in a way to lead up to the fact. "Isabel," I said, "Tedham is out at last." I had it on my tongue to say poor Tedham, but I suppressed the qualification in actual speech as likely to prove unavailing, or worse.

"Is that what kept you!" she demanded, instantly. "Have you seen him?"

"Yes," I admitted. I added, "Though I am afraid I was rather late, anyway."

"I knew it was he, the moment you spoke," she said, rising on the lounge where she had been lying, and sitting up on it; with the book she had been reading shut on her thumb, she faced me across the table where her lamp stood. "I had a presentiment when the children said there was some strange-looking man here, asking for you, and that they had told him where to find you. I couldn't help feeling a little uneasy about it. What did he want with you, Basil?"

"Well, he wanted to know where his daughter was."

"You didn't tell him!"

"I didn't know. Then he wanted me to go to Mrs. Hasketh and find out."

"You didn't say you would?"

"I said most decidedly I wouldn't," I returned, and I recalled my severity to Tedham in refusing his prayer with more satisfaction than it had given me at the time. "I told him that I had no business to interfere, and that I was not sure it would be right even for me to meddle with the course things had taken." I was aware of weakening my case as I went on; I had better left her with a dramatic conception of a downright and relentless refusal.

"I don't see why you felt called upon to make excuses to him, Basil. His impudence in coming to you, of all men, is perfectly intolerable. I suppose it was that sentimental letter you wrote him."

"You didn't think it sentimental at the time, my dear. You approved of it."

"I didn't approve of it, Basil; but if you felt so strongly that you ought to do it, I felt that I ought to let you. I have never interfered with your sense of duty, and I never will. But I am glad that you didn't feel it your duty to that wretch to go and make more trouble on his account. He has made quite enough already; and it wasn't his fault that you were not tried and convicted in his place."

"There wasn't the slightest danger of that—"

"He tried to put the suspicion on you, and to bring the disgrace on your wife and children."

"Well, my dear, we agreed to forget all that long ago. And I don't think—I never thought—that Tedham would have let the suspicion rest on me. He merely wanted to give it that turn, when the investigation began, so as to gain time to get out to Canada."

My wife looked at me with a glance in which I saw tender affection dangerously near contempt. "You are a very forgiving man, Basil," she said, and I looked down sheepishly. "Well, at any rate, you have had the sense not to mix yourself up in his business. Did he pretend that he came straight to you, as soon as he got out? I suppose he wanted you to believe that he appealed to you before he tried anybody else."

"Yes, he stopped at the Reciprocity office to ask for my address, and after he had visited the cemetery he came on out here. And, if you must know, I think Tedham is still the old Tedham. Put him behind a good horse, with a pocketful of some one else's money, in a handsome suit of clothes, and a game-and-fish dinner at Tafft's in immediate prospect, and you couldn't see any difference between the Tedham of to-day and the Tedham of ten years ago, except that the actual Tedham is clean-shaved and wears his hair cut rather close."

"Basil!"

"Why do you object to the fact? Did you imagine he had changed inwardly?"

"He must have suffered."

"But does suffering change people? I doubt it. Certain material accessories of Tedham's have changed. But why should that change Tedham? Of course, he has suffered, and he suffers still. He threw out some hints of what he had been through that would have broken my heart if I hadn't hardened it against him. And he loves his daughter still, and he wants to see her, poor wretch."

"I suppose he does!" sighed my wife.

"He would hardly take no for an answer from me, when I said I wouldn't go to the Haskeths for him; and when I fairly shook him off, he wanted me to ask you to go."

"And what did you say?" she asked, not at all with the resentment I had counted upon equally with the possible pathos; you never can tell in the least how any woman will take anything, which is perhaps the reason why men do not trust women more.

"I told him that it would not be the smallest use to ask you; that you had forgiven that old affair as well as I had, but that

William Dean Howells

women were different, and that I knew you wouldn't even see him."

"Well, Basil, I don't know what right you had to put me in that odious light," said my wife.

"Why, good heavens! *Would* you have seen him?"

"I don't know whether I would or not. That's neither here nor there. I don't think it was very nice of you to shift the whole responsibility on me."

"How did I do that? It seems to me that I kept the whole responsibility myself."

"Yes, altogether too much. What became of him, then?"

"We walked along a little farther, and then—"

"Then, what? Where is the man?"

"He's down in the parlor," I answered hardily, in the voice of some one else.

My wife stood up from the lounge, and I rose, too, for whatever penalty she chose to inflict.

"Well, Basil, that is what I call a very cowardly thing."

"Yes, my dear, it is; I ought to have protected you against his appeal. But you needn't see him. It's practically the same as if he had not come here. I can send him away."

"And you call that practically the same! No, *I* am the one that will have to do the refusing now, and it is all off your shoulders. And you knew I was not feeling very well, either! Basil, how could you?"

"I don't know. The abject creature drove me out of my senses.

I suppose that if I had respected him more, or believed in him more, I should have had more strength to refuse him. But his limpness seemed to impart itself to me, and I—I gave way. But really you needn't see him, Isabel. I can tell him we have talked it over, and I concluded, entirely of myself, that it was best for you not to meet him, and—"

"He would see through that in an instant. And if he is still the false creature you think he is, we owe him the truth, more than any other kind of man. You must understand *that*, Basil!"

"Then you are going to—"

"Don't speak to me, Basil, please," she said, and with an air of high offence she swept out of the room, and out to the landing of the stairs. There she hesitated a moment, and put her hand to her hair, mechanically, to feel if it were in order, and then she went on downstairs without further faltering. It was I who descended slowly, and with many misgivings.

IV

Tedham was sitting in the chair I had shown him when I brought him in, and in the half-light of one gas-burner in the chandelier he looked, with his rough, clean clothes, and his slouch hat lying in his lap, like some sort of decent working-man; his features, refined by the mental suffering he had undergone, and the pallor of a complexion so seldom exposed to the open air, gave him the effect of a workingman just out of the hospital. His eyes were deep in their sockets, and showed fine shadows in the overhead light, and I must say he looked very interesting.

At the threshold my wife paused again; then she went forward, turning the gas up full as she passed under the chandelier, and gave him her hand, where he had risen from his chair.

"I am glad to see you, Mr. Tedham," she said; and I should have found my astonishment overpowering, I dare say, if I had not felt that I was so completely in the hands of Providence, when she added, "Won't you come out to dinner with us? We were just going to sit down, when Mr. March came in. I never know when he will be back, when he starts off on these Saturday afternoon tramps of his."

The children seemed considerably mystified at the appearance of our guest, but they had that superior interest in the dinner appropriate to their years, and we got through the ordeal, in which, I believe, I suffered more than any one else, much better than I could have hoped. I could not help noting in Tedham a certain strangeness to the use of a four-pronged fork, at first, but he rapidly overcame this; and if it had not been for a terrible moment when, after one of the courses, he began, mechanically, to scrape his plate with his knife, there would not have been anything very odd in his behavior, or anything to show that it was the first dinner in polite society that he had taken for so many years.

The man's mind had apparently stiffened more than his body. It used to be very agile, if light, but it was not agile now. It worked slowly toward the topics which we found with difficulty, in our necessity of avoiding the only topics of real interest between us, and I could perceive that his original egotism, intensified by the long years in which he had only himself for company, now stood in the way of his entering into the matters brought forward, though he tried to do so. They were mostly in the form of reminiscences of this person and that whom we had known in common, and even in this shape they had to be very carefully handled so as not to develop anything leading. The thing that did most to relieve the embarrassment of the time was the sturdy hunger Tedham showed, and his delight in the cooking; I suppose that I cannot make others feel the pathos I found in this.

After dinner we shut the children into the library, and kept Tedham with us in the parlor.

My wife began at once to say, "Mr. March has told me why you wanted to see me, Mr. Tedham."

"Yes," he said, as if he were afraid to say more lest he should injure his cause.

"I think that it would not be the least use for me to go to Mrs. Hasketh. In the first place I do not know her very well, and I have not seen her for years, I am not certain she would see me."

Tedham turned the hollows of his eyes upon my wife, and asked, huskily, "Won't you try?"

"Yes," she answered, most unexpectedly to me, "I will try to see her. But if I do see her, and she refuses to tell me anything about your daughter, what will you do? Of course, I shall have to tell her I come from you, and for you."

"I thought," Tedham ventured, with a sort of timorous slyness, "that perhaps you might approach it casually, without any reference to me."

"No, I couldn't do that," my wife said.

He went on as if he had not heard her: "If she did not know that the inquiries were made in my behalf, she might be willing to say whether my daughter was with her."

There was in this suggestion a quality of Tedham's old insinuation, but coarser, inferior, as if his insinuation had degenerated into something like mere animal cunning. I felt rather ashamed for him, but to my surprise, my wife seemed only to feel sorry, and did not repel his suggestion in the way I had thought she would.

"No," she said, "that wouldn't do. She has kept account of the time, you may be sure, and she would ask me at once if I was inquiring in your behalf, and I should have to tell her the truth."

"I didn't know," he returned, "but you might evade the point, somehow. So much being at stake," he added, as if explaining.

Still my wife was not severe with him. "I don't understand, quite," she said.

"Being the turning-point in my life, I can't begin to do anything, to be anything, till I have seen my daughter. I don't know where to find myself. If I could see her, and she did not cast me off, then I should know where I was. Or, if she did, I should. You understand that."

"But, of course, there is another point of view."

"My daughter's?"

"Mrs. Hasketh's."

"I don't care for Mrs. Hasketh. She did what she has done for the child's sake. It was the best thing for the child at the time—the only thing; I know that. But I agreed to it because I had to."

He continued: "I consider that I have expiated the wrong I did. There is no sense in the whole thing, if I haven't. They might as well have let me go in the beginning. Don't you think that ten years out of my life is enough for a thing that I never intended to go as far as it did, and a thing that I was led into, partly, for the sake of others? I have tried to reason it out, and not from my own point of view at all, and that is the way I feel about it. Is it to go on forever, and am I never to be rid of the consequences of a single act? If you and Mr. March could condone—"

"Oh, you mustn't reason from us," my wife broke in. "We are very silly people, and we do not look at a great many things as others do. You have got to reckon with the world at large."

"I *have* reckoned with the world at large, and I have paid the reckoning. But why shouldn't my daughter look at this thing as you do?"

Instead of answering, my wife asked, "When did you hear from her last?"

Tedham took a few thin, worn letters from his breast-pocket "There is Mr. March's letter," he said, laying one on his knee. He handed my wife another.

She read it, and asked, "May Mr. March see it?"

Tedham nodded, and I took the little paper in turn. The letter was written in a child's stiff, awkward hand. It was hardly more than a piteous cry of despairing love. The address was Mrs. Hasketh's, in Somerville, and the date was about three months after Tedham's punishment began. "Is that the last you have heard from her?" I asked.

Tedham nodded as he took the letter from me.

"But surely you have heard something more about her in all this time?" my wife pursued.

"Once from Mrs. Hasketh, to make me promise that I would leave the child to her altogether, and not write to her, or ask to see her. When I went to the cemetery to-day, I did not know but I should find her grave, too."

"Well, it is cruel!" cried my wife. "I will go and see Mrs. Hasketh, but—you ought to feel yourself that it's hopeless."

"Yes," he admitted. "There isn't much chance unless she should happen to think the same way you do: that I had suffered enough, and that it was time to stop punishing me."

My wife looked compassionately at him, and she began with a sympathy that I have not always known her to show more deserving people, "If it were a question of that alone it would be very easy. But suppose your daughter were so situated that it would be—disadvantageous to her to have it known that you were her father?"

"You mean that I have no right to mend my broken-up life— what there is left of it—by spoiling hers? I have said that to myself. But then, on the other hand, I have had to ask myself whether I had any right to keep her from choosing for herself about it. I sha'n't force myself on her. I expect to leave her free. But if the child cares for me, as she used to, hasn't that love— not mine for her, but hers for me—got some rights too?"

His voice sank almost to a hush, and the last word was scarcely more than a breathing. "All I want is to know where she is, and to let her know that I am in the world, and where she can find me. I think she ought to have a chance to decide."

"I am afraid Mrs. Hasketh may think it would be better, for her sake, *not* to have the chance," my wife sighed, and she turned her look from Tedham upon me, as if she wished me rather than him to answer.

"The only way to find out is to ask her," I answered, non-committally, and rather more lightly than I felt about it. In fact, the turn the affair had taken interested me greatly. It involved that awful mystery of the ties by which, unless we are born of our fathers and mothers for nothing more than the animals are, we are bound to them in all the things of life, in duty and in love transcending every question of interest and happiness. The parents' duty to the children is obvious and plain, but the child's duty to its parents is something subtler and more spiritual. It is to be more delicately, more religiously, regarded. No one, without impiety, can meddle with it from the outside, or interfere in its fulfilment. This and much more I said to my wife when we came to talk the matter over after Tedham left us. Above all, I urged something that came to me so forcibly at the moment that I said I had always thought it, and perhaps I really believed that I had. "Why should we try to shield people from fate? Isn't that always wrong? One is fated to be born the child of a certain father, and one can no more escape the consequences of his father's misdeeds than the doer himself can. Perhaps the pain and the shame come from the wish and the attempt to do so, more than from the fact itself. The sins of the fathers shall be visited upon the children. But the children are innocent of evil, and this visitation must be for their good, and will be, if they bear it willingly."

"Well, don't try to be that sort of blessing to *your* children, Basil," said my wife, personalizing the case, as a woman must.

After that we tried to account to each other for having consented to do what Tedham asked us. Perhaps we accused each other somewhat for doing it.

"I didn't know, my dear, but you were going to ask him to come and stay with us," I said.

"I did want to," she replied. "It seemed so forlorn, letting him go out into the night, and find a place for himself, when we could just as well have let him stay as not. Why shouldn't we have offered him a bed for the night, as we would any other acquaintance?"

"Well, you must allow that the circumstances were peculiar!"

"But if he was sentenced to pay a certain penalty, and has paid it, why, as he said, shouldn't we stop punishing him?"

"I suppose we can't. There seems to be an instinctive demand for eternal perdition, for hell, in the human heart," I suggested.

"Well, then, I believe that your instinct, Basil—"

"Oh, *I* don't claim it, exclusively!"

"Is a survival of savagery, and the sooner we get rid of it the better. How queer he seems. It is the old Tedham, but all faded in—or out."

"Yes, he affected me like an etching of himself from a wornout plate. Still, I'm afraid there's likeness enough left to make trouble, yet. I hope you realize what you have gone in for, Isabel?"

She answered from the effort that I could see she was making, to brace herself already for the work before us:

"Well, we must do this because we can't help doing it, and because, whatever happens, we had no right to refuse. You must come with me, Basil!"

"I? To Mrs. Hasketh's?"

"Certainly. I will do the talking, but I shall depend upon your moral support. We will go over to Somerville to-morrow afternoon. We had better not lose any time."

"To-morrow is Sunday."

"So much the better. They will be sure to be at home, if they're there at all, yet."

She said they, but I knew that she did not expect poor old Hasketh really to count in the matter, any more than she expected me to do so.

V

The Haskeths lived in a house that withdrew itself behind tall garden trees in a large lot sloping down the hillside, in one of the quieter old streets of their suburb. The trees were belted in by a board fence, painted a wornout white, as far as it was solid, which was to the height of one's shoulder; there it opened into a panel work of sticks crossed X-wise, which wore a coat of aged green; the strip above them was set with a bristling row of rusty nails, which were supposed to keep out people who could perfectly well have gone in at the gate as we did. There was a brick walk from the gate to the door, which was not so far back as I remembered it (perhaps because the leaves were now off the trees), and there was a border of box on either side of the walk. Altogether there was an old-fashioned keeping in the place which I should have rather enjoyed if I had been coming on any other errand; but now it imparted to me a notion of people set in their ways, of something severe, something hopelessly forbidding.

I do not think there had ever been much intimacy between the Tedhams and the Haskeths, before Tedham's calamity came upon him. But Mrs. Hasketh did not refuse her share of it. She came forward, and probably made her husband come forward, in Tedham's behalf, and do what hopelessly could be done to defend him where there was really no defence, and the only thing to be attempted was to show circumstances that might perhaps tend to the mitigation of his sentence. I do not think they did. Tedham had confessed himself and had been proven such a thorough rogue, and the company had lately suffered so much through operations like his, that, even if it could have had mercy, as an individual may, mercy was felt to be bad morals, and the case was unrelentingly pushed. His sentence was of those sentences which an eminent jurist once characterized as rather dramatic; it was pronounced not so much in relation to his particular offence, as with the purpose of striking terror into all offenders like him, who were becoming altogether too common. He was made to suffer for many other peculators, who had been, or were about to be, and was given the full penalty. I was in court when it was pronounced with great solemnity by the judge, who read him a lecture in doing so; I could have read the judge another, for I could not help feeling that it was, more than all the sentences I had ever heard pronounced, wholly out of keeping with the offence. I met Hasketh coming out of the court-room, and I said that I thought it was terribly severe. He agreed with me, and as I knew that he and Tedham had never liked each other, I inferred a kindliness in him which made me his friend, in the way one is the friend of a man one never meets. He was a man of few words, and he now simply said, "It was unjust," and we parted.

For several months after Tedham's conviction, I did not think we ought to intrude upon the Haskeths; but then my wife and I both felt that we ought, in decency, to make some effort to see them. They seemed pleased, but they made us no formal invitation to come again, and we never did. That day, however, I caught a glimpse of Tedham's little girl, as she flitted through the hall, after we were seated in the parlor; she was in black, a forlorn little shadow in the shadow; and I recalled now, as we stood once more on the threshold of the rather dreary house, a certain gentleness of bearing in the child, which I found infinitely pathetic, at that early moment of her desolation. She had something of poor Tedham's own style and grace, too, which had served him so ill, and this heightened the pathos for me. In that figure I had thought of his daughter ever since, as often as I had thought of her at all; which was not very often, to tell the truth, after the first painful impression of Tedham's affair began to die away in me, or to be effaced by the accumulating cares and concerns of my own life. But now that we had returned into the presence of that bitter sorrow, as it were, the little thing reappeared vividly to me in just the way I had seen her so long ago. My sense of her forlornness, of her most hapless orphanhood, was intensified by the implacable hate with which Mrs. Hasketh had then spoken of her father, in telling us that the child was henceforth to bear her husband's name, and had resentfully scorned the merit Tedham tried to make of giving her up to them. "And if I can help it," she had ended, with a fierceness I had never forgotten, "she shall not hear him mentioned again, or see him as long as I live."

My wife and I now involuntarily dropped our voices, or rather they sank into our throats, as we sat waiting in the dim parlor, after the maid took our cards to Mr. and Mrs. Hasketh. We tried to make talk, but we could not, and we were funereally quiet, when Hasketh came pottering and peering in, and shook hands with both of us. He threw open half a blind at one of the windows, and employed himself in trying to put up the shade, to gain time, as I thought, before he should be obliged to tell us that his wife could not see us. Then he came to me, and asked, "Won't you let me take your hat?" as such people do, in expression of a vague hospitality; and I let him take it, and put it mouth down on the marble centre-table, beside the large, gilt-edged, black-bound family Bible. He drew a chair near me, in a row with my wife and myself, and said, "It is quite a number of years since we met, Mrs. March," and he looked across me at her.

"Yes, I am almost afraid to think how many," she answered.

"Family well?"

"Yes, our children are both very well, Mr. Hasketh. You seem to be looking very well, too."

"Thank you, I have nothing to complain of. I am not so young as I was. But that is about all."

"I hope Mrs. Hasketh is well?"

"Yes, thank you, she is quite well, for her. She is never very strong. She will be down in a moment."

"Oh, I shall be so glad to see her."

The conversation, which might be said to have flagged from the beginning, stopped altogether at this point, and though I was prompted by several looks from my wife to urge it forward, I could think of nothing to do so with, and we sat without speaking till we heard the stir of skirts on the stairs in the hall outside, and then my wife said, "Ah, that is Mrs. Hasketh."

I should have known it was Mrs. Hasketh without this sort of anticipation, I think, even if I had never seen her before, she was so like my expectation of what that sort of woman would be in the lapse of time, with her experience of life. The severity that I had seen come and go in her countenance in former days was now so seated that she had no other expression, and I may say without caricature that she gave us a frown of welcome. That is, she made us feel, in spite of a darkened countenance, that she was really willing to see us in her house, and that she took our coming as a sign of amity. I suppose that the induration of her spirit was the condition of her being able to bear at all what had been laid on her to bear, and her burden had certainly not been light.

At her appearance her husband, without really stirring at all, had the effect of withdrawing into the background, where, indeed, I tacitly joined him; and the two ladies remained in charge of the drama, while he and I conversed, as it were, in dumb show. Apart from my sympathy with her in the matter, I was very curious to see how my wife would play her part, which seemed to me far the more difficult of the two, since she must make all the positive movements.

After some civilities so obviously perfunctory that I admired the force of mind in the women who uttered them, my wife said, "Mrs. Hasketh, we have come on an errand that I know will cause you pain, and I needn't say that we haven't come willingly."

"Is it about Mr. Tedham?" asked Mrs. Hasketh, and I remembered now that she had always used as much ceremony in

William Dean Howells

speaking of him; it seemed rather droll now, but still it would not have been in character with her to call him simply Tedham, as we did, in speaking of him.

"Yes," said my wife. "I don't know whether you had kept exact account of the time. It was a surprise to us, for we hadn't. He is out, you know."

"Yes—at noon, yesterday. I wasn't likely to forget the day, or the hour, or the minute." Mrs. Hasketh said this without relaxing the severity of her face at all, and I confess my heart went down.

But my wife seemed not to have lost such courage as she had come with, at least. "He has been to see us—"

"I presumed so," said Mrs. Hasketh, and as she said nothing more, Mrs. March took the word again.

"I shall have to tell you why he came—why *we* came. It was something that we did not wish to enter into, and at first my husband refused outright. But when I saw him, and thought it over, I did not see how we could refuse. After all, it is something you must have expected, and that you must have been expecting at once, if you say—"

"I presume," Mrs. Hasketh said, "that he wished you to ask after his daughter. I can understand why he did not come to us." She let one of those dreadful silences follow, and again my wife was forced to speak.

"It is something that we didn't mean to press at all, Mrs. Hasketh, and I won't say anything more. Only, if you care to send any word to him he will be at our house this evening again, and I will give him your message." She rose, not in resentment, as I could see (and I knew that she had not come upon this errand without making herself Tedham's partisan in some measure) but with sincere good feeling and appreciation of Mrs. Hasketh's position. I rose with her, and Hasketh rose too.

"Oh, don't go!" Mrs. Hasketh broke out, as if surprised. "You couldn't help coming, and I don't blame you at all. I don't blame Mr. Tedham even. I didn't suppose I should ever forgive him. But there! that's all long ago, and the years do change us. They change us all, Mrs. March, and I don't feel as if I had the right to judge anybody the way I used to judge *him*. Sometimes it surprises me. I did hate him, and I don't presume I've got very much love for him now, but I don't want to punish him any more. That's gone out of me. I don't know how it came to go, but it went. I wish he hadn't ever got anything more to do with us, but I'm afraid we haven't had all our punishment yet, whatever *he* has. It seems to me as if the sight of Mr. Tedham would make me sick."

I found such an insufficiency in this statement of feeling that I wanted to laugh, but I perceived that it did not appeal to my wife's sense of humor. She said, "I can understand how you feel about it, Mrs. Hasketh."

Mrs. Hasketh seemed grateful for the sympathy. "I presume," she went on, and I noted how often she used the quaint old-fashioned Yankee word, "that you feel as if you had almost as much right to hate him as I had, and that if you could overlook what he tried to do to you, I might overlook what he did do to his own family. But as I see it, the case is different. He failed when he tried to put the blame on Mr. March, and he succeeded only too well in putting the shame on his own family. You could forgive it, and it would be all the more to your credit because you forgave it, but his family might have forgiven it ten times over, and still they would be in disgrace through him. That is the way I looked at it."

"And I assure you, Mrs. Hasketh, that is the way I looked at it, too," said my wife.

"So, when it seems hard that I should have taken his child from him," the woman continued, as if still arguing her case, and she probably was arguing it with herself, "and did what I could to make her forget him, I think it had better be considered whose sake I was doing it for, and whether I had any right to do different. I did not think I had at the time, or when I had to begin to act. I knew how I felt toward Mr. Tedham; I never liked him; I never wanted my sister to marry him; and when his trouble came, I told Mr. Hasketh that it was no more than I had expected all along. He was that kind of a man, and he was sure to show it, one way or other, sooner or later; and I was not disappointed when he did what he did. I had to guard against my own feeling, and to put myself out of the question, and that was what I tried to do when I got him to give up the child to us and let her take our name. It was the same as a legal adoption, and he freely consented to it, or as freely as he could, considering where he was. But he knew it was for her good as well as we did. There was nobody for her to look to but us, and he knew that; his own family had no means, and, in fact, he *had* no family but his father and mother, and when they died, that same first year, there was no one left to suffer from him but his child. The question was how much she ought to be allowed to suffer, and whether she should be allowed to suffer at all, if it could be helped. If it was to be prevented, it was to be by deadening her to him, by killing out her affection for him, and much as I hated Mr. Tedham, I could not bring myself to do that, though I used to think I would do it. He was very fond of her, I don't deny that; I don't think it was any merit in him to love such a child, but it was the best thing about him, and I was willing it should count. But then there was another thing that I couldn't bring myself to, and that was to tell the child, up and down, all about it; and I presume that there I was weak. Well, you may say I *was* weak! But I couldn't, I simply couldn't. She was only between seven and eight when it happened—"

"I thought she was older," I ventured to put in, remembering my impressions as to her age the last time I saw her with her father.

"No," said Mrs. Hasketh, "she always appeared rather old for her age, and that made me all the more anxious to know just how much of the trouble she had taken in. I suppose it was all a kind of awful mystery to her, as most of our trials are to children; but when her father was taken from her, she seemed to think it was something she mustn't ask about; there are a good many things in the world that children feel that way about—how they come into it, for one thing, and how they go out of it; and by and by she didn't speak of it. She had some of his lightness, and I presume that helped her through; I was afraid it did sometimes. Then, at other times, I thought she had got the notion he was in for life, and that was the reason she didn't speak of him; she had given him up. Then I used to wonder whether it wasn't my duty to take her to see him— where he was. But when I came to find out that you had to see them through the bars, and with the kind of clothes they wear, I felt that I might as well kill the child at once; it was for her sake I didn't take her. You may be sure I wasn't anxious for the responsibility of *not* doing it either, the way I knew I felt toward Mr. Tedham."

I did not like her protesting so much as this; but I saw that it was a condition of her being able to deal with herself in the matter, and I had no doubt she was telling the truth.

"You never can know just how much of a thing children have taken in, or how much they have understood," she continued, repeating herself, as she did throughout, "and I had to keep this in mind when I had my talks with Fay about her father. She wanted to write to him at first, and of course I let her—"

My wife and I could not forbear exchanging a glance of intelligence, which Mrs. Hasketh intercepted.

"I presume he told you?" she asked.

"Yes," I said, "he showed us the letter."

"Well, it was something that had to be done. As long as she questioned me about him, I put her off the best way I could, and after a while she seemed to give up questioning me of her own accord. Perhaps she really began to understand it, or some of the cruel little things she played with said something. I was always afraid of the other children throwing it up to her, and that was one reason we went away for three or four years and let our place here."

"I didn't know you were gone," I said toward Hasketh, who cleared his throat to explain:

"I had some interests at that time in Canada. We were at Quebec."

"It shows what a rush our life is," I philosophized, with the implication that Hasketh and I had been old friends, and I ought to have noticed that I had not met him during the time of his absence. The fact was we had never come so near intimacy as when we exchanged confidences concerning the severity of Tedham's sentence in coming out of the court-room together.

"*I* hadn't any interest in Canada, except to get the child away," said Mrs. Hasketh. "Sometimes it seemed strange *we* should be in Canada, and not Mr. Tedham! She got acquainted with some little girls who were going to a convent school there as externes—outside pupils, you know," Mrs. Hasketh explained to my wife. "She got very fond of one of them—she is a child of very warm affections. I never denied that Mr. Tedham had warm *affections*—and when her little girl friend went into the convent to go on with her education there, Fay wanted to go too, and—we let her. That was when she was twelve, and Mr. Hasketh felt that he ought to come back and look after his business here; and we left her in the convent. Just as soon as she was out of the way, and out of the question, it seemed as if I got to feeling differently toward Mr. Tedham. I don't mean to say I ever got to like him, or that I do to this day; but I saw that he had some rights, too, and for years and years I wanted to take the child and tell her when he was coming out. I used to ask myself what right I even had to keep the child from the suffering. The suffering was hers by rights, and she ought to go through it. I got almost crazy thinking it over. I got to thinking that her share of her father's shame might be the very thing, of all things, that was to discipline her and make her a good and useful woman; and that's much more than being a happy one, Mrs. March; we can't any of us be truly happy, no matter what's done for us. I tried to make believe that I was sparing her alone, but I knew I was sparing myself, too, and that made it harder to decide." She suddenly addressed herself to us both: "What would *you* have done?"

My wife and I looked at each other in a dismay in which a glance from old Hasketh assured us that we had his sympathy. It would have been far simpler if Mrs. Hasketh had been up and down with us as Tedham's emissaries, and refused to tell us anything of his daughter, and left us to report to him that he must find her for himself if he found her at all. This was what we had both expected, and we had come prepared to take back that answer to Tedham, and discharge our whole duty towards him in its delivery. This change in the woman who had hated him so fiercely, but whose passion had worn itself down to the underlying conscience with the lapse of time, certainly complicated the case. I was silent; my wife said: "I don't know *what* I should have done, Mrs. Hasketh;" and Mrs. Hasketh resumed:

"If I did wrong in trying to separate her life from her father's, I was punished for it, because when I wanted to undo my work, I didn't know how to begin; I presume that's the worst of a wrong thing. Well, I never did begin; but now I've got to. The time's come, and I presume it's as easy now as it ever could be; easier. He's out and it's over, as far as the law is concerned; and if she chooses she can see him. I'll prepare her for it as well as I can, and he can come if she wishes it."

"Do you mean that he can see her *here*?" my wife asked.

"Yes," said Mrs. Hasketh, with a sort of strong submission.

"At once? To-day?"

"No," Mrs. Hasketh faltered. "I didn't want him to see her just the first day, or before I saw him; and I thought he might try to. She's visiting at some friends in Providence; but she'll be back to-morrow. He can come to-morrow night, if she says so. He can come and find out. But if he was anything of a man he wouldn't want to."

"I'm afraid," I ventured, "he isn't anything of *that* kind of man."

VI

"Now, how unhandsome life is!" I broke out, at one point on our way home, after we had turned the affair over in every light, and then dropped it, and then taken it up again. "It's so graceless, so tasteless! Why didn't Tedham die before the expiration of his term and solve all this knotty problem with dignity? Why should he have lived on in this shabby way and come out and wished to see his daughter? If there had been anything dramatic, anything artistic in the man's nature, he would have renounced the claim his mere paternity gives him on her love, and left word with me that he had gone away and would never be heard of any more. That was the least he could have done. If he had wanted to do the thing heroically—and I wouldn't have denied him that satisfaction—he would have walked into that pool in the old cockpit and lain down among the autumn leaves on its surface, and made an end of the whole trouble with his own burdensome and worthless existence. That would truly have put an end to the evil he began."

"I wouldn't be—impious, Basil," said my wife, with a moment's hesitation for the word. Then she sighed and added, "Yes, it seems as if that would be the only thing that could end it. There doesn't really seem to be any provision in life for ending such things. He will have to go on and make more and more trouble. Poor man! I feel almost as sorry for him as I do for her. I guess he hasn't expiated his sin yet, as fully as he thinks he has."

"And then," I went on, with a strange pleasure I always get out of the poignancy of a despair not my own, "suppose that this isn't all. Suppose that the girl has met some one who has become interested in her, and whom she will have to tell of this stain upon her name?"

"Basil!" cried my wife, "that is cruel of you! You *knew* I was keeping away from that point, and it seems as if you tried to make it as afflicting as you could—the whole affair."

"Well, I don't believe it's as bad as that. Probably she hasn't met any one in that way; at any rate, it's pure conjecture on my part, and my conjecture doesn't make it so."

"It doesn't unmake it, either, for you to say that now," my wife lamented.

"Well, well! Don't let's think about it, then. The case is bad enough as it stands, Heaven knows, and we've got to grapple with it as soon as we get home. We shall find Tedham waiting for us, I dare say, unless something has happened to him. I wonder if anything can have been good enough to happen to Tedham, overnight."

I got a little miserable fun out of this, but my wife would not laugh; she would not be placated in any way; she held me in a sort responsible for the dilemma I had conjectured, and inculpated me in some measure for that which had really presented itself.

When we reached home she went directly to her room and had a cup of tea sent to her there, and the children and I had rather a solemn time at the table together. A Sunday tea-table is solemn enough at the best, with its ghastly substitution of cold dishes or thin sliced things for the warm abundance of the week-day dinner; with the gloom of Mrs. March's absence added, this was a very funereal feast indeed.

We went on quite silently for a while, for the children saw I was preoccupied; but at last I asked, "Has anybody called this afternoon?"

"I don't know exactly whether it was a call or not," said my daughter, with a nice feeling for the social proprieties which would have amused me at another time. "But that strange person who was here last night, was here again."

"Oh!"

"He said he would come in the evening. I forgot to tell you. Papa, what kind of person is he?"

"I don't know. What makes you ask?"

"Why, we think he wasn't always a workingman. Tom says he looks as if he had been in some kind of business, and then failed."

"What makes you think that, Tom?" I asked the boy.

"Oh, I don't know. He speaks so well."

"He always spoke well, poor fellow," I said with a vague amusement. "And you're quite right, Tom. He was in business once and he failed—badly."

I went up to my wife's room and told her what the children had said of Tedham's call, and that he was coming back again.

"Well, then, I think I shall let you see him alone, Basil. I'm completely worn out, and besides there's no reason why I should see him. I hope you'll get through with him quickly. There isn't really anything for you to say, except that we have seen the Haskeths, and that if he is still bent upon it he can find his daughter there to-morrow evening. I want you to promise me that you will confine yourself to that, Basil, and not say a single word more. There is no sense in our involving ourselves in the affair. We have done all we could, and more than he had any right to ask of us, and now I am determined that he shall not get anything more out of you. Will you promise?"

"You may be sure, my dear, that I don't wish to get any more involved in this coil of sin and misery than you do," I began.

"That isn't promising," she interrupted. "I want you to promise you'll say just that and no more."

"Oh, I'll promise fast enough, if that's all you want," I said.

"I don't trust you a bit, Basil," she lamented. "Now, I will explain to you all about it. I've thought the whole thing over."

She did explain, at much greater length than she needed, and she was still giving me some very solemn charges when the bell rang, and I knew that Tedham had come. "Now, remember what I've told you," she called after me, as I went to the door, "and be sure to tell me, when you come back, just how he takes it and every word he says. Oh, dear, I know you'll make the most dreadful mess of it!"

By this time I expected to do no less, but I was so curious to see Tedham again that I should have been willing to do much worse, rather than forego my meeting with him. I hope that there was some better feeling than curiosity in my heart, but I will, for the present, call it curiosity.

I met him in the hall at the foot of the stairs, and put a witless cheeriness into the voice I bade him good-evening with, while I gave him my hand and led the way into the parlor.

The twenty-four hours that had elapsed since I saw him there before had estranged him in a way that I find it rather hard to describe. He had shrunk from the approach to equality in which we had parted, and there was a sort of consciousness of disgrace in his look, such as might have shown itself if he had passed the time in a low debauch. But undoubtedly he had done nothing of the kind, and this effect in him was from a purely moral cause. He sat down on the edge of a chair, instead of leaning back, as he had done the night before.

"Well, Tedham," I began, "we have seen your sister-in-law, and I may as well tell you at once that, so far as she is concerned, there will be nothing in the way of your meeting your daughter. The Haskeths are living at their old place in Somerville, and your daughter will be with them there to-morrow night—just at this moment she is away—and you can find her there, then, if you wish."

Tedham kept those deep eye-hollows of his bent upon me, and listened with a passivity which did not end when I ceased to speak. I had said all that my wife had permitted me to say in her charge to me, and the incident ought to have been closed, as far as we were concerned. But Tedham's not speaking threw me off my guard. I could not let the matter end so bluntly, and I added, in the same spirit one makes a scrawl at the bottom of a page, "Of course, it's for you to decide whether you will or not."

"What do you mean?" asked Tedham, feebly, but as if he were physically laying hold of me for help.

"Why, I mean—I mean—my dear fellow, you know what I mean! Whether you had better do it." This was the very thing I had not intended to do, for I saw how wise my wife's plan was, and how we really had nothing more to do with the matter, after having satisfied the utmost demands of humanity.

"You think I had better not," said Tedham.

"No," I said, but I felt that I was saying it too late, "I don't think anything about it."

"I have been thinking about it, too," said Tedham, as if I had confessed and not denied having an opinion in the matter. "I have been thinking about it ever since I saw you last night, and I don't believe I have slept, for thinking of it. I know how you and Mrs. March feel about it, and I have tried to see it from your point of view, and now I believe I do. I am not going to see my daughter; I am going away."

He stood up, in token of his purpose, and at the same moment my wife entered the room. She must have been hurrying to do so from the moment I left her, for she had on a fresh dress, and her hair had the effect of being suddenly, if very effectively, massed for the interview from the dispersion in which I had lately seen it. She swept me with a glance of reproach, as she went up to Tedham, in the pretence that he had risen to meet her, and gave him her hand. I knew that she divined all that had passed between us, but she said:

"Mr. March has told you that we have seen Mrs. Hasketh, and that you can find your daughter at her house to-morrow evening?"

"Yes, and I have just been telling him that I am not going to see her."

"That is very foolish—very wrong!" my wife began.

"I know you must say so," Tedham replied, with more dignity and force than I could have expected, "and I know how kind you and Mr. March have been. But you must see that I am right—that she is the only one to be considered at all."

"Right! How are you right? Have *you* been suggesting that, my dear?" demanded my wife, with a gentle despair of me in her voice.

It almost seemed to me that I had, but Tedham came to my rescue most unexpectedly.

"No, Mrs. March, he hasn't said anything of the kind to me; or, if he has, I haven't heard it. But you intimated, yourself, last night, that she might be so situated—"

"I was a wicked simpleton," cried my wife, and I forebore to triumph, even by a glance at her; "to put my doubts between you and your daughter in any way. It was romantic, and—and—disgusting. It's not only your right to see her, it's your *duty*. At least it's your duty to let her decide whether she will let you see her. What nonsense! Of course she will! She must bear her part in it. She ought not to escape it, even if she could. Now you must just drop all idea of going away, and you must stay, and you must go to see your daughter. There is no other way to do."

Tedham shook his head stubbornly. "She has borne her share, already, and I won't inflict my penalty on her innocence—"

"Innocence? It's *because* she is innocent that it must be inflicted upon her! That is what innocence is in the world for!"

Tedham looked back at her in a dull bewilderment. "I can't get back to that. It seemed so once; but now it looks selfish, and I'm afraid of it. I am not the one to take that ground. It might do for you—"

"Well, then, let it do for me!" I confess that I was astonished at this turn, or should have been, if I could be astonished at any turn a woman takes. "I will see her for you, if you wish, and I will tell her just how it is with you, and then she can decide for herself. You have certainly no right to decide for her, whether she will see you or not, have you?"

"No," Tedham admitted.

"Well, then, sit down and listen."

He sat down, and my wife reasoned it all out with him. She convinced me, perfectly, so that what Tedham proposed to do seemed not only sentimental and foolish, but unnatural and impious. I confess that I admired her casuistry, and gave it my full support. She was a woman who, in the small affairs of the tastes and the nerves and the prejudices could be as illogical as the best of her sex, but with a question large enough to engage the hereditary powers of her New England nature she showed herself a dialectician worthy of her Puritan ancestry.

Tedham rose when she had made an end; and when we both expected him to agree with her and obey her, he said, "Very likely you are right. I once saw it all that way myself, but I don't see it so now, and I can't do it. Perhaps we shouldn't care for each other; at any rate, it's too much to risk, and I can't do it. Good-by." He began sidling toward the door.

I would have detained him, but my wife made me a sign not to interfere. "But surely, Mr. Tedham," she pleaded, "you are going to leave some word for her—or for Mrs. Hasketh to give her?"

"No," he answered, "I don't think I will. If I don't appear, then she won't see me, and that will be all there is of it."

"Yes, but Mrs. Hasketh will probably tell her that you have asked about her, and will prepare her for your coming, and then if you don't come—"

"What time is it, March?" Tedham asked.

I took out my watch. "It's nine o'clock." I was surprised to find it no later.

"I can get over to Somerville before ten, can't I? I'll go and tell Mrs. Hasketh I am not coming."

We could not prevent his getting away, by force, and we had used all the arguments we could have hoped to detain him with. As he opened the door to go out into the night, "But, Tedham!" I called to him, "if anything happens, where are we to find you, hear of you?"

He hesitated. "I will let you know. Well, good-night."

"I suppose this isn't the end, Isabel," I said, after we had turned from looking blankly at the closed door, and listening to Tedham's steps, fainter and fainter on the board-walk to the gate.

"There never is an end to a thing like this!" she returned, with a passionate sigh of pity. "Oh, what a terrible thing an evil deed is! It *can't* end. It has to go on and on forever. Poor wretch! He thought he had got to the end of his misdeed, when he had suffered the punishment for it, but it was only just beginning then! Now, you see, it has a perfectly new lease of life. It's as if it had just happened, as far as the worst consequences are concerned."

"Yes," I assented. "By the way, that was a great idea of yours about the office of innocence in the world, Isabel!"

"Why, Basil!" she cried, "you don't suppose I believed in such a monstrous thing as that, do you?"

"You made me believe in it."

"Well, then, I can tell you that I merely said it so as to convince him that he ought to let his daughter decide whether she would see him or not, and it had nothing whatever to do with the matter. Do you think you could find me anything to eat, dear? I'm perfectly famishing, and it doesn't seem as if I could stir a step till I've had a bite of something."

She sank down on the sofa in the hall in proof of her statement, and I went out into the culinary regions (deserted of their dwellers after our early tea) and made her up a sandwich along with the one I had the Sunday-night habit of myself. I found some half-bottles of ale on the ice, and I brought one of them, too. Before we had emptied it we resigned ourselves to what we could not help in Tedham's case; perhaps we even saw it in a more hopeful light.

William Dean Howells

VII

The next day was one of those lax Mondays which come before the Tuesdays and Wednesdays when business has girded itself up for the week, and I got home from the office rather earlier than usual. My wife met me with, "Why, what has happened?"

"Nothing," I said; "I had a sort of presentiment that something had happened here."

"Well, nothing at all has happened, and you have had your presentiment for your pains, if that's what you hurried home for."

I justified myself as well as I could, and I added, "That wretched Tedham has been in my mind all day. I think he has made a ridiculous mistake. As if he could stop the harm by taking himself off! The harm goes on independently of him; it is hardly his harm any more."

"That is the way it has seemed to me, too, all day," said my wife. "You don't suppose he has been out of my mind either? I wish we had never had anything to do with him."

A husband likes to abuse his victory, when he has his wife quite at his mercy, but the case was so entirely in my favor that for once I forbore. I could see that she was suffering for having put into Tedham's head the notion which had resulted in this error, and I considered that she was probably suffering enough. Besides, I was afraid that if I said anything it would bring out the fact that I had myself intimated the question again which his course had answered so mistakenly. I could well imagine that she was grateful for my forbearance, and I left her to this admirable state of mind while I went off to put myself a little in shape after my day's work and my journey out of town. I kept thinking how perfectly right in the affair Tedham's simple, selfish instinct had been, and how our several consciences had darkened counsel; that quaint Tuscan proverb came into ray mind: *Lascia fare Iddio, ch' e un buon vecchio.* We had not been willing to let God alone, or to trust his leading; we had thought to improve on his management of the case, and to invent a principle for poor Tedham that should be better for him to act upon than the love of his child, which God had put into the man's heart, and which was probably the best thing that had ever been there. Well, we had got our come-uppings, as the country people say, and however we might reason it away we had made ourselves responsible for the event.

There came a ring at the door that made my own heart jump into my mouth. I knew it was Tedham come back again, and I was still in the throes of buttoning on my collar when my wife burst into my room. I smiled round at her as gayly as I could with the collar-buttoning grimace on my face. "All right, I'll be down in a minute. You just go and talk to him till—"

"*Him?*" she gasped back; and I have never been quite sure of her syntax to this day. "*Them!* It's Mr. and Mrs. Hasketh, and some young lady! I saw them through the window coming up the walk."

"Good Lord! You don't suppose it's Tedham's daughter?"

"How do I know? Oh, how *could* you be dressing at a time like this!"

It did seem to me rather heinous, and I did not try to defend myself, even when she added, from her access of nervousness, in something like a whimper, "It seems to me you're *always* dressing, Basil!"

"I'll be right with you, my dear," I answered, penitently; and, in fact, by the time the maid brought up the Haskeths' cards I was ready to go down. We certainly needed each other's support, and I do not know but we descended the stairs hand in hand, and entered the parlor leaning upon each other's

shoulders. The Haskeths, who were much more deeply concerned, were not apparently so much moved. We shook hands
with them, and then Mrs. Hasketh said to us in succession,
"My niece, Mrs. March; Mr. March, my niece."

The young girl had risen, and stood veiled before us, and a sort
of heart-breaking appeal expressed itself in the gentle droop of
her figure, which did the whole office of her hidden face. The
Haskeths were dressed, as became their years, in a composite
fashion of no particular period; but I noticed at once, with the
fondness I have for what is pretty in the modes, that Miss
Tedham wore one of the latest costumes, and that she was not
only a young girl, but a young lady, with all that belongs to the
outward seeming of one of the gentlest of the kind. It struck
me as the more monstrous, therefore, that she should be
involved in the coil of her father's inexpiable offence, which
entangled her whether he stayed or whether he went. It was
well enough that the Haskeths should still be made miserable
through him; it belonged to their years and experience; they
would soon end, at any rate, and it did not matter whether
their remnant of life was dark or bright. But this child had a
right to a long stretch of unbroken sunshine. As I stood and
looked at her I felt the heart-burning, the indefinable indignation that we feel in the presence of death when it is the young
and fair who have died. Here is a miscalculation, a mistake. It
ought not to have been.

I thought that my wife, in the effusion of sympathy, would
have perhaps taken the girl in her arms; but probably she knew
that the dropped veil was a sign that there was to be no
embracing. She put out her hand, and the girl took it with her
gloved hand; but though the outward forms of their greeting
were so cold, I fancied an instant understanding and kindness
between them.

"My niece," Mrs. Hasketh explained, when we were all seated,
"came home this afternoon, instead of this morning, when we
expected her."

My wife said, "Oh, yes," and after a moment, a very painful moment, in which I think we all tried to imagine something that would delay the real business, Mrs. Hasketh began again.

"Mrs. March," she said, in a low voice, and with a curious, apologetic kind of embarrassment, "we have come—Fay wanted we should come and ask if you knew about her father—"

"Why, didn't he come to you last night?" my wife began.

"Yes, he did," said Mrs. Hasketh, in a crest-fallen sort, "But we thought—we thought—you might know where he was. And Fay—Did he tell you what he was going to do?"

"Yes," my wife gasped back.

The young girl put aside her veil in turning to my wife, and showed a face which had all the ill-starred beauty of poor Tedham, with something more in it that she never got from that handsome reprobate—conscience, soul—whatever we choose to call a certain effluence of heaven which blesses us with rest and faith whenever we behold it in any human countenance. She was very young-looking, and her voice had a wistful innocence.

"Do you think my father will be here again to-night? Oh, I must see him!"

I perceived that my wife could not speak, and I said, to gain time, "Why, I've been expecting him to come in at any moment;" and this was true enough.

"I guess he's not very far off," said old Hasketh. "I don't believe but what he'll turn up." Within the comfort these words were outwardly intended to convey to the anxious child, I felt an inner contempt of Tedham, a tacit doubt of the man's nature, which was more to me than the explicit faith in his return. For some reason Hasketh had not trusted Tedham's decision, and he might very well have done this without

William Dean Howells

impugning anything but the weakness of his will.

My wife now joined our side, apparently because it was the only theory of the case that could be openly urged. "Oh, yes, I am sure. In fact he promised my husband to let him know later where he was. Didn't you understand him so, my dear?"

I had not understood him precisely to this effect, but I answered, "Yes, certainly," and we began to reassure one another more and more. We talked on and on to one another, but all the time we talked at the young girl, or for her encouragement; but I suppose the rest felt as I did, that we were talking provisionally, or without any stable ground of conviction. For my part, though I indulged that contempt of Tedham, I still had a lurking fear that the wretch had finally and forever disappeared, and I had a vision, very disagreeable and definite, of Tedham lying face downward in the pool of the old cockpit and shone on by the stars in the hushed circle of the woods. Simultaneously I heard his daughter saying, "I can't understand why he shouldn't have come to us, or should have put it off. He couldn't think I didn't wish to see him." And now I looked at my wife aghast, for I perceived that the Haskeths must have lacked the courage to tell her that her father had decided himself not to see her again, and that they had brought her to us that we might stay her with some hopes, false or true, of meeting him soon. "I don't know what they mean," she went on, appealing from them to us, "by saying that it might be better if I never saw him again!"

"I don't say that any more, child," said Mrs. Hasketh, with affecting humility. "I'm sure there isn't any one in the whole world that I would bless the sight of half as much."

"I could have come before, if I'd known where he was; or, if I had only known, I might have been here Saturday!" She broke into a piteous lamentation, with tears and sobs that wrung my heart and made me feel like one of a conspiracy of monsters. "But he couldn't—he couldn't—have thought I didn't *want* to see him!"

It was a very trying moment for us all, and I think that if we had, any of us, had our choice, we should have preferred to be in her place rather than our own. We miserably did what we could to comfort her, and we at last silenced her with I do not know what pretences. The affair was quite too much for me, and I made a feint of having heard the children calling me, and I went out into the hall. I felt that there was a sort of indecency in my witnessing that poor young thing's emotion; women might see it, but a man ought not. Perhaps old Hasketh felt the same; he followed me out, and when we were beyond hearing, even if he had spoken aloud, he dropped his voice to a thick murmur and said, "This has all been a mistake. We have had to get out of it with the girl the best we could; and we don't dare to let her know that Tedham isn't coming back any more. You noticed from what she said that my wife tried to make believe it might be well if he didn't; but she had to drop *that*; it set the girl wild. She hasn't got anything but the one idea: that she and her father belong to each other, and that they must be together for the rest of their lives. A curious thing about it is," and Hasketh sank his voice still lower to say this, "that she thinks that if he's taken the punishment that was put upon him he has atoned for what he did; and if any one tries to make him suffer more he does worse than Tedham did, and he's flying in the face of Providence. Perhaps it's so. I'm afraid," Hasketh continued, with the satisfaction men take in blaming their wives under the cover of sympathy, "that Mrs. Hasketh is going to feel it more and more, as time goes on, unless Tedham turns up. I was never in favor of trying to have the child forget him, or be separated from him in any way. That kind of thing can't be made to work, and I don't suppose, when you come to boil it down, that it's essentially right. This universe, I take it, isn't an accident in any particular, and if she's his daughter it's because she was meant to be, and to bear and share with him. You see it was a great mistake not to prepare the child for it sooner, and tell her just when Tedham would be out, so that if she wanted to see him she could. She thinks she ought to have been there at the prison waiting to speak to him the first one. I thought it was a mistake to have her away, and I guess that's the way Mrs.

Hasketh looks at it herself, now."

A stir of garments made itself heard from the parlor at last, and we knew the ladies had risen. In a loud voice Hasketh began to say that they had a carriage down at the gate, and I said they had better let me show them the way down; and as my wife followed the others into the hall, I pulled open the outer door for them. On the threshold stood a man about to ring, who let his hand drop from the bell-pull. "Why, Tedham!" I shouted, joyfully.

The light from the hall-lamp struck full on his face; we all involuntarily shrank back, except the girl, who looked, not at the man before her, but first at her aunt and then at her uncle, timorously, and murmured some inaudible question. They did not answer, and now Tedham and his daughter looked at each other, with what feeling no one can ever fully say.

VIII

It always seemed to me as if we had witnessed something like the return of one from the dead, in this meeting. We were talking it over one evening some weeks later, and "It would be all very well," I philosophized, "if the dead came back at once, but if one came back after ten years, it would be difficult."

"It was worse than coming back from the dead," said my wife. "But I hope that is the end of it so far as we are concerned. I am sure I am glad to be out of it, and I don't wish to see any of them ever again."

"Why, I don't know about that," I returned, and I began to laugh. "You know Hubbell, our inspector of agencies?"

"What has he got to do with it?"

"Hubbell has had a romantic moment. He thinks that in view of the restitution Tedham made as far as he could, and his excellent record—elsewhere—it would be a fine thing for the Reciprocity to employ him again in our office, and he wanted to suggest it to the actuary."

"Basil! You didn't allow him to do such a cruel thing as that?"

"No, my dear, I am happy to say that I sat upon that dramatic climax."

This measurably consoled my wife, but she did not cease to denounce the idea for some moments. When she ended, I asked her if she would allow the company to employ Tedham in a subordinate place in another city, and when she signified that this might be suffered, I said that this was what would probably be done. Then I added, seriously, that I thoroughly liked the notion of it, and that I took it for a testimony that poor old Tedham was right, and that he had at last fully expiated his offence against society.

His daughter continued to live with her aunt and uncle, but Tedham used to spend his holidays with them, and, however incongruously, they got on together very well, I believe. The girl kept the name of Hasketh, and I do not suppose that many people knew her relation to Tedham. It appeared that our little romantic supposition of a love affair, which the reunion of father and child must shatter, was for the present quite gratuitous. But if it should ever come to that, my wife and I had made up our minds to let God manage. We said that we had already had one narrow escape in proposing to better the divine way of doing, and we should not interfere again. Still I cannot truly say that we gave Providence our entire confidence as long as there remained the chance of further evil through the sort of romance we had dreaded for the girl. Till she was married there was an incompleteness, a potentiality of trouble, in the incident apparently closed that haunted us with a distrustful anxiety. We had to wait several years for the end, but it came eventually, and she was married to a young Englishman whom she had met in Canada, and whom she told all about her unhappy family history before she permitted herself to accept him.

During the one brief interview I had with him, for the purpose of further blackening her father's character (for so I understood her insistence that I should see the young man), he seemed not only wholly unmoved by the facts, but was apparently sorry that poor Tedham had not done much worse things, and many more of them, that he might forgive him for her sake.

They went to live abroad after they were married; and by and by Tedham joined them. So far now as human vision can perceive, the trouble he made, the evil he did, is really at an end. Love, which can alone arrest the consequences of wrong, had ended it, and in certain luminous moments it seemed to us that we had glimpsed, in our witness of this experience, an infinite compassion encompassing our whole being like a sea, where every trouble of our sins and sorrows must cease at last like a circle in the water.

ABOUT THE AUTHOR

 **William Dean Howells** (March 1, 1837 – May 11, 1920) was an American realist author and literary critic.

Born in Martins Ferry, Ohio, originally Martinsville, to William Cooper and Mary Dean Howells, Howells was the second of eight children. His father was a newspaper editor and printer, and the father moved frequently around Ohio. Howells began to help his father with typesetting and printing work at an early age. In 1852, his father arranged to have one of Howells' poems published in the Ohio State Journal without telling him.

He wrote his first novel, The Wedding Journey, in 1872, but his literary reputation took off with the realist novel, A Modern Instance, published in 1882, which described the decay of a marriage. His 1885 novel The Rise of Silas Lapham is perhaps his best known, describing the rise and fall of an American entrepreneur in the paint business. His social views were also strongly reflected in the novels Annie Kilburn (1888) and A Hazard of New Fortunes (1890). He was particularly outraged by the trials resulting from the Haymarket Riot.

In 1904, he was one of the first seven chosen for membership in the American Academy of Arts and Letters, of which he became president.

Choose from Thousands of 1stWorldLibrary Classics By

A. M. Barnard
Ada Leverson
Adolphus William Ward
Aesop
Agatha Christie
Alexander Aaronsohn
Alexander Kielland
Alexandre Dumas
Alfred Gatty
Alfred Ollivant
Alice Duer Miller
Alice Turner Curtis
Alice Dunbar
Allen Chapman
Alleyne Ireland
Ambrose Bierce
Amelia E. Barr
Amory H. Bradford
Andrew Lang
Andrew McFarland Davis
Andy Adams
Angela Brazil
Anna Alice Chapin
Anna Sewell
Annie Besant
Annie Hamilton Donnell
Annie Payson Call
Annie Roe Carr
Annonaymous
Anton Chekhov
Archibald Lee Fletcher
Arnold Bennett
Arthur C. Benson
Arthur Conan Doyle
Arthur M. Winfield
Arthur Ransome
Arthur Schnitzler
Arthur Train
Atticus
B.H. Baden-Powell
B. M. Bower
B. C. Chatterjee
Baroness Emmuska Orczy
Baroness Orczy
Basil King
Bayard Taylor
Ben Macomber
Bertha Muzzy Bower
Bjornstjerne Bjornson

Booth Tarkington
Boyd Cable
Bram Stoker
C. Collodi
C. E. Orr
C. M. Ingleby
Carolyn Wells
Catherine Parr Traill
Charles A. Eastman
Charles Amory Beach
Charles Dickens
Charles Dudley Warner
Charles Farrar Browne
Charles Ives
Charles Kingsley
Charles Klein
Charles Hanson Towne
Charles Lathrop Pack
Charles Romyn Dake
Charles Whibley
Charles Willing Beale
Charlotte M. Braeme
Charlotte M. Yonge
Charlotte Perkins Stetson
Clair W. Hayes
Clarence Day Jr.
Clarence E. Mulford
Clemence Housman
Confucius
Coningsby Dawson
Cornelis DeWitt Wilcox
Cyril Burleigh
D. H. Lawrence
Daniel Defoe
David Garnett
Dinah Craik
Don Carlos Janes
Donald Keyhoe
Dorothy Kilner
Dougan Clark
Douglas Fairbanks
E. Nesbit
E. P. Roe
E. Phillips Oppenheim
E. S. Brooks
Earl Barnes
Edgar Rice Burroughs
Edith Van Dyne
Edith Wharton

Edward Everett Hale
Edward J. O'Biren
Edward S. Ellis
Edwin L. Arnold
Eleanor Atkins
Eleanor Hallowell Abbott
Eliot Gregory
Elizabeth Gaskel
Elizabeth McCracken
Elizabeth Von Arnim
Ellem Key
Emerson Hough
Emilie F. Carlen
Emily Bronte
Emily Dickinson
Enid Bagnold
Enilor Macartney Lane
Erasmus W. Jones
Ernie Howard Pie
Ethel May Dell
Ethel Turner
Ethel Watts Mumford
Eugene Sue
Eugenie Foa
Eugene Wood
Eustace Hale Ball
Evelyn Everett-green
Everard Cotes
F. H. Cheley
F. J. Cross
F. Marion Crawford
Fannie E. Newberry
Federick Austin Ogg
Ferdinand Ossendowski
Fergus Hume
Florence A. Kilpatrick
Fremont B. Deering
Francis Bacon
Francis Darwin
Frances Hodgson Burnett
Frances Parkinson Keyes
Frank Gee Patchin
Frank Harris
Frank Jewett Mather
Frank L. Packard
Frank V. Webster
Frederic Stewart Isham
Frederick Trevor Hill
Frederick Winslow Taylor

Friedrich Kerst
Friedrich Nietzsche
Fyodor Dostoyevsky
G.A. Henty
G.K. Chesterton
Gabrielle E. Jackson
Garrett P. Serviss
Gaston Leroux
George A. Warren
George Ade
Geroge Bernard Shaw
George Cary Eggleston
George Durston
George Ebers
George Eliot
George Gissing
George MacDonald
George Meredith
George Orwell
George Sylvester Viereck
George Tucker
George W. Cable
George Wharton James
Gertrude Atherton
Gordon Casserly
Grace E. King
Grace Gallatin
Grace Greenwood
Grant Allen
Guillermo A. Sherwell
Gulielma Zollinger
Gustav Flaubert
H. A. Cody
H. B. Irving
H.C. Bailey
H. G. Wells
H. H. Munro
H. Irving Hancock
H. R. Naylor
H. Rider Haggard
H. W. C. Davis
Haldeman Julius
Hall Caine
Hamilton Wright Mabie
Hans Christian Andersen
Harold Avery
Harold McGrath
Harriet Beecher Stowe
Harry Castlemon
Harry Coghill
Harry Houidini

Hayden Carruth
Helent Hunt Jackson
Helen Nicolay
Hendrik Conscience
Hendy David Thoreau
Henri Barbusse
Henrik Ibsen
Henry Adams
Henry Ford
Henry Frost
Henry James
Henry Jones Ford
Henry Seton Merriman
Henry W Longfellow
Herbert A. Giles
Herbert Carter
Herbert N. Casson
Herman Hesse
Hildegard G. Frey
Homer
Honore De Balzac
Horace B. Day
Horace Walpole
Horatio Alger Jr.
Howard Pyle
Howard R. Garis
Hugh Lofting
Hugh Walpole
Humphry Ward
Ian Maclaren
Inez Haynes Gillmore
Irving Bacheller
Isabel Cecilia Williams
Isabel Hornibrook
Israel Abrahams
Ivan Turgenev
J.G.Austin
J. Henri Fabre
J. M. Barrie
J. M. Walsh
J. Macdonald Oxley
J. R. Miller
J. S. Fletcher
J. S. Knowles
J. Storer Clouston
J. W. Duffield
Jack London
Jacob Abbott
James Allen
James Andrews
James Baldwin

James Branch Cabell
James DeMille
James Joyce
James Lane Allen
James Lane Allen
James Oliver Curwood
James Oppenheim
James Otis
James R. Driscoll
Jane Abbott
Jane Austen
Jane L. Stewart
Janet Aldridge
Jens Peter Jacobsen
Jerome K. Jerome
Jessie Graham Flower
John Buchan
John Burroughs
John Cournos
John F. Kennedy
John Gay
John Glasworthy
John Habberton
John Joy Bell
John Kendrick Bangs
John Milton
John Philip Sousa
John Taintor Foote
Jonas Lauritz Idemil Lie
Jonathan Swift
Joseph A. Altsheler
Joseph Carey
Joseph Conrad
Joseph E. Badger Jr
Joseph Hergesheimer
Joseph Jacobs
Jules Vernes
Julian Hawthrone
Julie A Lippmann
Justin Huntly McCarthy
Kakuzo Okakura
Karle Wilson Baker
Kate Chopin
Kenneth Grahame
Kenneth McGaffey
Kate Langley Bosher
Kate Langley Bosher
Katherine Cecil Thurston
Katherine Stokes
L. A. Abbot
L. T. Meade

L. Frank Baum
Latta Griswold
Laura Dent Crane
Laura Lee Hope
Laurence Housman
Lawrence Beasley
Leo Tolstoy
Leonid Andreyev
Lewis Carroll
Lewis Sperry Chafer
Lilian Bell
Lloyd Osbourne
Louis Hughes
Louis Joseph Vance
Louis Tracy
Louisa May Alcott
Lucy Fitch Perkins
Lucy Maud Montgomery
Luther Benson
Lydia Miller Middleton
Lyndon Orr
M. Corvus
M. H. Adams
Margaret E. Sangster
Margret Howth
Margaret Vandercook
Margaret W. Hungerford
Margret Penrose
Maria Edgeworth
Maria Thompson Daviess
Mariano Azuela
Marion Polk Angellotti
Mark Overton
Mark Twain
Mary Austin
Mary Catherine Crowley
Mary Cole
Mary Hastings Bradley
Mary Roberts Rinehart
Mary Rowlandson
M. Wollstonecraft Shelley
Maud Lindsay
Max Beerbohm
Myra Kelly
Nathaniel Hawthrone
Nicolo Machiavelli
O. F. Walton
Oscar Wilde

Owen Johnson
P.G. Wodehouse
Paul and Mabel Thorne
Paul G. Tomlinson
Paul Severing
Percy Brebner
Percy Keese Fitzhugh
Peter B. Kyne
Plato
Quincy Allen
R. Derby Holmes
R. L. Stevenson
R. S. Ball
Rabindranath Tagore
Rahul Alvares
Ralph Bonehill
Ralph Henry Barbour
Ralph Victor
Ralph Waldo Emmerson
Rene Descartes
Ray Cummings
Rex Beach
Rex E. Beach
Richard Harding Davis
Richard Jefferies
Richard Le Gallienne
Robert Barr
Robert Frost
Robert Gordon Anderson
Robert L. Drake
Robert Lansing
Robert Lynd
Robert Michael Ballantyne
Robert W. Chambers
Rosa Nouchette Carey
Rudyard Kipling
Saint Augustine
Samuel B. Allison
Samuel Hopkins Adams
Sarah Bernhardt
Sarah C. Hallowell
Selma Lagerlof
Sherwood Anderson
Sigmund Freud
Standish O'Grady
Stanley Weyman
Stella Benson
Stella M. Francis

Stephen Crane
Stewart Edward White
Stijn Streuvels
Swami Abhedananda
Swami Parmananda
T. S. Ackland
T. S. Arthur
The Princess Der Ling
Thomas A. Janvier
Thomas A Kempis
Thomas Anderton
Thomas Bailey Aldrich
Thomas Bulfinch
Thomas De Quincey
Thomas Dixon
Thomas H. Huxley
Thomas Hardy
Thomas More
Thornton W. Burgess
U. S. Grant
Upton Sinclair
Valentine Williams
Various Authors
Vaughan Kester
Victor Appleton
Victor G. Durham
Victoria Cross
Virginia Woolf
Wadsworth Camp
Walter Camp
Walter Scott
Washington Irving
Wilbur Lawton
Wilkie Collins
Willa Cather
Willard F. Baker
William Dean Howells
William le Queux
W. Makepeace Thackeray
William W. Walter
William Shakespeare
Winston Churchill
Yei Theodora Czaki
Yogi Ramacharaka
Young E. Allison
Zane Grey